Also by Val Chanda

Zorn and Grayall Find Murder by the Way

and

The *Psy Mind* series:

Deadly Reckoning
Calculated Risks
Judgment Called

ZORN AND GRAYALL

ENCOUNTER THE ELEMENTS OF MURDER

VAL CHANDA

Wasteland Press
Shelbyville, KY USA
www.wastelandpress.net

Zorn and Grayall Encounter the Elements of Murder:
An Elsewhere Mystery
by Val Chanda

First Printing – July 2015
ISBN: 978-1-68111-040-0
Map designed by Denis Proulx | www.shangrila-studio.com

Printed in the U.S.A.

0   1   2   3   4   5   6

To Barry for advice on the elements

And

To Sandy for elemental advice

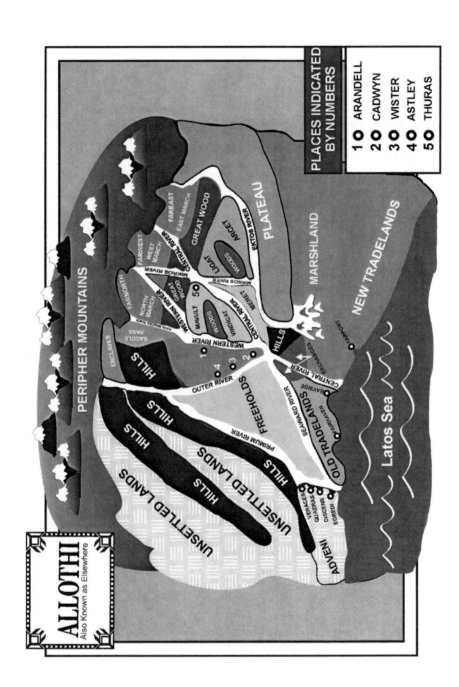

THE REGIONS OF ALLOTHI, KNOWN TO SOME AS ELSEWHERE

The Realm, or Regeren

North of the Great Wood, the Marches: Northmarch and Farnorth, Westmarch and Farwest, Eastmarch and Fareast

South of the Great Wood, the Domains: Mavult, Vindicat, Meret, Ligat, Arcet

The Coastal Lands: Adveni, Old Tradelands, New Tradelands

Inland: the Freeholds, the Exchanges, the Borderlands with the villages of Arandell, Cadwyn, Wister, and Astley

The Enclaves

The Rivers: Primum, Seaward, Outer, Western, Katabantes, Central, Mikros, Ektos

THE PEOPLE WHO ARE NAMED

Visitors to the Exchanges
Zorn of Northmarch, dispossessed ariston, last Warder of Farnorth in the Realm
Grayall of Wellworth, formerly a trader, had intended to marry Jarrell of Truware
Patric of Truware, Jarrell's brother
Lucian, representative of the insurgency's Provisional Authority, former servitor in the Realm

The Household of Gwynedd's Securing House
Gwynedd, owner
Torvan, her husband
Evane, their daughter
Haslen, house chamberlain
Caled, gatekeeper
Larit, household attendant

Other residents of the Exchanges
Arne Bennetson, trader
Carsten of Wrightwork, trader
Tirze Volsted, trader
Daniel Oletto, District Constable
Denon, clothier at Merchantplace

At Arandell
Traina, village physician
Brandon, her ward
Bertel, Presider to the village of Arandell
Rolf, an itinerant trader, deceased

Zorn's Alphaen Order-kin
Zarath, last Archon of Northmarch
Zered, one-time Warder of Farnorth, had abdicated prior to the dissolution
Zirel, eligible for, but not granted, a governance position

Others
Karel of Wellworth, Grayall's brother, currently in the New Tradelands
Jarrell of Truware, killed in one of the last battles in the Realm

After reading my first narrative, *someone* suggested—actually it was more like insisted—that in the interest of greater accuracy, if I should decide to pick up my pen again, I ought to include certain additional information. I am doing so although I had to restrain myself from telling her, if she's not satisfied with my accounts, she should write her own.
—**GW**

On the physical traits of the people of Allothi:
An attentive reader of Grayall's previous effort may notice that she describes people selectively. She tends to direct her attention to aspects relating to emotion and expression and to neglect, with one notable exception, factual details like eye, hair, and skin color.

Thus these additional comments may prove instructive and, perhaps, useful.

Allothi was settled as a result of two major migrations. One that came down over the mountains in the north, the other that came across the sea from the south.

The mixture of these two influxes of peoples undoubtedly produced the variations in physical characteristics that mark the Allothian populations.

Among the peoples of Allothi, the most common eye colors are brown, green, and gray. Blue is relatively rare. Hair is generally either black or some shade of brown. Red hair and blonde hair are uncommon. As for natural texture, hair may be straight, wavy, or tightly curled. Skin colors range from light pinkish-tan, through neutral and darker tans, to true brown. Very fair skin is not often seen. —**ZN**

Tan, pinkish tan, darker tans, brown, black—what kind of words are those to use for descriptions? Skin colors could be peach or blush, tawny or olive, copper or chocolate. Hair could be jet or sable; auburn, chestnut, or fawn. Those are the kinds of words I would choose. —**GW**

Of course you would. And doubtless, despite anything I might recommend, at some point you will. —**ZN**

CHAPTER ONE

It would have been hard, I think, to imagine two more unlikely traveling companions in all of Allothi than Grayall, formerly of the now-defunct trading enterprise of Wellworth, and Zorn of Northmarch, dispossessed traditional ariston of the Realm. Of course, if you'd seen us, in our nondescript clothing, riding along the Western River that morning, you would never have placed us for what we had been. Nor would you have guessed how we had been brought together. First, by me saving Zorn's life when I had found her along the road, bleeding, burned, and staked out kneeling between two trees, left by one of her own people to suffer a slow death. And then, her returning the favor by clearing from a charge of murder, the murder of an itinerant trader named Rolf, the young ward of my friend Traina, physician to the borderland village of Arandell.

You would also not have guessed that Zorn carried, in the worn leather pouch secured to her belt next to the scabbard of her knife, a fortune in ariston insignia. Insignia which had been the emblems of her order and ruling authority when she had governed as Warder of Farnorth. And which had played a central role in the events that had unfolded at Arandell. The journey we were on now would take us to the Exchanges where Zorn intended to convert those insignia into a more practical form of wealth by offering them for sale.

Located at the confluence of the Outer, the Western, and the Central Rivers, the Exchanges had long served as the commercial center for all the regions of Allothi. All the trading activity which came up from the coastal ports, that of both the Old and New Tradelands, funneled to the Exchanges where well-established vending enterprises provided a reliable market for the sale of merchandise. In addition, securing houses offered a protective haven for resources, issued bills of guarantee, and oversaw the auctioning of certain specialty goods. The Exchanges had also been the gateway to all trading with the Realm before its dissolution.

For me, the journey to the Exchanges was inevitable. And would have been, even without Zorn's business to transact. Such assets as I still possessed were lodged there with one of the securing houses, Gwynedd's. That establishment had served my family's trading enterprise for years in a relationship founded in trust and mutual benefit. But it wasn't just Gwynedd's Securing House with its reliability in commercial matters that I sought. I was drawn by personal ties, as well. Gwynedd, her husband Torvan, and their daughter Evane were friends. More than that, they were a second family to me. Not just their House, but their *home* promised a place of refuge, a place to regroup.

As for Zorn of Northmarch, she seemed to have no doubts about the decision she had made at Arandell that I act as agent for the sale of her insignia and she had accepted the Exchanges and Gwynedd's as her own destination as well.

Although Zorn never acknowledged any difficulties, I could tell she continued to feel the effects of the brutal treatment she had endured. Her external injuries, the burns on her hands, the wounds around her wrists, the knife cuts that had carved the identifying letters AR into her forehead, had all healed. Still, she often looked over-tired and maybe even feverish. And whenever we were off our horses, I could see, her right knee still bothered her. I thought the pace we kept was not comfortable for her. But if I suggested we allow ourselves longer rests, she declined in a way which seemed to leave no room for dispute. Or at least, none that I was willing to look for.

And it was true that the season was well advanced. We were fortunate not to have encountered any real weather yet, although heavy clouds loomed over the plateau lands to the east, clouds which had undoubtedly dropped the first snow on the higher ground. Any day now one of those storms would move far enough westward to bring the real start of the rainy winter season here. Both of us wanted to get to the

Exchanges before that, so Zorn took the analgesics which Traina had provided and we kept going.

We hoped to reach the vicinity of Cadwyn, the southernmost of the borderland villages, no later than our fourth day on the road. Just beyond it was the ferry that would carry us across the Central River and into the Exchanges.

Our steady rate of travel left us little room for conversation or further acquaintance. We rose early, ate, cleared camp, and rode. Broke for a meal and to rest the horses at midday, then went on. About six dusk set in, so by four-thirty we were usually looking for a place to spend the night. After the time it took to settle in, see to the horses, prepare and eat some dinner, we were both ready for sleep.

And so our journey was uneventful, uneventful that is until almost its end, when something occurred which took me a long time to reconcile.

It was going to be our last night's camp. We had stopped to overnight around the usual time and had followed our normal routine. All along I would have been willing to take on most of the work because I judged that our long days on the move were a strain for Zorn. But she had overruled any such suggestion simply by ignoring it and taking on a reasonable share of the load. So that late afternoon, when we had finished eating, I had cleaned up after us and Zorn had tended to the horses. Then, happily I settled down to relax, assuming Zorn would do the same. But she announced that she was going to walk a little which seemed to me less than sensible, since she was already limping.

"You should rest," I said. I was comfortably sprawled on a blanket I had spread over my saddle and on the ground. Zorn stood gazing down at me briefly, then headed off. "You should rest," I called after her, but it was only a gesture.

I guess I must have half dozed. You know, one of those cases when you would swear you haven't slept, except for the slight dislocation of time and awareness which says you must have. I remember a sharp sound like a very dry twig breaking and then suddenly awakening from a state which I had thought was wakefulness all along. A man was standing just a few feet away. I took in a lot of things at once. From the way he was dressed, he looked like the kind of odd-lot trader the murdered Rolf had been, but I knew immediately he wasn't. In the first place, he was well-armed, a large wicked-looking knife in his belt, a rifle cradled in his arm, and a full bandolier across his chest. In his hand, he held my own gun. The pack it had been in lay open at his feet. The sound that had awakened me had undoubtedly been the clicking shut of the cylinder after he had checked to see if it was loaded. It was equally clear, that as silently as he had done everything else, that one sure noise had been intentional.

In the second place, from the soundlessness of his approach and the set of his expression, there was no mistaking his intent. He intended to take whatever he wanted. The only question was, how much did he want. It's pointless to say how stupid I felt, with my own gun resting casually in the bandit's grip, his nonchalance proclaiming how confident he was that I presented no threat.

"Where's the other one?" he asked. His voice was a gritty growl. I started to get up. He shook his head, slightly, and I stopped. I sank back to the ground. My reaction amused him. With an ugly smile, he asked again, "Where is she?"

"I'm alone," I said.

I don't think I actually finished the words when something came hurtling at me. I threw myself back and whatever it was flew over me, barely missing my head. When it landed with a thud behind me, I realized he had kicked my pack, so swiftly and forcefully that nothing had flown out of it. As a demonstration of his speed and strength, it had been most effective. Fear, like a solid lump, rose in my throat. My heart seemed to be thumping against my rib cage. And he could see it all in my face. Watching me, he looked amused again. No, not just amused. He looked pleased. He said, "Lie to me, I'll kick your head in." He glanced around, never taking his attention off me for more than a second. Everything seemed abnormally still. "Doesn't matter," he said at last. "Time for her later. After you."

He stared down at me. I braced myself for his advance, but instead suddenly his head went up. Although I hadn't heard anything, I knew that he had, or seen something, perhaps a flicker of movement in the trees behind me. Zorn, I thought with futile insistence, stay back, stay out of sight. Then there was a small whisk of sound, followed by a thunk. And the bandit was standing with the hilt of a knife sticking out of his throat, Zorn's knife, thrown with unerring accuracy. His arms jerked convulsively and he gave a strangled, gasping sound, almost as if he would draw the knife deeper into him. Blood welled out of his mouth and burst from the edges of his wound in a fine spray. I scrambled away backwards, getting tangled in my saddle, but desperate to keep moving. The bandit fell, first to his knees, then he tumbled over to his side. I think he was dead before he hit the ground.

But I was no longer looking at him. I had turned my head and was staring, dumb-struck and horrified, at Zorn.

CHAPTER TWO

My gaze still fixed on Zorn, I staggered to my feet. In that moment, I was as terrified of her as I had been of the bandit. I think she started to say something, maybe to ask if I was all right, but my face must have shown what I was feeling. She watched me long enough to read my expression, to read it well. I turned away, back to the body lying curled before us. Blood stained down from his chin and throat like a bib. I stumbled to the side a step or two, then dropped to my knees and vomited. As I crawled away from my own stench, I felt the touch of a hand on my back. I jerked as if I had been burned. "Don't touch me." My words were involuntary. They rang with hysteria and revulsion.

Although I did not look at her to see, Zorn must have stepped away. I heard a slight rustle of movement, then a blanket dropped over my shoulders. Trembling, I clutched it to me. I don't know how long I huddled there, shaking. Surely only a few moments but, for me, time had changed its measure. It might as well have been hours before I realized Zorn had come to stand in front of me. "Grayall." Her voice held not the slightest tinge of emotion.

I raised my head and she held out a canteen of water which I took. I washed the taste of vomit from my mouth, but did not swallow. I was afraid my heaving stomach would simply throw it up again. My head hanging, bent almost to the ground, I whispered, "You killed him."

"Grayall," she began again. She waited until I looked up. "Of course I killed him. He would have…" Uncharacteristically she stopped, reconsidering her words. "A threat like that. It leaves no other possibility. You understand that."

I shook my head groggily. "But so quick, without warning."

"Warning." Her voice actually rose a little. She seemed about to add something but instead, with a minimal shake of her head, she walked away. I watched her cross over to the humped shape on the ground.

She looked back at me, I thought, perhaps scornfully. "Turn away," she said. But I didn't. I continued to watch as she eased the dead bandit onto his back with her foot, then stooped and pulled her knife out of his throat. The soft tissue of his neck had yielded to the knife going in and appeared to relinquish it with as little resistance. Zorn had flung it with such accuracy that it had found the hollow at the base of the bandit's throat, just above the top of the breast bone. If her aim had been off even slightly, the bone might have deflected the knife. But her aim had been flawless, just as I had seen her practice it so often on a fence post at Arandell.

At last I shifted my gaze and, for a few moments, stared sightlessly into the trees beyond our campsite. The light was fading rapidly. I heard Zorn move away, but when I looked back she had returned to the body. Her knife was again in its scabbard on her belt. I hadn't noticed her put it away, or wipe it, which she must have done. Which I hoped she'd done. She knelt beside the body, slowly on her achy knees, and began to strip him of his bandolier, his belt and knife. Her hands were steady, but I could see, as she rolled his body from side to side, his weight caused her to strain with the effort.

I got up and came forward the few steps necessary to join her. I felt like someone walking from one world to another. "I'll help," I said weakly, but she continued to search him, as quickly and as efficiently as she had slain him. She found nothing else.

When she finished, she looked up at me. I could imagine what she saw in my face, but I said again, "I'll help." My voice was hoarse. And so, together, we pulled him across the small clearing of our camp. He was heavy. He had been tall and strong, but it was the dead weight of a dead body, I had always heard. It was true. Some low shrubbery ringed our campsite. We dragged him there.

When I had stood up, the blanket had slipped from my shoulders. I went back for it. "To cover him," I said and started to drape it over the body, but Zorn caught the blanket from my hand.

"We have nothing to spare," she said and walked back into the clearing.

"We can't just leave him like that," I cried out, but Zorn ignored me. She retrieved my gun. Without looking around, she extended her arm behind her. I hesitated a moment, then stepped over and took the gun from her. I shoved it into my pack. Zorn, in the meantime, picked up the canteen I had left on the ground. She drank, then put the canteen back in her pack. After that, she got the bandit's rifle, which had fallen with him, checked it, and laid it across her saddle next to his knife and ammunition belt. All her movements were deliberate. They betrayed no trace of a reaction to having just killed someone.

I still wanted to say something more to her, but everything in me seemed frozen. Zorn waited for a few moments, then said, "The last hour or so that we rode, something bothered me. But I couldn't place it."

As if moving on its own, my head bobbed vaguely up and down. Somewhere in my mind, I grasped the point. She was explaining why she had gone off by herself, trying to satisfy her uneasiness. But I was utterly disconnected from myself and found nothing to say.

Into my silence, Zorn added, "I should have attended more closely." She gave one curt, authoritative nod in the direction of the body. "Fortunately he was overconfident, therefore just careless enough. Fortunate, too, he was alone."

All I could do was stare at her dumbly. In return, she studied me awhile longer but when it became clear I was not going to respond, she settled herself, apparently to sleep.

I settled, too, but with no expectation of sleep. The last light of dusk dwindled into darkness and I lay awake. I felt caught between two oppressive presences, both for the moment equally still. The dead bandit and my friend. I had started to think of Zorn that way, hadn't I? As a friend. She now seemed as alien to me as if another wandering predator had arrived to share my camp.

I was being unfair. I knew that. But feelings don't measure themselves against fairness. And it wasn't just that I had seen someone killed in front of my face. My real shock was at the graphic demonstration of Zorn's own lethality. I thought I had confronted some pretty harsh realities in the last months, but nothing like being in the presence of the ability to kill that efficiently, that unhesitatingly. It appalled me. And it frightened me.

All at once, the sounds of Zorn shifting position cut into my thoughts. She had sat up. "Tell me, Grayall, do you have any doubt about the man? About what he intended to do?" Her voice wasn't alien at all. It held that flat, calm, confident delivery which had become so familiar to me.

"I thought you were asleep," I croaked.

"Answer my question."

I sat up as well. I could barely make out her shape in the darkness. I considered for a moment and then said with reasonable firmness, "No, Zorn, I don't have any doubts."

"Then I ask you again, what else would you have had me do?"

"It's not…" I stumbled over my words. "It's not that I don't believe what you did was necessary." I got that much out, but came to a stop. Zorn waited. She was not one for prompting. All I could do was repeat what I had already said, "But, Zorn, you killed him. You just…killed him." I could hear a note of pleading in my voice.

"You have offered that observation previously."

"It's just…" But I was at a loss to fully explain what I felt, even to myself, much less to her. "Look," I said at last, "I know you saved my life…" My words trailed off.

"He might have settled for less than that." The lack of intonation in her voice was more unsettling than anger would have been. I heard her move again and her shape disappeared. I, too, lay back down. Then Zorn added, her voice now slightly muffled because she was no longer sitting up, "If you wish to alter our arrangements upon reaching the Exchanges, you are free to do so."

CHAPTER THREE

In the morning, I knew I should have answered Zorn at the time, but I simply hadn't been able to. We broke camp, me studiously avoiding that one place on the perimeter of our campsite where the bandit's body lay, Zorn appearing to pay it no heed at all. We had saddled the horses and were about ready to mount when I finally managed the overdue words. "What you said last night, I don't want to alter anything."

Zorn rested her hand on her saddle, to which I noticed she had tied the bandit's rifle, securing it by its strap. She looked at me steadily. "You might consider that decision more carefully."

Evading her gaze, I said, "I know you acted to defend me. And I don't much like to think what would have happened if you hadn't… done what you did."

"If I hadn't killed him," she corrected.

"All right, yes, if you hadn't killed him. I'll deal with it, Zorn, but give me some time."

"You'll deal with it. That's generous of you." Her voice held an edge, but it sounded deliberate and controlled. I searched for something to say, but she added, "I am a traditional ariston of Regeren. We are different. You should know that by now." She turned away abruptly, mounted, and rode out. I followed. Perversely I took one glance back, scarcely able to make out the dark shape lying at the edge of the campsite behind me.

In a couple of hours, we struck a road, the first paved road in our long miles of travel. It skirted the village of Cadwyn, then continued on to the ferry by which we would cross over into the Exchanges. We had no desire to delay so we didn't take the turning that led to the village. When the road forked, we kept going. Even when it got close to noon, we didn't bother to stop to eat. Perhaps neither of us was very hungry.

After a while, a fine mist came up. We had not outrun the weather by much. We met no one else on the road, and had nothing to say to each other. The only sound was the hollow clop of the horses' hooves on the wet pavement.

By the time we reached the ferry point, the mist had become a steady rain. It obscured the view across the river, turning the solid buildings and towers of the Exchanges into shadows. I paid the ferryman for both of us and we embarked. As we led the horses on board, Zorn's ornery roan fussed but her mastery won the argument with him and soon both our mounts were secured in the stalls provided. The roan clattered his hooves as the ferry started but he calmed down fairly quickly.

Zorn and I took shelter under a roofed area fitted with rough backless benches. We were the only passengers and we seated ourselves with a little distance between us. I watched the rain-pocked water flow past us, wishing I could throw my emotional baggage into it and watch it drift away.

I looked over at Zorn. She had turned sideways on the bench, resting her back against one of the posts holding up the roof. Her legs were extended in front of her, her right knee, the one that troubled her more, drawn up. She had placed her pack under it as a support. Her eyes were closed. Even in repose, her face looked severe, its planes set by the long lines from her cheek bones to her sharply angled chin.

She must have sensed me watching her because she opened her eyes. Dark against her tan skin, deep set, and slightly hooded, they always seemed to me better suited to hide rather than reveal any expression.

"I'm ready to see the end of this journey," I said. I knew I wanted to break the strain of silence that lay between us, but it was an effort to get the words out. I just hoped the effort didn't show too much.

Zorn adjusted the pack to ease her knee. She turned her head and I followed her gaze to the rain-blurred outlines of the buildings on the opposite shore. I could have named the business of many of them, identified whose securing house, whose enterprise. I wondered what it would be like to see them as Zorn must, as an unknown and untried environment. And then it occurred to me, for her that was probably true of any place beyond the borders of the Realm. Even among the non-traditionals of the south, for an ariston to travel outside the Realm would have been highly unusual. From what I understood, it simply wasn't done at all among the traditionalists from the Marches.

Still trying for a way back into conversation, I remarked, "I don't guess you've ever spent any time away from the Realm before."

Zorn shifted her gaze back to me and swung to sit upright. By now we were almost to the dock. We both stood up and walked over to the horses. As we slipped off the halters we had put on over the bridles, she said, "Almost five years. But that was some time ago."

As I tended to my horse, I didn't immediately connect what she said as a response to my comment. And, in my weariness and anxiety about how Zorn would be received in the Exchanges, I buried that fragment of information. It would not rise to the surface of my memory again for some time.

Chapter Four

It was very late in the afternoon but there was still some light left in the day, if you could find it through the rain, when Zorn and I rode up to the gate of Gwynedd's Securing House. The gate was still open. We passed through it and into the shelter of the portico that extended between the gate and the gatekeeper's lodge. Our horses came to a drooping halt and I dismounted wearily but, before I could approach the lodge, the gatekeeper himself appeared in his doorway. Without coming forward, he said, "The business of this House is closing for the day." His tone didn't quite make it to rudeness, but plainly he intended to be discouraging.

I didn't recognize him. He must have been hired during the time I had been away. More important, he obviously didn't recognize me nor, I guess, much like the look of us. And for that, I couldn't blame him. We were worn and muddy, and we must have appeared entirely unprosperous.

"My name is Grayall of Wellworth. That enterprise is known to you, I presume." I tried for an impressive tone, but it's a little tough when you're soaking wet and dripping puddles.

"Known? Yes. I know *that* enterprise no longer operates." Nonetheless, he came out to meet us. "Still your name has been given to me." He said it grudgingly. Maybe good gatekeepers are supposed to be suspicious, but I could have done with something more welcoming. "And this other?" He jutted his chin in Zorn's direction.

"A friend of mine. I'll make the introductions."

I thought he gave a cluck of disapproval, but he didn't argue. He disappeared back inside the lodge.

I glanced at Zorn who had sat unmoving through all this. "He's new since I was here last," I said.

She slowly swung out of the saddle. As she slid to the ground, her legs seemed to buckle, but she steadied herself quickly.

With little delay, a couple of youngsters who obviously did messenger duty came hurrying out of the lodge. One headed toward the main house, the other hurried off toward the stable.

The gatekeeper reappeared. He reached to take our horses' reins. "Your animals and gear will be attended to. Do you need assistance to the house?"

"No, I know the way." And I did. I knew the way, I knew the whole house. It was laid out in the shape of an H and business and personal life were intermixed within it. The top and bottom of the H created two bays, one facing forward, the other facing back toward the Central River, which ran through the Exchanges.

Here in the front bay, the wing on this side held, on the ground floor, Gwynedd's office, the library, and Torvan's study. On the floor above were the guest rooms. The wing across from us had a large, formal drawing room at the front. Behind that, a smaller, more comfortable parlor, and then the dining room. On that side, the family's rooms occupied the floor above.

At the back, the bay overlooking the river housed the kitchens, the employees' quarters, and various offices and workrooms devoted to the business of the house.

Although each wing had its own entrance, the main door to the house was set in the middle of the H's crosspiece. It opened onto an entry which led to a large hall.

Everything on this side of the house was dark but across the front bay, lights gleamed in the windows of the small parlor. I didn't want to troop in through the main entrance, sloppy as we were, so I led the way down the walk that ran beside the house, thinking I would try the nearest of the side doors. It was locked, however. I continued along the walkway intending to follow it around to the other side when the front door burst open and Gwynedd's daughter Evane came flying out to meet us.

"Grayall, by all that's precious, you're back. Thank heavens." Ignoring the wet, she embraced me.

"You'll get soaked," I protested.

"Don't be ridiculous. But come in, come in." She nodded at Zorn to include her in the invitation. "Time enough for introductions when you're in and dry." She led the way inside.

As we stepped into the entry, with the light and elegance of the hall looming before us, I found myself again uncomfortably aware of my bedraggled state. And Zorn's.

"Sorry for the mess," I started to apologize.

Evane smiled indulgently at me. "Grayall, I said, don't be ridiculous."

The house chamberlain, who I knew, a man named Haslen, came forward with an attendant to help us. They relieved us of our sodden jackets which the attendant gingerly carried away. To Haslen, who as chamberlain oversaw the entire household, Evane said, "See that one of the sets of rooms for guests is prepared." He glided away, up the stairs on our left.

"Come on," Evane said. "They're all in the parlor. You both need a glass of wine and a warm fire."

"All?" I repeated fretfully. I wasn't much in the mood for company, either business or social.

"Don't worry. It's just Arne and Carsten." She grinned and said to Zorn, "Old acquaintances, well accustomed to Grayall's eccentricities."

Zorn had not opened her mouth since we rode through the gate. And she didn't acknowledge Evane's explanation now. If Evane noticed the lack of response, she didn't show it. We followed her into the small parlor.

CHAPTER FIVE

Seeing the three people gathered in that room, I felt like I had slipped back to an earlier time, a time when life held sure and familiar patterns. Like this one. Arne, Carsten, and Gwynedd, comfortable with wine and firelight, and with the successful completion of some piece of business. I could even read the outcome. Carsten, triumphant. He had won whatever had been at stake in this encounter. Arne, appearing good-natured in defeat, not because he took losing lightly but because he won more often than he lost in his longstanding rivalry with Carsten. And Gwynedd, her face alight with satisfaction at business well-conducted, the rich brown of her skin shining like polished bronze.

We had hardly stepped through the door, when they all rose in a cluster and came forward with greetings and embraces. Arne, first, with an exuberant hug for me. I had known for a long time that such a demonstration by Arne of hearty good nature was a bit of a show but I enjoyed it anyway. Carsten, as always, more restrained, not as outgoing, shook hands. And then Gwynedd, nodding slightly as if to confirm it was really me, drew me to her and said quietly but with genuine emotion, "Grayall. This is a welcome arrival. We've been worried about you."

"Sure," I said. "Show up unexpectedly in the pouring rain. Interrupt business. I'm the perfect guest."

"Business is finished for the night," Gwynedd said lightly. Then added, more seriously, "And you know you're not a guest in this house, Grayall. You're part of us."

She glanced at the others and I knew she was uncertain whether to ask the question that was in her mind. But the people in the room were no strangers to my affairs, and the sooner the better I supposed, so I said, "You all may as well know first off, Jarrell is dead." There was that moment of stillness which news like that always brings, followed by murmurs of condolence.

Only Evane's voice stood out, full with quick sympathy. "Oh, Grayall. No."

I didn't want to make elaborate explanations, not then and there. I shrugged and said, "He died almost two months ago and I've known for a while."

Gwynedd tactfully pulled Evane back a step. Arne thrust a glass of wine into my hand and then handed one to Zorn.

"You must be exhausted," Gwynedd said.

I noticed her words included Zorn as well. I also noticed the swiveling of heads in Zorn's direction. I looked at her, too. To me her appearance, the angular face, the tan skin, the deep-set black-brown eyes, marked her, unmistakably, as a traditional Realm ariston, but maybe that was only because I had seen others of her kind back in my family's trading days, memories which had been reinforced by my acquaintance with her. I could also, behind her fringe of thick, black hair, catch a glimpse of the scar on her forehead. But probably that, too, was only because I knew to look for it.

Sentiment over Jarrell had prevailed over curiosity about Zorn so far, but that wouldn't last much longer in the face of her silent and unidentified presence. So, answering the others' expectations rather than any actual inquiry, I finally introduced her. "May I present Zorn of Northmarch." The distinctive set of her features the rest of them might not place, but her name and designation brought a quiver of reactions. Gwynedd, Arne, and Carsten exchanged glances. And out of the corner of my eye, I saw Evane stiffen with evident distaste.

But whatever undercurrents my naming of Zorn had provoked, Gwynedd seemed intent on ignoring them. She simply stepped forward and said smoothly, "Any friend of Grayall's is welcome in this house."

Zorn inclined her head slightly, a spare gesture of acknowledgment, then said in her distinctly level voice, "Grayall brought me here as a client." She didn't add, not as a friend, but that's what it sounded like.

"Well, new clients too are always welcome. At least when they come well recommended." Gwynedd gave me a raised-eyebrow look that mixed doubt with inquisitiveness. Still, without missing a beat, she continued, "And may I present my daughter Evane. And also Arne Bennetson and Carsten of Wrightwork. The proprietors of two of our most successful enterprises."

Carsten nodded. He seemed unsure how to react, but Arne stepped forward, bowed slightly, and said, "We are honored to have you with us, Your Excellency." His deference amused me. It was quick, it was politic, and it was actually his way of taking charge, of regaining whatever edge he had lost this evening over Carsten who clearly had been perplexed about how to offer a greeting to Zorn.

But Evane had no such uncertainties. She turned away from Zorn, glared at Arne and her mother, and said with all the bite she could muster, "I decline the introduction." Then she favored me with a look. The welcome of greeting, the light of friendship in her eyes, the generous sympathy, they had all gone. In their place was a chill and rejecting anger. Without another word, she stalked out of the room.

My first impulse was to follow her, to challenge that anger, my second was to glance nervously at Zorn. But if she had any reaction to Evane's insulting behavior, it did not surface. Her expression remained unaltered, her dark, hooded eyes remained opaque.

As for the others, they continued to stare after Evane. Arne and Carsten were startled, I think. Gwynedd upset. Into the awkwardness of the moment, Zorn said, "Grayall claims her recommendation is worth having." With that, all they could do was bring their attention back to her.

Gwynedd, obviously nonplussed but with no opening for apologies, replied, "Yes, that it is." She seemed to be searching for additional words to recover civility. But evidently she couldn't find them.

Whatever else Evane had accomplished, the uncomplicated tone of homecoming had vanished.

Arne stepped in again to smooth over the break in social niceties caused by Evane's rudeness. "Well, we are not staying the night, are we?" He gestured to include Carsten.

Carsten accepted the cue. He extended his hand to Gwynedd. "Yes, you have things to attend to. Thank you. A good piece of business." The reserve in his voice could not hide his satisfaction.

Arne clapped him on the shoulder. "I have to let him win once in a while. To keep things interesting."

"I win when I wish to win," Carsten said, but his voice lacked Arne's good humor. Still they went out in apparent companionship.

I gazed after them. "They never change, do they?"

Gwynedd didn't bother with that. She had regained her composure. "Time to get you both settled in. What first? Food?"

I was hungry but I wanted to clean up before eating and Zorn offered no objection, so Gwynedd led the way across the hall and up the stairs. Before we reached the top, it was obvious Zorn was limping. "Are you injured?" Gwynedd asked her. "I'll summon a physician."

"There is no need," Zorn said.

Gwynedd regarded me quizzically. I shrugged. "Well, if you're sure," she said. When Zorn didn't respond, Gwynedd continued up the stairs, slowly.

She led us, not to ordinary guest rooms, but to one of the sets of rooms designed for the convenience of business associates who might want a place for private conference. There were two of them, one looking down into the front courtyard, the other facing out toward the gardens on the west side of the house. They were composed of a central sitting room with a sleeping chamber on either side. Zorn and I had the set overlooking the gardens.

The rooms, as expected, were warm and inviting. A stove in the sitting room had dispelled the chill, and our travel-worn packs had been stowed in the bedrooms. Fresh clothes had also been laid out for both of us. In addition, in Zorn's room, the rifle, the one the bandit had carried, was leaning in a corner. I wondered what the house attendants had thought about that. Gwynedd, as she checked that everything was in order, appeared to pay it no attention at all.

When she had satisfied herself, she said, "Haslen will see to anything else you need. I hope you'll join me later. Or I can have some food brought up if you're too tired to come down again." I knew the first of those two invitations was for me. The second, I assumed, was for Zorn.

CHAPTER SIX

Within the hour, I had bathed and changed. Although I had stored my remaining belongings with Gwynedd before I had gone in search of Jarrell, the clothes laid out for me were new, and tailored to my measurements. Trousers and jacket of fine burgundy-colored wool, cream shirt of cotton broadcloth woven smooth as silk. Even a pair of boots of wine-colored leather. Gwynedd had obviously had them all made up for me in anticipation of my return. I flushed with pleasure and a little embarrassment at her generosity. It had been so long since I'd worn civilized clothing that, as I dressed, I had an awkward first-day-of-school feeling. But it felt good nonetheless.

When I was ready, I came out into the sitting room of the set, but Zorn wasn't there, so I knocked on the door of her room. She said, "Enter," and I did. Gwynedd had mustered a set of clothes for her as well, probably from the household stores which were kept for the use of clients and other visitors. Jacket, trousers, and shirt were carefully folded across a chair. But Zorn herself was sitting back against the head of the bed. She was wearing a dressing gown. Behind her usual expression of self-contained alertness, her eyes glittered with unnatural brightness. She seemed to me worn out and feverish.

"I think Gwynedd was right about the physician," I said.

"I need rest, not a physician," Zorn rejoined shortly.

"Well, that's a concession anyway."

"My weariness aside, you might find explanations, and continued reunions, easier in my absence."

I thought for a moment, particularly about Evane's behavior. "You're probably right," I said. "You want some food sent up?"

"Yes."

"No physician?"

"Yes." She waited a moment for my confusion to register, then added, "That is correct. No physician."

"All right. There's not much sense in arguing with you anyway." On a bedside table sat the pouch that held the insignia. I reached for it. "I'll take these down. Have Gwynedd put them in the safe."

Zorn didn't stop me, but she said, "You have things to consider. Or perhaps, reconsider."

"I told you, nothing has changed…in that regard." Unfortunately, the pause and the addition were noticeable.

Zorn gave me one of her impassive stares and then a barely perceptible nod which I took for a dismissal. But as I turned to leave, she said, "While you are arranging matters, bear in mind, I am in no humor to be called a liar."

It took me a long moment to figure out what she meant. When I did, I said, "What you told me at Arandell, about helping renegade servitors flee, I believed you then. I still do."

"I owed you that confidence. For the rest, I prefer to be judged as I am found. Remember that when you narrate your recent experiences."

"Don't worry, I won't hold you up as an insurgent sympathizer, no matter what the provocation." It came out sounding more sarcastic than I intended but I was irritated that, as all too typical of her, she had issued what amounted to an order.

She studied me. "As one person's reaction to my presence has already demonstrated, you will be busy enough answering for your own sympathies." She inclined her head again. This time it did signal the end of our conversation. So I left her and went down.

I wasn't best pleased with Zorn's attitude, her unwillingness to make known the actions she had taken in the Realm and the terrible price Archon Zarath had exacted from her for what she'd done. But I was reluctant to press her on that point. After all, the decision to make revelations about herself rightly belonged to her, not to me. And the more I reflected on our exchange, the more it struck me, maybe she hadn't so much given me an order as asked for my consideration. She was probably correct that at least some people would doubt her word about assisting runaway servs, taking any such claims as a bid to curry favor with those sympathetic to the insurgency, which was certainly the majority opinion in the Exchanges. As for myself, even if I had been tempted to defy her wishes in this matter, I suspected the same would hold true for me. Any defense of her on my part would only sound like a self-serving attempt to justify my association with her.

Besides I had other concealments to worry about. I had taken the death of the bandit and pushed it somewhere. But that death, that killing, pushed back at me, refusing to stay tucked away. It frustrated me that I couldn't just put it aside, that I needed to talk to someone about it. Worse, I probably needed to talk about it with Zorn. But what was there to say? She had killed the bandit to save me. And all I could feel was revulsion that she had the ability, and the will, to do it. Also I couldn't decide whether it was something I should tell Gwynedd. Or for that matter, could tell Gwynedd.

As I started across the hall, Haslen intercepted me and I told him to send some food up for Zorn.

"She is … or was … Her Excellency of Northmarch, as I understand," he said.

"Is that a problem?" I asked sharply.

"I should know whether etiquette demands any particular decorum or mode of address." There was mild rebuke in his voice.

"Sorry. But you'll have to use your own judgment on that. Anyway, you've had some experience dealing with ariston. You used to do some trading in the Realm yourself, if I remember correctly."

He gave me a patient smile. "Many of us did. But that was some years ago. Before I took employment here. And of course, as in the case of your family's enterprise, I traded only in the south. With the non-traditional houses of the Domains."

We were being very polite to each other but, out of my own defensiveness, I had reminded him of his dealings with the Realm and he had parried it nicely by reminding me of mine.

"Well, Haslen, I'm no expert on the protocol of social interactions with dispossessed ariston. As for Zorn, I call her by her name."

"But then, you are her friend." His smile broadened. I don't think I imagined the insinuating tone in his voice. He knew he had the better of our exchange. With a courteous nod, he wandered off to attend to his duties.

CHAPTER SEVEN

I found Gwynedd waiting for me in the parlor, sitting at a small table. As I walked in, I raised my hands to indicate my clothes. "Thanks for all this."

Gwynedd smiled. "The tailors did a good job. Now come over here and have some food." She had set out a tray for me. Joining her, I ate and drank with more enthusiasm than manners. When I finished, she poured me another glass of wine.

I raised it in a mock toast. "I told you I was the perfect guest."

She ignored my flippancy. "I wish I knew what to say to you about Jarrell."

I shook my head, indicating that I wished I knew what to say as well. Finally I managed, "The news I got, it wasn't exactly unexpected. And at least, now I'm sure." My voice thickened. Tears would have come much too easily. I cleared my throat and added, "It's what I went for, after all. To get certain word of what happened to him."

Gwynedd leaned forward and laid one of her hands over mine. She let it rest there in silent consolation. After a while, she straightened and said, "I'm very glad you came back to us. Safely."

It was as good an opening as any. "Even with complications." I gestured toward the other side of the house.

Gwynedd's eyes widened with interest. "Zorn of Northmarch," she said pensively.

"Zorn, of the Alphaen Order of Northmarch, last Warder of Farnorth. To be precise."

Gwynedd raised an arm and rested her chin between her thumb and index finger. She waited. When I didn't say anything else, she folded her arms and settled back in her chair. "You going to tell me about all this?"

"Yeah, I guess." So briefly I told her how I had found Zorn, roped between two trees and left to die. I told her about Traina's ward Brandon and how Zorn had saved him from a false judgment. But beyond the basic facts, I didn't elaborate. For now at least, I kept both Zorn's confidences and my own. I didn't say anything about who had tortured her, nor the reasons for it. And at the last, I didn't say anything about the bandit, dead with a knife in his throat. I meant to, but when it came to it, the words just weren't there.

When I gave my account of finding Zorn, a shadow had passed over Gwynedd's face, darkening her warm-brown skin, but otherwise she had listened quietly enough. When I finished, she said, "You surprise me a little. Oh, not that you saved the ariston's life. That's completely in character."

"It was hardly a great moral decision. I just couldn't do anything else."

"Don't make it sound like a flaw in your character. What surprises me is the continued association. Maybe the friendship?"

"I don't know. I don't know if we're truly friends or not. Let's just say there's some mutual indebtedness. But to get to a less perplexing point, I really did bring Zorn here as a client." I pulled out the pouch containing the insignia and handed it to Gwynedd. "See what you think of this." Gwynedd opened the pouch and let its contents slip out onto the table. I had the satisfaction of hearing a distinct intake of breath. "We might not look very promising," I said, "but maybe that's business worth your consideration."

Ignoring my teasing, Gwynedd took up each piece of the insignia for careful examination. The twisted neck collar with its heavy pendant, the beautifully worked gold chain, the medallion belt, the seal ring, the two pins, one large enough to serve as a cloak fastener, the other, smaller, suitable to secure a neckcloth. Their gold gleamed in the firelight and their polished onyx reflected like black mirrors.

When Gwynedd had laid the last piece back down, she said, "Ariston insignia. Traditional house insignia." Her voice sounded almost reverent.

"I'm glad you're a little impressed."

"Grayall," she chided me.

"Anyway Zorn wants to sell them. With me acting as agent. Naturally I recommended you as the securer for the sale."

"Sell them," Gwynedd repeated as if she hadn't paid attention to anything past my first words.

"Yeah. They're all she has left, except for what she's picked up on the way."

A familiar glint came into Gwynedd's eyes. "This would be quite a coup. The biggest thing of the season. Probably of several seasons."

"I thought you might like it."

"But still, even in these circumstances, for a traditional ariston to deal commercially in items like these," Gwynedd passed a graceful sweep of her hand above the insignia, "it's…unexpected."

"Out of character," I amended. Gwynedd nodded her agreement. "Look," I said, "I don't pretend to know Zorn very well. And I certainly don't pretend to understand her. Traditional ariston, they are…" The shadow of the death on the road overtook me as I groped for what I wanted to say, and I finished lamely. "They aren't like us." Well, it was what Zorn herself had said, more or less. Dissatisfied, however, I added, "But I think there's more to her than that ariston manner, that ariston persona. I have reason to think that."

Gwynedd studied the insignia laid out before her. "You don't need to excuse her to me. This house has done a lot of business with people who traded with the Realm." She regarded me slyly. "People like your own parents. And Jarrell's."

"Maybe you should make this speech to Evane." I hadn't planned to say that. The words were out of my mouth before I knew it.

Gwynedd paused, then said, "I do want to apologize for her."

I shook my head. "No. That's pointless. You can't apologize for what she feels. But…" I felt my jaw clench. "She looked at me like…she looked at me like she hated me." To cover the moment, I reached over for the pouch and slowly began putting the insignia back into it.

Gwynedd let out a long deliberate sigh. "Yes, well, we still do business with the Realm. Only now it's the Provisional Authority for Reorganization. That's the temporary administrative apparatus the insurgents have recently set up, trying to establish some degree of order, at least in the south. This House is acting as guarantor for them. We're working with one of their representatives. His name is Lucian. He had been a servitor, of course. When the Realm was the Realm." She stopped to consider. "He's very intense, very bitter. Also very good looking. And Evane likes him. She likes him a lot."

"Oh, shit," I burst out. It might not have been eloquent but it was heartfelt. "Is he staying here?"

"He has been. At present, he's off in the Freeholds, negotiating for the things he's come for. Enough grain to get them through this winter. And he wants birds, if he can get them."

By birds, Gwynedd meant messenger birds, carrier pigeons, or peristeri as they were called in the Realm. The ariston had used them as a fast and effective means of long distance communication. Something the founders of the new regime urgently needed access to as well. But the retreating ariston hadn't left their birds behind, not alive anyway. They were too valuable a resource to leave to their enemies, so they'd slaughtered them as they fled. Getting a new stock of them would be almost as important to the reorganization efforts as getting grain for the winter.

Gwynedd continued, "As for Lucian, actually I expected him today, so things could be worse. But he'll probably be back here tomorrow. It'll take him some time to complete his transactions and make shipping arrangements." She closed her hand over the pouch which still sat before us on the table. "About as long as it will take to arrange *this* transaction."

"Listen, I can make other plans."

Gwynedd raised her hand. "Grayall, this is no favor to you. Gwynedd's Securing House is pleased to have this commission. Let there be no doubt about that. This is business. In Zorn of Northmarch, you have brought me a very good client. Very good indeed. And that is something I expect Evane to understand. And Lucian, as well, if he wishes to do business with this House."

"In other words, if it comes to a choice between Lucian's business and Zorn's, you'll take Zorn's."

"Let's just say, I cannot allow one client to dictate my interactions with another." She lifted the pouch and settled it in the palm of her hand. "Of course, the other client may have objections of her own. If Lucian does remain, Zorn of Northmarch may change *her* mind about using this securing house. She would have good reason, given what was done to her."

I knew Gwynedd was assuming it was a band of insurgents who had dealt so brutally with Zorn. I didn't correct that impression. I said, "No. She won't do that." And despite my own confusions about Zorn's character, I was sure I was right about that. She would not allow Lucian's presence to change her intentions. She would not condescend to let herself be so influenced.

"Still," Gwynedd insisted, "she's entitled to know and make her choice. Before all this is made official." She sat in thoughtful silence for a few moments. "They have a reputation for not tolerating offenses. Be they major or minor."

"Ariston, you mean, I suppose. Not former servitors, not insurgents."

Gwynedd smiled. "Don't be a smartass. As for Zorn and Lucian, they need to understand, with regard to the functions and hospitality of this house, both of them are welcome. But any quarrels between them are not. Those would interfere with business."

I nodded and then smothered a yawn behind my hand. Our discussion was important but my weariness was winning out. Gwynedd took pity on me. "We won't settle everything tonight. You handle Zorn. I'll manage Evane."

And presumably Evane would manage Lucian, I thought, but didn't say it.

We stood up. Gwynedd came over and embraced me. "We'll deal with all of this. I just want to say again, I'm so glad you're back safe."

My getting back safe. It was the second time she had referred to that. "It wasn't all that dangerous," I said. "The insurgents were pretty careful of me when I was with them."

"Actually I've been thinking of something closer to home. There've been reports of bad outbreaks of brigandage in the country between the outland villages. Almost as far south as Cadwyn. Not just robbery, but assault and murder, as well. You and Zorn came that way. I think you were fortunate."

"Yeah, I suppose we were." She must have heard something peculiar in my tone.

"You *are* all right? You didn't have any trouble?" Her voice filled with concern.

"Let's just say, whatever trouble we had, we took care of it."

Gwynedd studied me. "Something did happen. Are you sure you're all right? Both of you?"

"I got a bit older on this trip. Otherwise, I'm OK."

"And Zorn of Northmarch?"

"Zorn is always all right. Just ask her."

CHAPTER EIGHT

I woke late the next morning, after a long hard sleep, and I woke feeling uncomfortable, and more than a little doubtful. You handle Zorn, Gwynedd had said. As if I could. I thought about the things Gwynedd didn't know, especially about the bandit, how quickly and efficiently Zorn had killed him. I thought about the things I didn't know either. Like what in the world really made Zorn tick and how little I actually knew about predicting her reactions. The pieces I had didn't seem to fit very well. She had betrayed the Realm, saved Brandon, rescued me. Yet, as far as I could tell, she remained every inch the traditional ariston. So what would she do if confronted with an angry and unforgiving former serv like Lucian? Not justify herself, that was for sure. Beyond that…I shut my mind to the image of that lightning knife and accused myself of melodrama. Still, just like at Arandell, I found myself accountable for Zorn's behavior, and nervous about that responsibility.

I washed, dressed, and came out into our sitting room. The door to Zorn's room was open, but she wasn't there. The bed was made and the clothing Gwynedd had provided for her was no longer draped over the chair. There wasn't much else in the room. The clothes she had worn traveling, like mine, had been taken away to be cleaned. The bandit's rifle was no longer in view, but it took only a little bit of snooping to find it. It was standing upright in a tall, narrow cabinet. I checked it. It was unloaded. The ammunition belt the bandit had worn lay curled on a shelf above it. His knife was there, too, but not the one Zorn had been given in Arandell, the one with which she had killed him.

I came downstairs to find the house quiet. Everyone else was evidently up and about their duties. I went to the dining room where some trays of breakfast food were keeping warm. It was the custom at Gwynedd's to put food out buffet style, an easier way than set mealtimes to accommodate a diversity of schedules, not to mention a diversity of clients.

I was hungry but I wanted to find Zorn, feeling an urgency which I kept trying to discount. I made a sandwich of bacon and bread, something I could eat while I searched for her. As I was doing so, one of the household attendants appeared with fresh coffee. I took some and drank a few sips, then asked, "You don't happen to know where my associate is, do you?" Associate, a nice discreet choice of words.

"Out walking around the grounds, I think."

"Thanks," I took my sandwich and headed out. The attendant politely ignored my irregular manners.

I went through the back wing of kitchens and offices, intending to check the dock behind the house. Outside, the air smelled fresh after the rain, but it was the smell of settled places, and it seemed strange to me after my long journey. The sky was streaked with clouds and the sunshine that contended with them seemed thin, but still the day was pleasant enough. At the dock, nothing was being loaded or unloaded, the river ran quietly, and Zorn was not there.

I came back to the house, went to the opposite wing and followed the corridor that ran its length. I went past the door to Torvan's study, which was closed, and past the library, which was empty. And finally reached Gwynedd's office. There I found a clerk filing papers. No. She hadn't seen the new client. Haslen might know. Gwynedd had gone out and wouldn't be back for a couple of hours. Evane was out, too. Sorry.

I thought of checking with Haslen but decided that most likely he would only be able to tell me what I already knew, that Zorn was wandering around the grounds somewhere, so I decided to keep searching on my own. But as I stepped back into the corridor I heard a dry voice say, "So, the wandering one returns." It was Torvan. He nodded toward his study. "Come in for a minute, if your business isn't too pressing." He grinned as he said it and then retreated.

Torvan had a long, loose-jointed body, and a long, pleasant face to match. He wasn't handsome but he was attractive. He smiled easily, but genuinely. He had watchful brown eyes which always gave you the feeling that he saw what was important, the substance rather than the surface of things, and of people.

Torvan's occupation was doing research in whatever interested him. It wasn't a profitable endeavor, but since the business of Gwynedd's Securing House more than adequately took care of the family income, he was free to follow his inclinations. And over the years, he had acquired a notable reputation as a scholar. Last year he had even been granted one of the rare visitor's admissions to do research at Veraces, the most select and prestigious of the scola, the centers of learning, in Adveni.

I came to the door of his study and peered in. "My business probably isn't as pressing as I think," I said. Torvan was already back at his desk, behind a fortification of books, notebooks, and papers. The bookshelves around the walls were full and stacks of books rose, like pillars, from the floor. Against one wall stood a worktable as cluttered as the desk. Beside it was a chair piled with papers.

I stepped carefully around a column of books, lifted the papers from the chair, and started to set them on the floor.

"If you disarrange things, I'll never find anything," Torvan said with mock dismay. He gestured to the papers I was holding. "Let me think. Notes on alkali metals, right?"

I glanced at the heading on the top sheet. "Right."

"Over there." He pointed to a corner of the worktable.

I added them to the stack of papers already there. "So glad I haven't ruined your filing system," I said as I sat down.

"Me too. It's taken years to perfect." He grinned again, a quick mobile show of teeth. "Besides theory grows in chaos. I reserve order for practice." It was true. Torvan had a small laboratory detached from the house. It was as organized as this room was not. "And speaking of order and chaos brings me to your homecoming." He pushed aside a pile of notebooks and rested his arms on the desk. "The client you brought. An interesting, if explosive, bit of matter." He contemplated me like I was an experiment about to yield results.

"I hope not," I said testily.

"Well, maybe not explosive in itself. More like a reagent." I regarded him doubtfully. "Something that causes a reaction," he said. "You really should pursue disinterested studies more often, Grayall."

"Look, Zorn is..."

"Oh, Gwynedd's given me the rundown. Besides your ariston has already impressed me. She spent the better part of the morning in the library. While others I could name were lying in bed all day."

"With the company I have to keep, I need all the rest I can get. I'll probably need a two hour nap, at least, just to recover from this conversation."

"Just like old times, isn't it? I'm glad you can still tease back. Despite everything you've gone through." Torvan had dropped his bantering tone abruptly. I nodded, feeling choked up and silly to feel that way. Seeing my emotion, he added quietly, "No point in saying much. You know how sorry I am. For your loss." The words were minimal but his concern was clear.

"Yeah. Thanks."

"Anyway I wanted to say, like Gwynedd, I'm really glad you've come back to us. And don't worry, she'll manage her clients. She always does. Besides, the ariston seems rather sensible."

"Sensible." I laughed. "It's not the first adjective I would have applied to Zorn. But if she is, it's on her own terms. And now I'd better go find her and see if I can figure out a bit more about what those are."

"That's the trouble with the commercial mind. It only seeks the knowledge it thinks is profitable." Torvan gave me one last grin of satisfaction and I left him.

I walked around the front corner of the house, passing between it and the lodge. Here alongside the house ran the strip of well-tended gardens which our windows overlooked. It all seemed somewhat bleak now, with the summer bloom gone and fall advancing to winter.

Beyond the gardens were the stable and paddocks, screened from the house by a line of trees. I angled off toward them and was told, yes,

Zorn, or rather the new client, as they called her, had been there earlier but no one knew where she was now, except she had not gone out riding. They would have known that, they assured me.

I came back up from the stable and followed a path that ran through the gardens. Among the plantings, benches were set. Any one of them would have provided an inviting spot from which to enjoy the late morning sunshine, but Zorn was not occupying any of them. At the end of the gardens, the path, now bordered with weeds and strewn with soggy leaves, turned left and curled away toward a pond, used for irrigation rather than decoration. As I trudged along, I reflected, if I didn't find her there, I'd about run out of places to look.

CHAPTER NINE

I couldn't remember the last time I'd been back to the pond, but now I followed the path to it. It was fed on the far side by a ditch which ran from the river. It had a built-up bank all around and, on the near side, a line of trees grew close to its edge. Their leaves looked tired like they wanted to fall and were only waiting for one more good storm to relieve them of further responsibility. A couple of the trees had been damaged at one time, probably struck by lightning. All that was left of one of them was a bare trunk with a splintered end pointing starkly at the sky. Just beyond it, the other, too, had been split. One of its main limbs had cracked so that on one side its branches arched, hanging down like the spray of a fountain.

As I climbed the slight incline leading to the bank, a cluster of ducks and geese swimming in the pond raised a ruckus of harsh honking sounds. Between the jagged, dead tree and its more gracefully damaged companion, some large logs had been stacked into an irregular pyramid. With its base broader than its off-center top, it formed a kind of rough bench. Zorn was sitting there, gazing out at the pond, or at least facing in that direction. She didn't move as I approached, nor did she turn her head when I came up to her. I saw in her no trace of the feverishness of the night before.

In fact she appeared utterly composed. She sat in a posture I came to know as typical of her, upright yet completely at ease. Watching her, I felt there was no mistaking she was someone who had carried authority for a long time.

I don't know, maybe it was just the clothes. After all, this was the first time I'd seen her dressed in civilized fashion. The torn and blood-stained ariston garb she'd been wearing when I found her certainly didn't count. For the rest, we'd both worn clothing suitable for rough travel. But now in the fine clothing Gwynedd had lent her, gray trousers and a jacket of darkest indigo, sober colors in keeping with the preference of a traditional ariston, she looked a lot more like a member of the Alphaen Order of Northmarch. Maybe too much so for my taste.

It seemed whenever I was uncomfortable with Zorn, I took refuge in abruptness. "I need to talk to you," I said, standing over her.

Slowly, arrogantly it seemed, she transferred her gaze to me. "Yes," she replied evenly. "As I said last night, you have things to consider."

Suddenly I wasn't standing over her but before her, an unsatisfactory servitor called to account. Anyway that's how it felt. To break that feeling, I stepped forward and sat down next to her. "It's not that," I protested. "There's something you don't know. One of Gwynedd's other clients…"

She interrupted me. "I spoke with Gwynedd this morning. Or rather, she spoke with me. About her other client. The representative of the insurgency's Provisional Authority, to be specific. For my part, I confirmed my intention to proceed with the commission for the sale of the insignia and I told her, I have no interest in the other business this house conducts. Nor in its other clients." She went back to surveying the pond.

I expelled some breath, a little too vigorously to be called a sigh. "Just as simple as that, is it?" Zorn didn't respond. I studied her profile. My scrutiny evidently caused her no self-consciousness whatever. I waited a moment. "And if it's not that simple for Lucian?"

"I leave that to Gwynedd," she said, as though the matter was scarcely worth consideration.

I wasn't going to allow her to dismiss my concerns so casually. I went directly to what she must know was preying on my mind. "You still carrying that knife?"

Instead of answering, Zorn leaned forward. She reached behind her and in one fluid movement drew the knife from under her jacket. There had been no hesitation, no catching of the knife in the cloth.

Considering that the fashion in the Exchanges favored an elegant jacket of almost tunic length, it was a pretty neat trick.

I glared at the knife which rested easily in her hand. "Going armed is hardly necessary here," I said tightly. Zorn didn't answer and she didn't change position. "And you must know, keeping that thing handy," I jabbed a finger at the knife, "is asking for trouble under these circumstances."

As smoothly as she had taken out the knife, Zorn put it away. Then she gave me her familiar, assessing stare. That look of detached observation that made me feel like a specimen under examination.

"Just what is it you fear, Grayall?" she said at last. "That I'll kill someone for insulting me."

"How am I supposed to know what you'll do after...?" I stopped myself.

A flicker of awareness gleamed in her eyes. "So that is what you fear." Her tone held a muted but unmistakable note of surprise. Maybe it held amusement as well.

The surprise I could live with, but the amusement angered me. "Shouldn't I?" My voice rose sharply.

"You think I do not know the difference between self-defense and self-indulgence?"

"And you're so sure you can always tell the difference, are you?"

"It only requires judgment and training."

"Yeah, I'll say one thing for you. You are well trained." My words were heavy with sarcasm.

Zorn responded as if the sarcasm had never existed. "Yes. I am. You have noted one of the more praise-worthy aspects of a traditional ariston upbringing. We are trained to act within the limits of our capabilities. And those of us who lack any particular stature or strength must acquire the skills necessary to compensate for those deficiencies."

Her persistent tone of superior detachment collided for me with the graphic image I could not get out of my mind. A knife in the throat, appearing so suddenly it might have burst from within rather than entered from the outside, and a shattered, astonished face closing in death. My emotions bubbled up and I burst out, "You traditional ariston, you're all just a bunch of cold-hearted bastards, aren't you?" I was on my feet, not even realizing I had risen. I turned to get away as quickly as possible, but Zorn reached up and grabbed my arm. Her grip was stronger than I expected.

"By any standards you know, yes, we are." She let her hand fall from my arm. "I owe you, Grayall, and I value your friendship, if that's what it is, but none of that changes who and what I am. I killed a predator who, given any chance, would have killed us. I am pleased I had the ability to do it. If it is cold-blooded to be content that you and I are alive and unharmed, and he is dead, then I will accept the label. Even from you. But do not mistake me for some undisciplined piece of rabble that cannot distinguish between the justifiable and the unconscionable. I will not accept that. Even from you." Through it all, her tone remained implacably neutral, as flat and cold as the words were not.

Without really intending to, I sat down again. Zorn's speech had drawn off my anger and left me feeling deflated. "I know you were right, to do it, to kill him. I know what the consequences would have been for me if you hadn't," I said shakily. "It's just…I don't know why I feel…I feel so revolted by it. And scared by it, too."

Zorn looked down and cocked her head to one side, apparently in contemplation. Finally she said, "Killing is a revolting act, no matter what the circumstances. As for your fear, I cannot alter that."

She considered me, the smooth composure of her face unbroken, and I couldn't tell whether my anxieties were relieved or not. The ambivalences Zorn stirred in me were deep and pervasive. I suspect she read my uncertainty in my face.

We sat in silence for a while. I thought about the degree of deliberate revelation she had just permitted herself, for that's what it had been. I had no doubt she had full control over every statement she had made. "I ask a lot of you, don't I?" I said eventually.

"You've earned the right to ask whatever you want of me. Not that I am necessarily capable of giving it."

I shook my head. "You've acquitted any claim you think I have on you in more ways than one. And you know it. Or should. As to my concerns, maybe you have convinced me. That you always know what you're doing."

"Now you overestimate me, Grayall." She stood up. "But if you have mastered your worries sufficiently to proceed with the sale of the insignia as we have arranged, Gwynedd would like to meet with us to discuss...business." She let the weight of her voice drop ironically on the last word.

I got up as well and with Zorn leading the way we headed back through the gardens toward the front of the house. But as we passed the stable, a loud, clear voice rang out, coming from the direction of the gate. "Gwynedd cannot expect me to stay in the same house with aristo shit like that." There was a sharp gasp of breath, but it came from me not from Zorn. The morning seemed to be progressing toward its inevitable conclusion.

CHAPTER TEN

More by instinct than by intent, my arm shot forward and I grasped Zorn's shoulder, trying to hold her back. She submitted long enough to glance at me. Her eyes glinted, but with what emotion I could not tell. Then she pulled free and kept walking. I followed close on her heels.

Standing before the gatekeeper's lodge were Evane and a young man who had evidently just arrived. He was gesturing with both hands in vigorous protest. Obviously he was Lucian.

Gwynedd's description of him had been correct. He was good looking. Of medium height, well-built without being overly muscled. His hair, halfway between brown and blonde, was an attractive old-gold color, a good match for his light brown eyes. His upraised hands were long and slender, graceful except for the last two fingers of his left hand. They jutted out at an awkward angle. As for intensity, his face was rigid with anger.

When Zorn and I came into view, he saw us immediately. Evane, who had her back to us, noticed his gaze and swung around to face us. She took a step, placing herself alongside him, and gripped his upper arm. I supposed it was a gesture of restraint, but it seemed oddly protective instead.

Even without Evane's reaction to guide him, Lucian had surely figured out who we were. I quickly moved in front of Zorn. If there'd been anyone around objective enough to appreciate it, it probably looked almost comic, so well did my movements mirror Evane's. I don't know what I expected. Maybe that Lucian would attack Zorn and she would retaliate. That I'd hear again that quiet swish of sound, and that he too would be dead with a knife in his throat.

I didn't really believe it would happen, not with any rational part of me, not after the conversation Zorn and I had just had. But something in me must have believed it, for in the moment we stood there, I felt sick, like I had when Zorn had killed the bandit, as if a second death had already occurred.

But nothing happened. Lucian, boiling with temper as far as I could tell, just stood there, staring at us. I couldn't see Zorn's face, but I could well picture it, remote and untouched by the other's hot anger.

And then Gwynedd appeared. She came hurrying over. I supposed she, too, had heard Lucian's voice. She stopped midway between our opposing camps. She glanced at each of us, undoubtedly taking the measure of the situation, and finally let her gaze settle on Zorn.

"Your Excellency of Northmarch. I was hoping to have our meeting now. If that is convenient for you." Gwynedd's tone was very formal, very courteous, yet some sense of demand lurked in it.

I kept watching Evane and Lucian. Gwynedd's exaggerated politeness to Zorn provoked him to look, if possible, angrier than ever and Evane's face was hard and set.

Zorn replied, "I have no other obligations. At present." Despite the levelness of her voice, she managed to make the last two words sound like a promise, or a threat, of future intentions.

"Let's go then," I added nervously, and needlessly, for Zorn had already started for the house.

Gwynedd lingered behind for a few words with Evane and Lucian. I didn't hear what she said to them.

Catching up with Zorn, I led the way to the side door and down the corridor to Gwynedd's office. The door was open. I just about threw myself into one of the big easy chairs that sat before Gwynedd's desk. I was surprised how shaky I felt. Only with the tension released did I realize how apprehensive I had been.

Zorn had walked over to a sidewall and was looking at the books shelved there. With her back to me, she said, "I thought perhaps I wouldn't kill him just yet."

I snapped forward in the chair. "That's not funny, Zorn."

"That depends on your point of view." She had taken a book down and was leafing through it.

"And what is your point of view? Your Excellency." It was Gwynedd who had come in quietly behind us, and she added Zorn's title like a conscious afterthought.

I wasn't pleased that she had overheard our exchange. "Don't encourage her, Gwynedd. Apparently Zorn enjoys watching other people be provoked. It enforces the contrast with that damnable ariston manner of hers."

Zorn replaced the book she had been examining, came over and sat in the other chair. "My point of view?" she said to Gwynedd, disregarding me completely. "That if I call to account everyone who despises me for having been a member of the ruling class of Regeren, I am likely to have a long and tedious work ahead of me."

Gwynedd came around and sat at her desk. "That sounds like a sensible and pragmatic approach. Although people in your situation have been known not always to be sensible and pragmatic."

Zorn gazed at her steadily. "Have you known many people in my situation?"

Gwynedd looked sheepish but she didn't give in completely. "Of course, I was only generalizing. Based on what one might expect. In the face of injury and the loss of one's entire way of life. Such things might overrule sense and practicality."

"They might. But they do not. As for protestations about my future behavior, those are pointless."

"Something about your past behavior might be in order," I said, under my breath.

"Grayall?" Gwynedd inquired.

"Never mind." I knew Zorn wasn't going to budge on explaining herself and I still wasn't ready to oppose her wishes on the matter. Even though Lucian's presence made it tempting to do so.

"I don't expect anyone to put up with insults under my roof," Gwynedd continued. "I will make that clear to Lucian."

"Just as you are now making it clear to me," Zorn said. "However, you will have less trouble with me than with your client from the Provisional Authority. But for all that, I cannot say you will have no trouble. I will not cause a disturbance in your house. I cannot state with equal assurance that I will not be a source of disturbance."

"A fine distinction you draw," Gwynedd said. Zorn just looked at her, so she went on, "In all fairness, I am in no position to dictate terms to you. You could go anywhere with the commission for your insignia. Sell them through any securer, any exchange. And set whatever terms you wanted. Grayall could still handle it."

"I will point out to you. The doubts in this matter are yours and Grayall's, not mine."

Gwynedd sighed. "All right, I'll not press you further. Now to our business."

She reached down, opened a desk drawer and took out three beautifully polished, flat wooden boxes. She set them on the desk, reached down again and brought out three smaller, square boxes. She slipped the catches on the boxes, opened them and turned them around to face us. They were lined with spotless cream-colored velvet. Distributed among them, the gold and onyx insignia, the torque with its pendant, the chain, the belt, the ring and two pins, all recently cleaned, looked magnificent nestled against the rich cloth.

If Zorn found her possessions impressive, she gave no indication, but Gwynedd's eyes shone with approval and appreciation. Leaning over to admire the insignia, I said, "Not bad merchandise."

Gwynedd shook her head at me. She turned the boxes back toward herself and stared at their contents. "They are splendid." She glanced over at Zorn. "You are sure you want to sell them?" She looked apologetic, as if the question had escaped her inadvertently. As with most questions she considered irrelevant, Zorn didn't bother to answer. "Well, yes, then, to proceed," Gwynedd said. She rang a call bell, and a clerk promptly appeared with documents and a witnessing seal. Zorn signed the authorization for Gwynedd's Securing House to guarantee and manage the sale of the insignia and I countersigned as agent. I also signed the statement of provenance and the attestation of Zorn's ownership. Gwynedd affixed the seals and the clerk went off with the documents and the insignia, all to be deposited in the safe.

Gwynedd confirmed the valuation I had put on the insignia, as a minimum. "As the first of their kind to come on the market, they will draw a lot of attention," she said. "Many will seek the prestige that will come with acquiring them."

"Want to make a side bet on whether they go to Arne or Carsten?" I said. I turned to Zorn. "Carsten specializes in fine metal work, gems. The insignia will suit him just fine."

"And the other?" she asked.

"Arne Bennetson?" He specializes in making sure Carsten doesn't forget who's really top dog. Arne's generally considered the most successful trader around here, the one with the widest ranging operation."

"A longstanding, friendly rivalry has its uses," Gwynedd added with quiet complacency.

"You really do expect the insignia to go higher than a thousand argen, don't you?" I asked.

"Let's just say the competition between Arne and Carsten shows no sign of slackening with the years."

"So what do you say to that bet? I'll take Arne."

Gwynedd laughed. "Grayall, you don't have enough left to gamble with."

"I'm due to receive a fee from an important commission. Soon. From a notable Securing House. Gwynedd's. You might have heard of it."

"Yes," Gwynedd acknowledged dryly. "Now, let's get the business done so you can collect it." She outlined to Zorn the usual procedure, that the insignia would be offered for sale at a bidding assembly which would draw the major traders and merchants. Before that took place, however, announcements needed to be sent out, applications to attend the bidding reviewed and approved, or rejected. As agent I would assist with those activities. Also the house had to be prepared for an onslaught of other guests. The evening before the bidding assembly, the bidders would gather at Gwynedd's for a reception. The most important of them would stay overnight.

"An event like this presents a good opportunity to show off status and influence," I explained to Zorn. "No one's going to let it go to waste."

Gwynedd nodded. "I will select a suitable date. I would estimate around three weeks from now should be about right. To complete the necessary arrangements and to allow enough time for interest to build. In the meantime," she said to Zorn, "my clerk has established a line of credit for you." And then to me, "I was thinking, Grayall, if neither of you are too worn from your travels, you might escort Zorn of Northmarch to Merchantplace this afternoon."

It was a reasonable suggestion. Zorn certainly needed to replenish her stock of goods. But I also figured Gwynedd would be happy to have us out of the house while she settled matters to her satisfaction with Evane and Lucian. Besides, the thought of accompanying Zorn on a shopping expedition held a certain perverse fascination. And of course I needed some things myself. "Resources for gambling aside, how does my account stand?" I asked Gwynedd.

"Depleted, but not exhausted. I'll have a statement drawn up for you."

"Well, your suggestion is all right with me. You feel up to it?" I said to Zorn.

"The proposed excursion does not sound strenuous."

The opening was too good to pass up. "You've never done much shopping, have you, Zorn?"

"No. I've had little opportunity to indulge in such commercial pastimes. And even less inclination. However," she paused like she was taking a weighty matter under consideration, "I submit myself to the demands of necessity." Satisfaction rippled in her voice like wind over water.

I should have known I wasn't going to get the final word.

CHAPTER ELEVEN

Before starting out for Merchantplace, Zorn and I went in to lunch. Whether because of or despite the morning's activities and anxieties, I was more than ready to do justice to Gwynedd's excellent kitchen. I ate roast lamb with mint sauce, creamed potatoes, vegetables which had been preserved from the summer gardens. For dessert, there was a lightly whipped confection of chocolate and cream. I gave serious attention to the meal.

Zorn evidently had a different notion of lavish dining. She took a slice of the lamb. Other than that her lunch consisted of cheese, some brown bread, and a couple of pieces of fruit. She consumed her food absent-mindedly as if she scarcely noticed, or cared, what she was eating. A gibing comment made it to the tip of my tongue, but I held it back. Still when I went for a second helping of the dessert, I couldn't resist asking her, "You want some of this?" She declined without paying any attention, I think, to what I was offering her.

We lingered over our coffee. My lunch, at least, needed to settle awhile. But we set out at last. Gwynedd had ordered two of her good saddle horses readied for us. Well-dressed and elegantly mounted, we rode out of the gate looking nothing like the ragtag pair that had ridden in yesterday. The gatekeeper stared at us, almost, it seemed to me, resenting the transformation.

Merchantplace was just over a mile from Gwynedd's, along the main road that paralleled the river which was mostly out of sight, hidden behind the impressive gates and facades of the various exchanges, securing houses, and other enterprises. There hadn't been much of a view of them in the pouring rain yesterday, but now the afternoon sun had overcome the few lingering clouds of the morning. It shone warmly on stone and brickwork and glinted off windows. It all seemed familiar to me and welcoming, finally.

We traveled along the first part of the road fairly peacefully. The noise and confusion of deliveries took place mostly on the river. But there were walkers and other riders going about their business. I didn't see anyone I knew, but some of the passersby, I guessed, recognized Gwynedd's horses and I also guessed that a trail of whispers followed us. Looks like new clients at Gwynedd's, the whispers would say. Information, or at least speculation, had always flowed through the Exchanges like a second river.

We soon reached the much livelier bustle of Merchantplace. It occupied a courtyard that opened off the street on the river side. Across the back and along both sides, the permanent and more prosperous merchants had their establishments. Along the front gate and spilling over into the road were the stalls and tents of the transient dealers.

As we turned toward the gate, a chorus of calls went up, trying to attract our attention to the wares laid out before us. Many of the gateway merchants employed youngsters to woo purchasers and a small group of them appeared beside us. "New goods, just arrived, from the coast. Come see. Come see." They jostled each other, each of them trying to get closest.

"Leave us be," I said firmly, but not too harshly. Gwynedd had given me some money before we left and I flipped a few coins to them. The youngsters stopped pestering us to chase the coins and we rode into the courtyard where business was conducted more sedately.

To my surprise, the noise and confusion at the gate had disconcerted me somewhat. The price, I supposed, of having journeyed too long in less populated places. I glanced at Zorn to see how she was reacting to things. She rode next to me in silence, observant of her surroundings but certainly not unsettled by them.

Once inside the courtyard, I led the way to a corner establishment. It was a clothier's shop my family had traded with for years. Two grooms appeared at our horses' heads before we even dismounted.

"I thought we'd start here," I said to Zorn.

As we stepped through the door, the proprietor came rushing to meet us. His name was Denon. He was younger than my parents' generation, having taken over the running of the business from his father.

"Grayall of Wellworth," he said, stretching out his hand. "We had word from Gwynedd this morning about your arrival. It is good to see you back in the Exchanges." He made a little formal bow toward Zorn. "And Your Excellency of Northmarch. An honor." I could tell Denon knew that, in Zorn, he had before him a customer with an excellent line of credit, backed by Gwynedd's Securing House.

She received his greeting with an unresponsive stare and Denon seemed flustered for a moment, probably wondering whether some other ceremony was appropriate. But he only bowed again and, inviting us to accompany him, led the way into one of his private customer rooms.

As we followed him, I came up behind Zorn and said into her ear, "Just don't forget, that's your line of credit talking, not your ariston status."

Naturally she ignored that.

We were soon pretty well surrounded with bolts of cloth and assistants taking measurements. Denon insisted on re-doing mine, since it had been so long. "You're too thin, Grayall. All this traveling so far afield is not good for the health." I thought his eyes widened when he noticed the scars on Zorn's hands and wrists, but he didn't say anything. The scar on her forehead, pretty well hidden behind her hair, I don't think he even noticed.

Denon and his people worked quickly and efficiently, writing up our orders. Zorn's included everything, outer and inner wear and accessories. But at least she could afford it. For myself, I planned to add a few things to the meager store of belongings I had left at Gwynedd's, but I had to do some selecting between need and want. As I watched the costs accumulate, I became increasingly grateful for the gift of new clothing Gwynedd had given me.

When we finished, Denon assured us, or rather particularly assured Zorn, since most of his attention was directed at her, that part of our orders would be delivered to Gwynedd's within a day or two with the rest to follow as soon as could be. When this failed to win any show of approval from her, he looked at me. "That's fine," I said. "We do appreciate it."

As Denon's assistants carried out the bolts of cloth, I noticed that the materials Zorn had selected for her jackets and trousers consisted of a dark slate gray, a muted silver gray, and black. On top of the pile was a bolt of good broadcloth, undoubtedly intended for shirts. That too was gray, a pale, still lighter shade of silver.

I noted the stack of cloth, all of the finest quality but all unremittingly somber, and felt annoyed. Denon had shown me a beautiful jacket, rich blue in color, somewhere between turquoise and royal. It was almost finished and easily alterable to my measurements. I wanted it. I found myself hungrier for finery that I had expected. But tempted or not, I knew I couldn't afford it. And here was Zorn who could buy what she wanted, settling for unrelenting gray and black. "Don't you know any other colors?" I gestured to the bolts of cloth. "Or should I say, any colors at all."

Zorn looked pointedly at the blue jacket, with its brilliant hue, still hanging over my arm. "I will wear them, Grayall, not you."

"That's a favor, anyway," I responded, laying aside the jacket.

When we finished at Denon's, I led the way to the bootmakers. It was only a short walk down the row of shops, so we left our horses. The shop had a new proprietor but we were greeted with an enthusiasm pretty much equal to Denon's. Here, too, word of who we were had obviously preceded us.

Zorn ordered two pair of fine leather boots, black of course. She also ordered a pair of boots sturdy enough for hard work or hard travel. They were to be of roughed-out medium brown leather. I fingered the sample as the clerk wrote up the orders. "You sure you want to be this adventurous?" I said to Zorn.

She gazed at me blankly, so I tossed the leather sample to her. "I mean...they're brown."

"Perhaps you'd like those in window, to match that jacket you were admiring."

I looked in the direction she indicated. Sure enough, the bootmakers had made up a display pair of boots to showcase their craft. These had been fashioned in bright blue leather and were intricately carved. As examples of leather work they were spectacular, but they were as ugly as they were gaudy. I doubted it was intended anyone would seriously consider wearing them.

"They're the wrong shade," I said sarcastically.

The clerk, who had been busy with the orders, evidently picked up our conversation just at that moment. Hastily she assured me that the boots could be done in any color I wished.

"Well?" Zorn said, amusement clear in her voice if not in her face.

"I concede. You've won this one."

Zorn nodded, the slightest move of her head. "Just so you admit it." She signed the orders the clerk had prepared for her.

"Will that be all that is required then?" the clerk asked, glancing between the two of us and sounding a little bewildered.

"Yes, I think we're quite done here, thank you," I said.

But we didn't make it to the door because we were stopped by a bluff, noisy voice raised in greeting. It was Arne. "Grayall, Grayall, glad to have tracked you down. Saw your horses at Denon's and they said they thought you'd come here." With a dignified bow, he turned to Zorn. "An honor again, Your Excellency."

Arne was at his most ingratiating, but Zorn received his courtesy, as she had that of the two shopkeepers, without acknowledgment. I could never tell whether she took it all as her due or couldn't care less. Still I was irritated by the deference shown to her. Which only shows consistency isn't my strong suit since I had been equally displeased with Lucian's insults.

"What do you mean, tracked us down?" I said to Arne.

He pulled his attention back to me. "Just that. Wanted to tell you. I did some checking this morning. Thought I'd remembered something. I was right. Patric is here. In the Exchanges. He's doing some contract work for a new trading operation. Rellards. I was pretty sure Gwynedd wasn't aware."

"No. She would have said." Arne's news surprised me. Patric was Jarrell's older brother. Last I heard, he had been doing some trading in the south, in the Old Tradelands. I hadn't expected him to turn up here.

"Thought you'd want to know," Arne said.

"Yeah. Sure." My mind had shifted suddenly to the unenviable task of bringing Patric the news of Jarrell's death. He had bitterly opposed Jarrell's decision to join the insurgency and they had quarreled vehemently over it. He had also let me know in no uncertain terms that I should have used my influence more forcefully to dissuade Jarrell.

"If there's anything I can do to help?" Arne said, his voice trailing into a question. He looked expectantly at Zorn.

I started to decline, but Zorn interrupted me. "Patric. Who is he?" I told her, without details. "Then you can be of assistance," she said to Arne. And against my expectation, she agreed to have him accompany her as she completed her provisioning. "You have other things to attend to, Grayall."

Arne was so completely pleased with these arrangements I suspected he'd planned this outcome all along. It was like him to dovetail a favor with some particular end he had in mind for himself. But I didn't fault him for that.

He volunteered to go back for my horse and when he was out of earshot I said to Zorn, "He's probably going to try to find out why you're here in the Exchanges."

"That had occurred to me. Should I tell him?"

"Word about the sale will be out soon. So you may as well, if he asks. Just don't let him inveigle any advantage for himself. Relative to the bidding, I mean."

"I fail to see what advantage he could gain. But don't be concerned. On any matters pertaining to business, I will refer him to you, Grayall. After all, you are my agent." She had assumed a drawling, dismissive tone.

Listening to her, I got the feeling she wasn't taking the commercial end of things as seriously as her situation warranted, that she still didn't fully grasp what having money meant in the Exchanges. Even more importantly, what *not* having it meant. My earlier irritation surfaced and

I said, "There wouldn't be all this bowing and scraping and 'Your Excellency-ing' if you'd come here penniless, you know."

"You've already reminded me of that once today. And you seem to overlook, if I'd been penniless, I might not have come here."

Arne's return with my horse left me no room for further comment. I mounted and headed for Rellards which Arne said was about a mile farther along from Merchantplace, down a side street. Arne, appearing very much the courtier, walked off with Zorn.

Chapter Twelve

Rellards turned out to be a middling enterprise, one of the many that straggled along the streets in the less prestigious section of the Exchanges. I went in, inquired and was directed to a room, more cubbyhole than office. Shelves full of heavy ledger and record books made it seem even more claustrophobic. There was, at least, a small window, which revealed the motes of dust that eddied in a shaft of sunlight.

Patric sat at a table working on accounts. He glanced up as I came in. A straight-backed chair stood just inside the door. I carried it the two or three steps to his table. I put it down across from him and sat.

He had started to get up but re-seated himself when I did.

There was a lot of Jarrell's look in Patric's face. It wasn't so much that they actually resembled each other. It was more the turn of expression they shared, the way some people might share a turn of phrase.

But any apparent similarity between them was misleading because they were really quite different. I had loved Jarrell, had felt for him whatever I understood by that word. Patric, I wasn't even sure I liked.

Sitting there and faced with saying what I had come to say, I could find no way to begin that didn't seem too abrupt. Patric didn't wait for me, however. Without any other greeting, he asked, "Is he dead?"

"Yes," I said hollowly. "About two months back from what I've been told. In a skirmish between the insurgents and the loyalist forces. One of the last, as I understand."

Patric looked down. He seemed to be trying to remember where he had put something. He set his left hand on the accounts he had been working on. As if he had lost control of it, his hand slid across the papers, scattering the top few sheets. His right hand still grasped the pencil he had been using. He clenched it in his fist, his thumb stiffly extended along its length. When he looked up at me, his face was set in hard lines of anger. His chest rose and fell heavily as if the air around him resisted each breath.

"Stupid." He hurled out the word. "And I told him. Told him. And he gets himself killed. For nothing." Patric seemed aware of what he was clutching in his hand and he dropped the pencil. "Incredibly stupid," he said again, more calmly. Then he stood up abruptly and turned away to face the window. "I told him, you know," he said with his back to me, "if he held to this decision I would never go after him."

Out of the deep well of my grief and frustration, some of my own anger seeped but I spoke quietly. "What I know is that Jarrell never expected any such thing. Never wanted anyone else involved in what he took on himself when he went to join the insurgents."

Patric swung around, rested his hands atop the back of his chair and leaned forward. "Never wanted anyone else involved. Don't you be stupid too, Grayall. You, me. Tell me we're not involved."

"I can't argue with you, Patric. It's too hard for me." I could feel the unwelcome catch in my voice. "Maybe I should have tried anything to stop him. But I couldn't do that."

Patric came back and sat down again. He straightened the papers he had disarranged, then picked up the pencil that had rolled away and set it carefully beside them. With an obvious effort at regaining his composure, he said, "I do appreciate you bringing me this news. Only…" He took a breath as though he still needed to steady himself. "Don't think I don't realize, I should have gone with you. Or gone in your place. I do know that."

I shook my head. "Going to find out about Jarrell. That was something I had to do. You couldn't have stopped me anymore than either of us could have stopped him. As for going with me, that would have been pointless."

Patric gave a scoffing chuckle. "You're just as stubborn as he was." Then he looked straight at me. With absolute seriousness, he said,

"Despite some of the things I told you before, I don't blame you. It was Jarrell's stupidity, not yours. Further argument with him wouldn't have helped."

I decided to let that pass. The weapon I could have used, but didn't, would not have been an argument. It would have been my relationship with Jarrell itself. If you love me, don't go. The one thing I never said. I was just as glad it didn't seem to occur to Patric.

We sat in silence for a while, each taken with our own thoughts, I guess. Finally in what seemed a deliberate attempt to move on to less emotionally charged topics, Patric asked, "When did you get back?"

"Yesterday. I spent some time in Arandell on the way. With Traina."

He nodded absently. "How did you know I was here?"

"Arne told me."

He nodded again. "Bennetson. Never misses much, does he?"

"Some things never change," I said. "Arne's one of them."

"Are you staying at Gwynedd's?"

"Yes."

"That's good. I probably should have stopped in by now, but I didn't want to seem..." Instead of finishing he gazed around the cramped, shabby room. "But I assume business will get me there. Eventually."

I understood the awkwardness he felt. As close as I was to Gwynedd, even for me it had felt a lot better coming back bringing a good commission rather than empty-handed. Even if that good commission was tied to another unpleasant piece of news I had to deliver to Patric.

"There's something else I should tell you," I said. The tone of my voice caught his attention. "I have a client. I met her on the road." Patric seemed genuinely surprised and I started to explain. "It wasn't anything I expected, nothing I was looking for..."

He anticipated me. "You don't have to make excuses about engaging in business in this situation. Certainly not to me. I give you credit." He watched my reaction. "I mean that, Grayall. You really didn't expect I'd consider it callous, did you? In times like these we do what we must and we take our opportunities as they come to us. I'm just surprised you were able to be that sensible."

This time I didn't wait to consider the problem of delivering my news too abruptly. I just plunged in. "My client is Zorn of the Alphaen Order of Northmarch. She was the Warder of Farnorth."

For a long moment, Patric stared at me. Then he whispered, "An aristo. A traditional aristo." He drew the words out into a long rasp of sound. I couldn't tell whether he was shocked, or angry, or disbelieving.

Defensively I blurted out, "Farnorth. That's a long way from where Jarrell died."

But Patric paid no mind to my attempt at justification. Instead he laughed, a harsh barking sound that carried no true mirth. "You!" The word burst out explosively. "Working for one of them."

"Look, Patric…" I began, but his laughter increased and he waved me to silence. I felt uncomfortable and increasingly angry.

When his laughter had subsided to a ripple in his voice, Patric asked, "And what are you doing for Her Excellency, the Warder of Farnorth?"

"Zorn isn't the Warder of Farnorth," I said sharply. "Not anymore."

"Of course not. My mistake. Jarrell and his insurgent friends took care of that, didn't they? So it's just plain Zorn, is it? Just another trading client." Unable to contain himself, he broke into laughter again. It still was not a happy sound.

I sat there, not knowing what to do and feeling the hot blush of anger and embarrassment on my face.

Patric must have read my expression because he finally mastered himself. "No. No. Grayall. I'm sorry. It's just, after you and Jarrell always being so self-righteous about our families' dealings with the Realm, it is funny. You have to admit that."

"I don't find it so," I said from a tight throat.

"OK. OK. I said, I'm sorry. Anyway answer my question. What are you doing for your…client?" If he'd laughed again, I think I would have walked out on him, but he didn't.

I explained as briefly as I could about acting as agent for the sale of the insignia. I left the impression that Zorn and I had met at Arandell and I didn't say anything about the actual circumstances under which I had found her. Every time I was faced with that, I found myself more reluctant to talk about it. Whether by now I was protecting Zorn's privacy or my own, I wasn't quite sure.

Patric listened intently, his mood of bleak amusement apparently broken, replaced by his interest in the insignia. It seemed no one in the Exchanges was going to prove immune to their allure.

"When will the bidding take place?" he asked when I finished.

"Gwynedd's arranging it. It'll be about three weeks."

"I don't think you'll like me better for it, Grayall, but I still approve. Aristo or no aristo, and despite what happened to Jarrell, it seems to me you've done the right thing. The Realm has cost you…us…quite a bit. We may as well get something back from it, if we can." He paused. "As you said, Jarrell died a long way from Farnorth." His eyes narrowed. "And it wasn't murder, after all. It was a battle."

The pragmatism of his response left me almost as uncomfortable as his previous burst of mocking laughter and I couldn't think of anything else to say. Ours had not been a conversation to finish with idle small talk. Besides Patric had to get back to his work. We left each other with mutual assurances that we would meet for lunch or dinner soon. Although, in honesty, I mostly wished that it would be awhile before I'd have to see Patric again.

CHAPTER THIRTEEN

When I got back to Gwynedd's, I went straight up to our rooms. There was no sign of Zorn, and I was glad for the solitude. My meeting with Patric had taken its toll. I went into my bedroom and lay down.

I found that my eyes kept filling. I didn't sob, it wasn't even really crying. I just couldn't stop the tears from welling up and overflowing. Damn Patric, I thought, and then tried to tamp down my anger and frustration. After all, it wasn't his fault I had to be the one to tell him about Jarrell. And thus stir up feelings over his loss that I had been suppressing.

When I'd returned, it had been well after four, the western sun had been slanting past the windows of my room. I don't know how long I lay there, the captive of my own futile tears. I must have dozed eventually because, when I finally heard a small bustle in the adjoining sitting room, my room was dim enough to call for a light. But I didn't get up. I didn't bother. I could still feel where the last of my tears had dried on my face.

Shortly, there was silence in the other room again. I kept telling myself I should muster some energy, but I didn't seem able to find any. After a while my door opened and I could see Zorn silhouetted against the light from the sitting room. That was unexpected because she was usually scrupulous about knocking if my door was closed. Without saying anything, she came in. She set a mug on my bedside table.

"I don't want anything," I said.

"That's up to you. It's coffee."

She lit the lamp, then turned and sat on a chair that stood against the wall. Curls of steam rose from the mug, the coffee smelled good, and my throat *was* dry. I elbowed myself into a sitting position, picked up the mug and sipped from it.

Zorn sat watching me, no, studying me. "Did you want something?" I demanded irritably.

"Your encounter with the brother was difficult." It was a flat observation. Nothing in Zorn's voice turned it into a question.

"You realize how often you don't answer what you've been asked? But yes, talking to Patric was difficult." I drank some more coffee. Zorn kept silent, leaving me room to talk if I wanted and I guess I did. "Too much guilt all around," I said. "Both of us feeling we should have found a way to stop Jarrell. And maybe trying not to blame each other. Patric defensive because he didn't go to find out what happened to his brother."

"As you did."

I shrugged. "Jarrell and Patric had at least one trait in common. They both knew how to dig in their heels. They fought bitterly over Jarrell's decision to join the insurgency. Patric swore he'd have nothing to do with it. And he kept his word."

"Having done so, he must live with the consequences. Just as you must live with the consequences of your decisions."

Zorn had only expressed what somewhere inside I had been thinking myself, but from her the thought seemed too absolute, unmixed with any emotional uncertainty. I shook my head. "You'd make a terrifying judge, Zorn."

"You think realism and compassion are incompatible?"

What seemed incompatible with compassion was the remote calm of Zorn's face. Yet her presence, and this conversation, came out of sympathy for me, I supposed. I drew myself more upright. "With regard to *my* decisions, Patric did have a few choice comments about me taking you on as a client."

"None you did not anticipate, I assume."

"He ended up deciding he approved. The business being too good to pass up. And Jarrell having been killed in what Patric seemed to consider a fair fight."

Zorn gave the slightest twist of a smile. "Those opinions should please you. But I surmise they do not."

"They're just so typically Patric." I vented my frustration with a long sigh. Then I said, abruptly, "Tell me something. The dissolution of the Realm. How do you really feel about it?"

The sudden shift of my question surprised Zorn, I think, but she was always quick. "It is done. We must live with the consequences." I was sure she had deliberately echoed her previous words.

I sipped my coffee, thinking I should have known better than to ask her to talk about herself. She might give such information at times, but only at her own choice.

But then she added, "However, I will answer your question by telling you what I think." She let her voice linger on the last word. "The dissolution of Regeren was due. Overdue, in fact."

With that, Zorn got up and walked out. But soon one of the household attendants came in with a tray of food. There was a warm damp towel too. If Zorn had asked me about eating, I would have said I wasn't hungry, but I was. I wiped my face and ate.

When I finished, I walked into our sitting room. Zorn wasn't there, nor in her room, the door to which was open. A flat leather case and an assortment of clothing, neatly folded, lay on her bed. Not the custom-tailored dress clothes I had watched her order at Denon's but sturdy ready-made garments. Trousers in the dark-blue twilled cloth known as denim, flannel shirts, neckerchiefs, and a sheepskin vest. A stack of similar clothing had been placed on one of the chairs in the sitting room. Atop it was a label. Deliver to Grayall of Wellworth. Draped across the back of the chair was the rich-blue dress jacket I had admired.

As I was standing there, Zorn came in. Laying my hand on the durable clothing, I asked, "What's all this?"

"Provision for the future."

"What's that supposed to mean?"

"It means, perhaps neither of us will remain in the Exchanges indefinitely."

I thought about the implications of her comment, then said, "I don't know. I may need to seek trading employment somewhere else but there's no reason you can't stay here. You could live in the Exchanges quite comfortably."

Zorn walked over, picked up the dress jacket, and handed it to me. "More precisely, I could afford to live here. Try this on."

The minor alterations the jacket required had been done and it fit me well. I looked down at it, then gestured to the other clothing. "You didn't have to do any of this." It was the usual lame response to an unexpected gift.

"There is not much I am required to do. In the present circumstances."

"In the present circumstances?" I repeated in mock protest. "I should think that's the story of your life. Doing what you want."

"That opinion, Grayall, reflects your considerable ignorance of Regeren and its customs. At least, in the Marches." With that pronouncement, Zorn went off to her room. Through the open door, I watched as she transferred the clothing there from the bed to a wardrobe. When she had finished, she picked up the flat case and walked over to the cabinet where she had stowed the bandit's rifle.

"Is that another purchase?" I asked from the doorway. I had a pretty good idea what it might be. "Is that part of the reason you were so willing to go off with Arne Bennetson today? Without having me around."

I came up beside her and she handed me the case. Inside was a new revolver. I'm no great expert, but it looked to be of fine quality, more impressive certainly than the weapon the insurgents had given me. And like all well-made guns, it looked both elegant and deadly.

Returning the case to her, I said, "You planning to wear this to dinner? To go with that knife you insist on carrying."

"Only if the company requires it." She put the gun away in the cabinet.

One of the problems with Zorn's teasing was that her tone of voice rarely varied, so it was hard to be sure when she was needling me. But I was getting more perceptive about it. "You know that's still a sore point with me to joke about."

"I believe you normally take the initiative in what passes for humor between us."

I smiled in concession. "OK, you're right about that. I started it."

We had come back to the sitting room. Zorn sat in one of the easy chairs. I pushed a hassock over to her, so she could ease her knee. I took the rest of the clothing she had purchased for me into my room and took off the blue jacket. I came back and sat in the other chair.

"I haven't thanked you. And I don't mean to be ungracious but...the dress jacket, the other clothing, well, you certainly don't owe me anything, any repayment."

"If you don't mean to be ungracious, don't be. As for thinking in terms of payment and repayment, that is a characteristic of your upbringing. Just as a preoccupation with readiness is a characteristic of mine."

I leaned back and gave an exaggerated sigh. "I'll say one thing for your company, Zorn. It certainly takes one's mind off other concerns."

Zorn stretched her leg across the hassock. Lazily she said, "To be of use is always gratifying."

CHAPTER FOURTEEN

In the ensuing days, notification that Gwynedd's Securing House would be offering for sale insignia from the Alphaen Order of Northmarch caused a suitable stir. Gwynedd had set the bidding for the last Friday of the month, which meant we had two and half weeks to get through. But either I'd exhausted my store of worry or I was lulled by the quiet that followed on that first encounter with Lucian because I actually started to relax.

In fact once Zorn's commission had been made official, I was free of immediate decisions and glad to be so. Gwynedd must have sensed my mood because she said to me, "Take your time, Grayall. You have nothing to rush for. Stay here, if you want. Even after the bidding." Still, despite her kindness I knew I'd have to face up to the future sometime soon. But for now, I took her advice and let my days shape themselves without much worry or planning.

Normally I would have spent some time with Evane, but given the way things stood between us, that was impossible. She avoided me. When we did meet, she was stiff, unforgiving, and she rebuffed any attempts at conversation. Lucian, I learned from Gwynedd, had at first insisted on leaving the house, but was eventually persuaded to put his mission before his angered pride. And fortunately, arranging his grain purchases and trying to locate suitable messenger birds kept him out of the way most of the time.

Gwynedd did make one concession to him. She found quarters for him in the opposite wing of the house, so the chances for unpleasant meetings were considerably lessened. And meals, which might have been a problem, were spared by the customs of the house. But although

I saw little of either Evane or Lucian, I was always aware of their presence, like a bitter core at the center of the household's activity.

The closest thing I had to a routine was joining Gwynedd for coffee and talk when she took her mid-morning break. Mostly we went over the preparations for the bidding assembly, although Gwynedd hardly overtaxed me in my role as agent. After the weeks of traveling, I enjoyed the long, leisurely mornings. I broke them occasionally to go riding with Zorn, who went out regularly every day.

Zorn, of course, organized her time differently. After an early breakfast, she disappeared into the library. By mid-morning, she was out riding. The afternoons she devoted to additional active pastimes. Especially in the first few days, she familiarized herself with the Exchanges. Her apparent detachment masked an acute facility for observation, as I discovered when I occasionally accompanied her and found out how quickly she had mastered this new environment. Within a short time, she seemed to know every major building and most of the enterprises in the surrounding area. She even corrected me about a couple of changes that had occurred since I had last been in the Exchanges.

I had no problem with Zorn's explorations, it was her other activities that disturbed me. Every afternoon, she took the gun she had purchased and went off by herself for what I assumed was target practice. At any rate, she went through a good bit of ammunition. For all I knew, she practiced advanced knife throwing, too.

I wasn't happy about any of it, but I had given up, for the time being, on further protests about Zorn's weapons and her proficiencies with them. Partly because Gwynedd hadn't raised any objections. When Zorn inquired of her about a suitable place to shoot, Gwynedd took her request calmly enough, seeming to treat it as the pursuit of a hobby. But I was convinced none of this was recreation with Zorn. It was deadly earnest. Maybe she was only trying to purge the demons of vulnerability that being left for dead had stirred in her. But I suspected it all went deeper than that. That maintaining her expertise with weapons was necessary to her sense of herself, her sense of, what was the word she had used, readiness. Well, I had seen an example of her readiness, and I didn't want any more demonstrations.

As for the rest of her activities, the only thing I could observe that passed for relaxation with Zorn was her appropriation of the spot by the pond she had visited on our first day at Gwynedd's. She fell into the habit of wandering off there in the late afternoon and, if I wanted her, I could usually find her there, sitting on the pile of logs. Despite its eccentricity, it seemed a fitting place for Zorn to take her rest rather than somewhere more sensibly comfortable. And it was an attractive spot, even if more homely than beautiful.

So to my content, initially the days passed quietly. Or so I thought. But an undercurrent of trouble was beginning its course. And it flowed, as I had feared all along, to Zorn.

The first ripple in the current didn't register on me at all. Zorn and I had gone out one afternoon. I had some copy to drop off at the printers for the announcements about the bidding assembly. After that we proceeded on one of our tours of the Exchanges. We got back fairly late in the day and the gatekeeper didn't appear, so we rode straight down to the stable without waiting for anyone to come and take our horses. Since no one was immediately to hand, we untacked the horses ourselves. I had already noticed something about Zorn, and it surprised me somewhat. She didn't seem overly fond of being waited on hand and foot, nor to expect it.

We had brought the horses back cool, which was another thing Zorn was careful about, so we led them to their stalls. Zorn's horse was stabled at the end of a row, past an opening to the loft. As she walked back up the stable aisle, I caught a blur of movement over her head. "Watch out," I cried, just as a bale of good heavy green hay fell through the opening. Fortunately Zorn reacted to the motion above her even before my warning and twisted out of the way. The bale grazed her shoulder and knocked her off balance a couple of steps, but that was all.

I shouted up to the opening. "You want to kill somebody!" But no apologetic head appeared. I climbed the ladder that was fixed to the wall until I could see into the loft, but no one was there. Three more bales remained piled at the edge of the opening, one precariously balanced on top of the other two. I climbed up the rest of the way and pushed the top bale back so it wouldn't fall as well. "Dumb thing to do, leaving them stacked that way," I said to Zorn as I came down the ladder. "You all right?"

She nodded and then belatedly someone came hurrying up. It was the stable manager who, noticing us and the fallen hay bale, demanded anxiously, "Has something happened?"

"Yeah. Zorn almost caught a hundred pounds of hay on her back." I pointed toward the loft. "Stack them like that, it's not surprising."

The stable manager looked exasperated. "I'm sorry. One of the horses got out and we were in a bit of a fuss. Still it's no excuse. Are you…?" she started to ask Zorn.

"It missed," Zorn said offhandedly, but I noticed she glanced up at the opening to the loft.

As we walked out, I said, "It didn't miss. You ducked."

"At least my reflexes are quicker than your alarms."

Behind us I could hear the stable manager chewing out one of the grooms who was futilely protesting that he hadn't piled the bales carelessly when he obviously had. As I looked back at them, I even felt a little sorry for the groom because Haslen showed up in the middle of the reprimand. Accumulating bad marks in front of the house chamberlain was not recommended.

Chapter Fifteen

I t was a couple of days later when something else happened to Zorn. I was in the dining room, dawdling over some coffee, trying to make headway with a letter to my brother Karel. I planned to send it with a trading party leaving at the end of the week for the New Tradelands. But my attention kept straying to a commitment I had made with Patric to finally get together with him again.

Shortly after my visit to him at Rellards, he had stopped at Gwynedd's on business for his employer, and then he had come by a couple of times after that. He had asked me more than once to have lunch or dinner with him, but I kept putting him off. But, on his last visit, it was the day Zorn almost got leveled by the hay bale, he'd pressed me to join him for lunch on this afternoon. I'd run out of excuses so I'd agreed. But I wasn't looking forward to it.

I had just picked up my pen to return to my letter when one of the house attendants popped his head in, searching for Haslen. One of the youngsters who assisted at the gate had brought a message. Someone had found a horse wandering riderless, recognized it as belonging to Gwynedd's, and brought it back. Only no one at the lodge knew where the gatekeeper was so they thought they'd better report it directly to the chamberlain.

Hastily I pushed aside my writing materials. Leaving the attendant to continue his hunt for Haslen, I ran out. Under the portico just inside the gate, I found Gwynedd and Evane, standing next to a tall bay with a nervous eye that I knew Zorn was in the habit of riding as a change from her roan. Gwynedd clucked disparagingly. "I've told Zorn not to bother with this one. He's so skittish," she said. "I'll get some help." She headed off toward the stable. Evane was holding the horse. It was the first time we'd been alone in each other's company since the evening Zorn and I had arrived.

I walked up to the bay. The sweat had dried on him, but it was obvious he had run hard. And probably through a thicket or something because he had scratches on his chest and front legs. His head drooped but he still managed to show a crescent of white at his eyes.

Evane stroked his neck and gave him a litany of reassurance. "Easy, boy, easy. It's all right." Preferable to speaking to me, I supposed, but the horse looked unconvinced. He sidled away as I drew alongside, and Evane steadied him. There was dirt on the saddle and across the cantle was a fresh gash.

"I think this horse has fallen," I said.

Evane flashed me a look. "Eager's a good horse." She continued to stroke his neck. "He just needs skillful riding." Her tone was caustic.

"Zorn's one of the best riders I've ever seen," I retorted. "And you don't have a horse in your stable as uncooperative as that roan she came in on." The tension between Evane and me seemed waiting to spark.

Fortunately Gwynedd reappeared and interrupted us. With her was one of the grooms, mounted and leading a horse. Gwynedd was leading two others. "I assume you know the most likely places, Grayall," she said, handing me the reins of one of the horses. She turned to Evane. "I have things I cannot leave right now. Will you go?"

For answer Evane silently handed the bay over to her mother and took the other horse from her. We both mounted and, with the groom still leading the spare horse, we all set out.

There were a couple of bridle paths that Zorn rode most often. To check first, I chose one that followed a circuit through a strip of woodland. It was covered with a layer of tanbark and its footing allowed for a good run. Zorn favored it. I sent Evane along it from one direction while the groom and I headed off the other way. If we didn't find Zorn, we'd meet in the middle and try elsewhere. But the groom and I found her. She was walking along the edge of the tanbark about a half mile in. She was limping slightly, but otherwise apparently uninjured. I dismounted and hurried to her.

Before I could ask her anything, she said, "If you're going to fall, pick soft ground."

"Only you didn't fall."

She shook her head. "No. The horse went down."

"Luckily not on top of you."

"Luckily," she repeated, with a distinct note of sarcasm.

Seeing that Zorn was unhurt, I took the extra horse from the groom and sent him off to intercept Evane. In a few minutes, they joined us.

Evane looked at Zorn and me disdainfully. "I'll ride ahead. Tell mother all the worry was for nothing." She didn't wait for a response, nor for that matter to see if she was right. The groom gave me a questioning glance. I nodded at him to follow her.

Gazing after Evane, I said, "Nothing if not gracious." Zorn mounted the spare horse, a bit laboriously for her, I thought. "You sure you're all right?" I asked.

"I had the breath knocked out of me, that's all."

Slowly we rode back to Gwynedd's. When we arrived at the house, Zorn went directly to the stable. She sought out the bay, checked him over, and ran her hands down his legs. She looked like she knew what she was doing. Seeing her, the stable manager came over and assured her the horse was fine. "No heat, no swelling, no lameness," the manager said. "A few scratches where he ran through some brambles, but that's all."

Evidently not satisfied, Zorn began picking up each of the horse's feet in turn. The stable manager peered over her shoulder as she examined the bottom of each hoof. The two of them might have been physicians consulting on a patient. When Zorn had set down the last foot, the stable manager said, "Shoes look all right. He just tripped and fell. It happens."

Zorn made a sound in her throat which might have been agreement but, from the faint crease of frown I saw in her face, I thought she was not happy with the diagnosis.

We were almost back to the house when Zorn murmured, "Something brought that horse down."

Startled, I blurted out, "Brought him down? What are you saying?"

But just then, Gwynedd came out of the house. She hastened to meet us, a concerned look on her face. Before she could make the inevitable inquiry, Zorn disposed of it. "The horse is not injured, nor am I."

Gwynedd seemed about to say something but I spoke first. "This business of the horse falling, Zorn thinks…"

Zorn cut me off. "I think I will clean up and reserve conversation for later." Without waiting for anything further from either of us, she continued through the door and headed up the stairs.

Gwynedd stared after her. "She never leaves much room for discussion, does she?"

I shrugged. "I see you've noticed. Zorn's great at the 'Her Excellency has spoken' routine."

Only this time I knew Zorn's abruptness had been purposeful. Clearly something was bothering her about the fall the horse had taken. Just as clearly, she had warned me off of saying anything about it in front of Gwynedd. I wanted to go after her and press her for an explanation but that would have to wait. Because of the morning's excitement, I was already overdue for the lunch I had arranged with Patric.

CHAPTER SIXTEEN

Patric and I were going to meet at an inn which adjoined Merchantplace. Fortunately he was late too and we arrived together, both of us appearing somewhat distracted. He apologized, saying something had come up at Rellards at the last minute. I said it was fine, I had been delayed as well, and then told him about Zorn's accident. He didn't have much reaction. The waiter came to seat us and we went into the dining room.

The room was busy with the clatter of plates and a confusion of voices, but a background of noise can create an odd sense of privacy. While we waited for our food, Patric asked about my plans. "Your brother Karel and the rest of your family, they're still in the New Tradelands?"

"As far as I know. I'm sending a letter to let them know where I am. And about what happened to Jarrell."

"I imagine you're planning to join them. When you're finished here."

"I don't know. Somehow, I don't have much enthusiasm for trying to rebuild the fortunes of Wellworth. Nor for much else right now. How about you?"

"I've done a few trips into the Tradelands, freelance, you know. And I pick up contract work, like now, with Rellards. I'm putting a little away. When I have enough to buy into an enterprise, I will." He traced invisible lines on the table covering with the tines of his fork. "You'll come back to it, Grayall, the trading world. Like me, it's all you know. You just need some time."

He seemed to think that was an optimistic forecast of my future. I decided not to argue with it, but Patric's plans, and my brother's, to try to re-capture the life our parents had led, I doubted I would come back to it.

Besides, Patric seemed restless to me like he was preoccupied with something. He kept toying with his knife and fork. "How's everything working out with your aristo?" he finally asked.

"She's not 'my' aristo."

"Your client, then," he said a bit smugly.

"Things are working out well enough, considering we're sharing the house with a representative of the insurgency's Provisional Authority."

"So I heard. Leave it to Gwynedd. But everyone is talking about the bidding on the insignia."

"Is Rellards going to file an application to participate?" I asked.

"I don't know. It seems too rich for them. But there's time until the deadline." Our food arrived and between bites, Patric said, "I suppose you think I owe you an apology. For laughing at you that first day. And you're right, I do. I was upset, you know. About Jarrell."

"It's all right," I said. "I understand."

He should have left it there, but that wasn't like Patric. He went on, "It's just that you and Jarrell were always so high and mighty about the Realm. An oppressive system of ruler and ruled, ariston and servitor, that amounted to slavery, you called it. Remember? And then like an idiot Jarrell gets himself killed fighting for the rebel cause. And you come back with an aristo in tow." He shook his head and gave his attention to his lunch.

We ate for a while in silence. As usual Patric had managed to make me uncomfortable. There wasn't much to say to his observations. They were all true enough, as far as they went. So I didn't say much. I don't think Patric noticed.

When he finished eating, he patted his mouth and settled back in his chair. With a musing expression on his face, he said, "Still, if you take the larger view, the aristos were the ones under attack. I mean it was their way of life being threatened. I'm sure I'd fight to protect what I had, too."

His manner provoked me. "Actually I don't think Zorn cries any tears for the downfall of the Realm," I said.

Patric smiled complacently. "Nor for anything else. Showing their feelings. That's against their principles, isn't it? Those traditional ariston." He paused. "One of them, it must be an interesting personality to observe. But as for your assertion about the ariston's attitude toward the downfall of the Realm, well... Can anyone lose that kind of power and status and not resent it?" He smiled again to show he thought the answer to his question was self-evident. "You believe what you need to believe, Grayall." It was a stance Patric had often taken with Jarrell and me, playing the shrewd man of affairs, instructing us, the young idealists. My irritation must have shown because he added, "But then again, so do we all."

We finished with coffee and a liqueur. But Patric still seemed to have something unspoken on his mind. He remained fidgety. This time he drew circles on the table with the base of his glass. "What's the matter?" I asked.

He looked at me in surprise but then he probably wasn't aware of the signals he'd been sending. "Nothing, everything's fine. Glad we had a chance to meet and talk. And let me say again, thank you. For bringing the word about Jarrell. I do know I was wrong not to do more about him."

Hearing that comment, I decided it explained the preoccupation I had noticed in Patric throughout our lunch. He was still feeling uneasy that he hadn't gone after Jarrell himself or, at least, gone with me. I would have liked to reassure him I much preferred things the way they were, but I could only do that by letting him know I was happier without large doses of his company. And I wasn't quite prepared to make that point to him. Not yet anyway.

As it turned out, Patric did have something other than guilt feelings about Jarrell on his mind that day. Maybe I should have realized at the time what it was, but I didn't. It would be awhile before I finally learned what was preoccupying him. When I did, I was glad I had not said more about my feelings for him. Or rather my lack of them.

Chapter Seventeen

After I left Patric, I needed to stop and see the trader who had agreed to carry the letter to my brother. Actually I was supposed to deliver the letter to him but, with chasing after Zorn in the morning, I hadn't finished it. I told him I'd bring it tomorrow. I had a few other errands to run as well and I didn't want to postpone them, but all afternoon the accident with the horse and Zorn's reaction to it continued to nag at me. I knew I wanted to speak with her about it before the day was out.

At last I finished the things I had to do and got back to Gwynedd's toward the end of the afternoon. As I rode into the courtyard, everything was quiet. The surly gatekeeper, who as far as I was concerned had not improved with further acquaintance, didn't appear from the lodge. He had gotten in the habit of ignoring our comings and goings, neglecting his normal duties of seeing to the horses and arranging for them to be taken down to the stable.

Since I didn't like him very much, I didn't consider his carelessness a great loss most of the time. But his slackness was becoming inconvenient. I had noticed, for example, that he'd been absent this morning when Zorn's horse had been brought in and he could have been of some use. And now, I was tired, I wanted to find Zorn, and I didn't want to bother with bringing my horse down to the stable myself. It seemed to me it was about time the gatekeeper attended to his responsibilities more conscientiously.

I rode over to the lodge and raised a shout which brought him to the door. He came out with a sour face but that was his normal expression. I dismounted and handed him the reins. He didn't exchange any word of greeting. I couldn't tell whether his grumpiness was intentional but, if it was, I wasn't going to be fazed by it. Unwilling or no, maybe he could save me a trip to the house to inquire after Zorn. "I'm looking for Zorn of Northmarch," I said. "Have you seen her?"

"The aristo?" He used the disparaging term. "Went out again earlier. Came back, maybe an hour ago, maybe longer. Don't know where she is now."

His answer was rude enough and grudging enough to irritate me further. "The aristo," I echoed him. "Not a very polite way to refer to a guest, and client, of the House."

His eyes blinked repeatedly. All at once, he looked more worried than sullen. "No offense," he mumbled. Maybe he figured I'd complain to Gwynedd.

And I might have, but from his reaction I judged he had probably chosen his words without thinking, as a matter of habit. "All right," I said. "But in future, mind your courtesy better."

He bobbed his head in affirmation and then busied himself with my horse.

Evidently I had reached the limit of his helpfulness. I glanced up at the house. I could see the windows of our rooms from where I stood, but they shone blankly in the late afternoon sun. I stood undecided for a moment, but concluded the pond was the best bet at this time of the day, so I wandered off through the gardens and followed the path to the back of the grounds.

I was right. Zorn was sitting in the familiar place, gazing out across the water, her head canted a little against the setting sun. The ducks and geese set up their usual raucous greeting at my approach, but they subsided quickly.

Instead of joining Zorn on the logs, I leaned against the spiky tree that stood beside them. My encounter with the gatekeeper hadn't improved my mood. Without offering any greeting, I began, "You said, you'd save conversation for later. It's later. So. What did you mean? Something brought the horse down."

Zorn looked me over judiciously. "Have you had a trying afternoon? Jarrell's brother seems to wear on you."

"He's not the only one." Her expression became more intent. "No. I don't mean you. I don't like that gatekeeper."

"Caled," Zorn said.

It often surprised me, the things Zorn knew or noticed. I hadn't ever found out the gatekeeper's name, but I wasn't going to be sidetracked. "I didn't come out here to talk about my day. Or about the household staff. What about the horse?"

Zorn seemed to have her answer prepared. "A decent horse, well-shod, does not normally fall. Certainly not on a clear path with a good surface."

"People trip, I guess horses can too. Even the stable manager said that."

Zorn took a moment before replying. "This afternoon I went back to the place. I also looked at the horse again."

"So. Did you find anything?"

"Slight abrasions on trees on either side of the path. Indicative, but not conclusive. And if something did trip the horse, any marks on him are lost among the scratches he sustained."

"Something like what?"

"Wire possibly. Rope or a stout cord perhaps." Zorn looked pensive. "The place was well chosen. At that hour of the morning, you go from bright sun to deep shade there. Easy to miss something stretched across the path." She took another thoughtful moment. "Of course, I should have examined the area then. But we fell hard. I was winded. By the time I recovered myself, the horse had struggled to his feet. I approached him, but he shied away and galloped off. I was not pleased."

"You don't mean to say you lost your temper?" I didn't attempt to keep the amusement out of my voice.

"Not so *you* would have noticed. But I was distracted. And didn't immediately consider whether the fall might be something other than an accident."

"You've got to work on that response time, Zorn."

"Yes, you're right." She had a knack of treating my sarcastic comments as if I'd meant them seriously. I hoped it amused her more than it did me.

I shook my head skeptically. "You really think somebody booby trapped you? On purpose."

"As opposed to what? Setting a trap unintentionally."

"Very funny." I mulled over everything Zorn had said. What she was suggesting didn't seem likely to me, although I knew she was hardly taken with a fanciful turn of mind. "You have any other reasons for suspecting this?" I asked. "Aside from the unexpectedness of the fall, I mean. And some bruised tree bark."

"It isn't the first thing that has happened." Zorn sounded thoughtful, but her voice betrayed no alarm. Then again, it wouldn't even if there was cause.

After a moment's consideration, I said, "The hay bale."

Zorn nodded. "And something else." She pointed to the ground on the far side of the log pile, the side overhung by the fountain-like tree. A dead-looking gnarled branch of good size, and probably of good weight, lay there. "That came down one afternoon. After we'd had heavy winds overnight."

I remembered. The windows had rattled all night long to an accompaniment of rumbling thunder and occasional flashes of lightning. I thought we would wake to a storm, but it had blown itself out by morning.

I stepped forward and looked up at the tree with its arching branches. Against its darker trunk, I could see jagged edges of light-colored wood where one of them had broken off.

"You sitting here at the time?" I asked.

Zorn unbuttoned her right cuff, turned it back, then pushed up the sleeve of her thin under-jersey. The yellow-green remnant of a bruise mottled her arm from mid-forearm to elbow.

"Lucky it didn't come down on your head," I said.

"That's the second time you've used that word today. Lucky with the branch, the horse." She paused to pull down her sleeves and re-button her cuff. "Lucky with the hay bale. Lucky I still know how to duck, it seems." I inadvertently glanced down at her knees and she caught me doing it. "I am not completely decrepit," she added.

I came around and bent to inspect the branch. The wood was dead and it had splintered badly. But if anyone had helped it along, I couldn't tell. "After it came down, did you see any marks to indicate it might have been cut? Or otherwise encouraged to break off?"

"I didn't check. I blamed the wind and my own carelessness for sitting under dead tree branches." She gazed down at the branch. "That remains the most likely explanation. And as you said, horses do lose their footing."

"Yeah, and hay bales topple out of lofts. But all three in one week?" Zorn didn't react but I did. "You know who it is and we have to tell Gwynedd."

"No." Zorn could make one word sound very emphatic when she wanted.

"Listen, Zorn," I said, with some emphasis of my own. "You owe it to Gwynedd to leave this to her. Lucian gave his word not to cause trouble and..."

Zorn returned one of her most repressive stares. "I have no evidence on which to base an accusation against Lucian."

"Damn it, Zorn, what have we been talking about?" My voice rose with exasperation.

"We have been considering whether coincidence has been stretched too far with these apparent accidents. If it has, that conclusion does not automatically lead to assigning blame."

"Who else if not him?" I demanded. "Who else hates you that much?"

She stood up. "I don't know. Perhaps anyone with contempt for Regeren and who sees me as a symbol of it. I suspect I could find more than one candidate who would qualify." She was right, of course. It wasn't far off as a description which could fit even me, and we both knew it. But I didn't give in.

"You're just being difficult. It comes natural to you. And Gwynedd should at least know about these so-called accidents. Eventually one of them's likely to be successful." Zorn started to answer but I cut her off.

"And so help me, Zorn, if you say, 'I can take care of myself,' I'll throw you in the lake."

Zorn mustered one of her almost smiles. "I thought that was precisely the source of your anxiety. My ability to take care of myself." She seemed to measure the couple of inches in height I had on her. "But it is tempting, just to see you try it. Then again, I may need you to cover my back sometime. For the present, I am going away. That should alleviate your immediate concerns." She started walking toward the house.

Caught off guard, I stood still for a few moments. Then I trotted after her. "Going away? Going where?"

"To the Freeholds. Bennetson is sending a trading expedition there tomorrow morning. I will accompany it."

"The Freeholds? What do you want there?"

"Knowledge," she said without stopping. "The kind that aids in making decisions." And with that unenlightening comment, she walked on ahead.

CHAPTER EIGHTEEN

Following Zorn more slowly, I pondered her unexpected announcement. The Freeholds occupied a large territory to the north of the Seaward River. They ran up to the Outer River on the east and to the Primum on the west.

They were made up of tracts of land owned outright. Some of them were huge, consisting of thousands of acres. These were owned by shareholding companies. However, most of them ran to a couple of hundred acres or so and were held by individuals.

The economic base of the Freeholds was primarily farming. They had long been a major supplier of wheat and other grains throughout Allothi. And a fair number of the holdings had operations in livestock, mainly cattle and horses.

All in all I couldn't think of any particular reason Zorn would have to journey there. Maybe she was just bored with waiting around for the bidding or maybe it was her way of taking precautions. No question, having her away from Gwynedd's for a few days had its advantages. Not that it would solve any problems, but it would postpone dealing with them.

As I came through the gardens, Zorn was already out of sight around the corner of the house. But Evane was coming up from the stable. Despite Zorn's unwillingness to point a finger at Lucian, I decided there was something I needed to ask Evane. She hesitated when she saw me, giving me time to pass by. But I waited for her. After a while, reluctantly she came toward me.

"I'd like a word with you," I said.

"If you must," she answered rigidly.

"For heaven's sake, Evane. We've known each other for years. Doesn't that count for anything with you?"

"Known each other? So I thought, Grayall. But then again I thought you loved Jarrell and felt about the Realm the same way he did. But what I've discovered is your principles can be bought. As for your love for Jarrell, that can be sold."

The scorn that drove her words was overwhelmingly genuine. And the best defense against hurt is anger. Mine flashed instantly and the tensions that had been accumulating in me served as tinder. My words blazed.

"You self-righteous bitch. You're right. You don't know me. And worse, you don't know her." I jerked my head in the direction Zorn had gone. "You're really good at making judgments, aren't you? You just don't care whether they're right." I was tired of Evane's contempt and now my anger, my frustration, overrode my intentions and Zorn's cautions. The long-withheld claim of justification came rushing out. "Those scars she carries. One of her own people, Zarath the Archon of Northmarch, did that to her. For helping renegade servs escape the Realm. Insurgent renegades." The old saying about trembling with emotion is true. A pulse beat in my jaw and my chin twitched.

But Evane's anger flowed with its own current and wasn't about to be deflected by mine. She glared at me, her eyes cold and spiteful. "Helped the insurgents? According to who, Grayall? Her? And you believe it? You're not that stupid. That self-serving, maybe, but not that stupid."

We were both of us riding runaway emotions and I should have just walked away. But I had a reason for stopping Evane in the first place, and my anger would not let go of it. "Where was Lucian this morning? When Zorn's horse went down." What I had planned, in the beginning, to ask as neutrally as possible now came out as an unmistakable accusation.

My question startled Evane, but only for as long as it took her to catch its implication. "How dare you," she said, straight out of melodrama, which I guess is what we were playing at. "You leave Lucian out of this." She threw the words at me, each one bitten off separately.

"Maybe that won't be so easy. If someone did arrange that fall, it's a criminal action. Zorn could have been badly hurt."

Our voices which had started low in their intensity had climbed to a shouting match. But now Evane's dropped again into a harsh whisper. "If she had been, I wouldn't have wept."

And then Gwynedd came around the side of the house. "What the hell do you two think you're doing?" she demanded in a quiet but frigid voice. "Evane?" Evane didn't answer, didn't wait for a reprimand. She turned her back on her mother and me and hurried to the house. Gwynedd turned to me. "I would have expected more sense from you at least, Grayall," she said wearily. "Why can't you two just stay out of each other's way."

It wasn't really a question. And pretty clearly, Gwynedd thought it was only the underlying friction between Evane and myself which had exploded. I was tempted to correct her impression by sharing with her my inquiry about Lucian's whereabouts this morning, but decided this was not the time or the place.

I noticed with embarrassment that my go-around with Evane had attracted attention. Caled the gatekeeper was standing in the doorway of the lodge and curious onlookers had appeared outside the stable. Besides I had done everything Zorn had asked, or maybe ordered, me not to do, and probably done it in the worst possible way. So I muttered, "I'm sorry," and walked off to the house.

Haslen was at the door, but he disappeared discreetly when I came in. Zorn was waiting for me at the bottom of the stairs. The angular planes of her face were carved in unrelenting lines. "I told you. When I need defending, I will do it myself. Or did you forget what I said?" Her voice could have frozen water.

"I didn't forget." My anger had turned sour and my tone was bitter. "Too bad we can't all manage your spectacular level of self-control."

Something in Zorn's expression changed. In a less icy voice she said, "I have cost you a friendship. I understand that. If I could buy it back for you, I would. But the only coin I have with which to do that is my word and that isn't worth much here."

All the emotion drained out of me. "I'm just tired of it, Zorn. Tired of it all. Tired of Evane and Lucian and…"

She nodded at my unfinished sentence. "Next time, be more careful where you stop to camp." Her dark, hooded eyes met mine knowingly for a moment. Then she started up the stairs.

I put my hand on her shoulder to stop her. "You read people pretty well and I won't say I haven't had that thought before. But no matter what, I would not take that back. That I stopped in that clearing. That I stopped in time. I am thankful for that." I let my hand fall, I had run out of things to say.

Zorn had looked back at me. "At least, that is something we have in common," she said. Then she continued up the stairs.

CHAPTER NINETEEN

When Zorn announced her intention to leave for the Freeholds the next day, Gwynedd was accommodating, but she was undoubtedly surprised as well. I suspected she did some quick figuring to calculate whether Zorn would be back in time for the bidding. But the journey Zorn was planning would leave time to spare. Arne's trading expedition would start traveling by boat along the Seaward. After making a series of stops, they'd pack inland for a good tour of the holdings along the river, then finish up back in the vicinity of the Exchanges.

In the morning, I got down to the gate ahead of Zorn. I had volunteered to ride with her to Arne's and bring her horse back. For a change, Caled the gatekeeper was ready at his post. While I waited, Haslen showed up. He fussed around, assuring me one of the grooms could go along to bring the horse back. I assured him in return that I didn't mind at all. As we talked, he seemed to be watching Caled. I wondered if Caled noticed.

In good time, Zorn appeared and we mounted. Haslen offered wishes for a safe journey. Caled opened the gate and we rode off. I glanced back at Haslen and confirmed another impression I'd had. He seemed relieved. In his post as chamberlain, the recent strains in the household must have fallen on him fairly heavily, although he was always too polite to show it.

I straightened in the saddle and said, "Looks like Haslen will be glad to see the back of you for a few days." As I had done, Zorn glanced behind her. "Can't blame him," I added. "Things have been a bit tense."

But Zorn no longer seemed to be listening. She had drawn rein and I thought she was going to turn around. "You forget something?" I asked.

She paused, then started forward again without answering. We rode on in silence for a while. Zorn seemed absorbed in her own thoughts. I looked at her. She was wearing one of the sets of workmanlike clothing she had purchased for both us. To the denim trousers, shirt, and vest, she had added gloves and a broad-brimmed hat with a high crown. She also wore a neckerchief, folded once to form a point in front and knotted loosely at the back of her neck. And of course, the brown boots I had teased her about. Her knife in its scabbard was visible under the vest. Her gun was not, but I knew she had a holster which fit snugly at the small of her back and I suspected she had not omitted that last and, to her, probably most crucial part of her outfit. And it suddenly occurred to me that all of this traveling kit had been ordered before any of the overly coincidental accidents had occurred. If that provided a clue to Zorn's decision to make this journey, I couldn't figure it out, so I took another stab at getting an answer from her.

"You going to get around to telling me why you're making this trip?" I asked. Still preoccupied, she didn't seem to hear me. "Zorn." I called her out of her abstraction and repeated the question.

"Eventually." She let the word hang. Her attention was still elsewhere.

"I'd like to credit your good sense." I thought that was a great opening for an explanation but Zorn didn't take it. I pressed on. "What I said yesterday, while you're gone, I think I should tell Gwynedd. About the so-called accidents."

That finally seemed to break through her concentration. "Leave it." Her tone was peremptory. I started to object but she raised her hand and said, "I will attend to that when I return. If it proves necessary."

"And when will that be? After Lucian succeeds in taking you out with one of these … accidents."

"You insist on placing blame on him with no evidence."

"Evidence or not, none of which we've looked for by the way, he has the obvious motive."

"He has a motive that makes sense to you. But obvious motives can obscure more subtle ones. People do things for reasons that do not always make sense, even to them."

Listening to Zorn pronounce on the role of the irrational and emotional in human behavior was delightfully ironic. However, I refrained from pointing that out. Instead I said, "That's all well and good. But it doesn't offer a convincing alternative to Lucian." We rode on in silence for a while and we were almost to Arne's when I said, "Whichever of us is right, whether it's Lucian or some general anti-ariston malice on someone's part, you could defuse it, at least a little." I glanced over at her, but her face, half-shadowed under the brim of her hat, was even more unreadable than usual. "You could tell someone besides me what really happened to you and why."

"Do you suggest I begin with Evane?" She spoke in the same sub-zero voice she had used on me yesterday.

"Look, I handled that stupidly..."

She stopped her horse and faced me. "Even my patience has its limits. If you want to minimize confrontations, do as I say. Leave things as they are." She turned and rode on ahead of me. I wanted to argue my point further, but I didn't. I had known Zorn long enough now to recognize that continued discussion would be pointless.

I caught up to her and was trying to think of a way to lighten the mood, when she said, with no noticeable change of voice, "Besides, you forget, I can take care of myself." The corners of her mouth twitched into a quirky half smile. "Too bad there's no lake handy," she added.

"It'll still be there when you get back."

"I look forward to any encounter you wish to initiate."

Chapter Twenty

When we arrived at Arne's, we found him reviewing inventory for the trip with his expedition chief. They were having some discussion about how much of a shipment of spring-traps they could include and they finally settled on half. I despised the ugly things, with their vicious serrated jaws, but there were trappers who plied the unsettled lands beyond the Primum River all the way to the tag end of the mountains in the west. And they wanted them. Some of the property owners in the Freeholds would buy them for re-sale.

Arne greeted us with his usual boisterous good humor and repeated how pleased he was to be able to oblige Her Excellency. The expedition chief acknowledged us politely, but more quietly. He seemed to take Zorn's presence in stride, managing to be neither obsequious nor insolent.

It didn't take long to complete the final preparations. Within half an hour, everything was done and we went down to the dock behind Arne's house. Zorn gave me an economical good-bye. She still didn't offer any comment about why she was going to the Freeholds. She had ducked my question about that and it was clear she wasn't going to elaborate, not for the present anyway. She went on board and the boat started down river. Arne and I stood watching it depart.

"Let's hope it's a profitable trip," Arne said.

I looked at him. He looked prosperous, almost glossy. "Oh, I don't guess you have much to worry about. Business must be good for you."

"It keeps fair," he said a bit smugly.

"A lot better than that, I think." The bulk of Arne's business was in the Freeholds and the Tradelands, so the collapse of the Realm had not much damaged his enterprise. If anything, it had helped. The enterprises, like my family's and Jarrell's, that had operated in the southern parts of the Realm had also done some trading with the Freeholds, and Arne had been able to pick up some of the business they had abandoned there. His position as the most successful trader in the Exchanges seemed assured.

"I can't complain," he said. "But you know, you have to keep after it. Business never takes care of itself." Arne was still watching the boat. "By the way, I'm glad you came into something." He made a small motion with his head. "The percentage you'll get from Gwynedd for the aristo's commission will give you a start anyway."

"The aristo? What happened to 'Her Excellency'?"

Arne smiled. "She's a mile down river by now."

"You've been pretty helpful. To Zorn."

Arne's face assumed a particularly knowing expression. "Zorn of Northmarch will clear a thousand argen, or likely more, on the sale of those insignia. Nothing wrong with cultivating a good prospect. As you should well know, Grayall. Besides if…" He broke off what he was saying and walked over to the extra boxes of traps that had been left behind. He squatted down, checked through them and said, "I think our insurgent Lucian will be interested in these. He won't find enough grain on the market to cover all the Provisional Authority will need this winter. They'll have to find some way to supplement their food stores. I expect they might be willing to try some trapping."

I came over and stood behind him. "Hateful things," I said gazing at the closed steel jaws of the traps.

Arne glanced back at me over his shoulder. "Commodities. Sometimes necessary. Therefore marketable." He stood up and we started to walk back toward his house.

"Therefore, good business," I said. "Anyway what were you going to say? You were talking about Zorn being a good prospect when you broke off."

At first I thought he was going to evade my question, but then he said, "I was going to say if, by cultivating the aristo, I can make Carsten nervous, so much the better. Is that nasty and cutthroat enough?" He grinned at me. "He thinks I have some ulterior motive in helping Zorn of Northmarch. Something to gain an advantage for myself in the bidding."

"Tell you the truth, Arne, I didn't think you'd be that interested in Zorn's insignia. Not enough to get in a bidding war with Carsten over them. After all, they seem more in his line."

"Maybe. Maybe not." He paused, then said, "I can do better than Carsten. In anything." His tone had changed, gotten harder, and he must have heard it himself because he laughed again and added, "Carsten and I have been competing with each other for twenty years. He can win some. Just so I win the important ones."

"Which you always do."

"Yes, always." The harder tone had crept back into his voice but he dispelled it again. "Anyway," he said with more typical heartiness, "if Carsten thinks I can get anything out of Her Excellency, he doesn't know her very well. Not like you."

I blew out a puff of air. "That's open to question." Arne raised his eyebrows at me. "This trip of hers, for example. It was news to me. When did she set it up with you?"

"I mentioned I was sending a party out. I think it was back on that day I took her around Merchantplace. She asked at the time about the possibility of her going along, but she only confirmed with me yesterday."

"You don't happen to know what she wants in the Freeholds, do you?"

"How should I know if you don't? After all, Her Excellency certainly doesn't confide in me." From his intonation, I had the feeling he was suggesting I could answer my question myself.

"She didn't tell me why she was going. I just thought she might have mentioned something to you."

Arne looked at me speculatively. "No. But what I don't know, I might be able to guess … " He let his voice trail off, insinuatingly.

"Yes, Arne," I said with studied patience. "Your guess. What would it be?"

"I would *guess*," he emphasized the word, "she might be considering the purchase of a property in the Freeholds." That brought me up short. It was a possibility that simply hadn't occurred to me.

"A property in the Freeholds. Why would she do that?"

Arne shrugged. "She has to live somewhere. I suspect the Exchanges wouldn't be her preferred choice. And unless she has some intention of seeking out the other aristos in the Enclaves..."

"No. She won't go there."

"Well, then. She'll certainly be able to afford something in the Freeholds. Oh, not one of the great properties, but something up to two-hundred and fifty acres or so. As I said though, it's just a guess. And leaving aside other reasons for her sudden departure."

"Other reasons like what?"

"You are being cautious." He put a tinge of mockery in his voice. "But if you want to keep things quiet, don't have shouting matches with Evane. Not out in the open anyway. I heard about that."

Arne tapped the gossip in the Exchanges as well as anyone, but I was still surprised and none too pleased. "That's fast work, even for you," I said.

He grinned appreciatively. "News of trouble usually spreads quickly. And I figured one purpose of this trip might be to put some distance between Her Excellency of Northmarch and our local insurgent representative. Not to mention Evane."

"I wouldn't exactly call it trouble," I said defensively.

Arne smiled his disbelief. "Whatever you say. But from what I heard, you confronted Evane and accused Lucian of trying to kill the aristo. Which ended up with the two of you screaming at each other out in front of the house."

"That's not what happened." My anger clipped the words, but made no headway against Arne's amused skepticism. "Zorn had been out riding," I explained. "Her horse went down. For no apparent reason. I only asked Evane where Lucian had been that morning."

"Oh, Grayall." Arne laughed out loud. "Such an innocent question. Can't think why Evane took it badly."

"Arne..." I started to protest but he didn't wait for me.

"I told you before, what I didn't know, I could guess. Well, I'm guessing. Yesterday's incident isn't the only thing that's happened and you're just as glad to see Zorn of Northmarch gone for a few days."

We had reached the house and Arne invited me in but I knew he was in the middle of his morning work, so I declined. But before I left, I decided on a cautionary word. "Arne, don't look for trouble. At Gwynedd's, I mean. A couple of other things have happened, accidents that were maybe just a little too convenient." I told him briefly about the hay bale and the branch. I knew him well enough to know he'd poke around if he thought there was something to be nosed out. It was better to treat him as a confidant. "But Zorn doesn't want to make a fuss about any of this, you understand."

He drew the lower part of his face down into a classic expression of complicity. "Don't worry, I'm an old hand at discretion."

I wasn't sure I was entirely satisfied with that, but it was the best I was going to get. Arne might not believe my disclaimers, but maybe I had given him enough information to satisfy him and keep him from spreading gossip, for the present anyway.

As for Arne's other speculation, the more I thought about it, the more sense it made. A property in the Freeholds might suit Zorn very well. A nice private patch of ground to control, maybe to retreat to. There was even a possible connection with something else about her. She knew horses and I recalled her arrangements to purchase Traina's colt. Maybe she'd planned this trip back in Arandell. Although my guess was Arne had hit the mark. Whatever Zorn's original intention, the timing of this trip probably owed something to recent events at Gwynedd's. However, those were notions I kept to myself. Arne didn't need to know how much I agreed with him.

CHAPTER TWENTY-ONE

I returned to Gwynedd's and found Caled still being attentive to his duties at the gate. I left my horse and walked over to the house. Haslen came out as soon as I entered the hall. He was fumbling with the substantial ring of keys he carried everywhere and which seemed to be the visible symbol of his responsibilities in the household.

He greeted me with his usual smooth courtesy, then said, "I hope Zorn of Northmarch got off in good order."

"Yes, thank you," I replied. He glanced down, confirming the key he had selected. I couldn't resist adding, "Makes one less thing for you to worry about for a few days, wouldn't you say?"

His head came up. "I might think it. I wouldn't say it." The politeness of his tone never varied but I was sure he was annoyed at my comment. He excused himself and started to walk away. But after a couple of steps he turned back to me. He was smiling, wryly. "You know this household too well, Grayall. For me to treat you only as a guest. You're right. It is one less worry."

I grinned at him. "Believe me, I know that feeling when it comes to Zorn."

He nodded sympathetically. Then with a more serious face, he said, "Still she is an important client. A very important one."

I laughed at his solemn tone. "Important enough to make up for the worry," I said lightly.

He smiled again, but this time it seemed more politic than genuine. Evidently he had unbent as far as he thought appropriate. He glanced at his keys again, as if reminding himself that he had things to attend to.

More likely reminding me. I waved him away. With a nod of farewell, he took himself off.

I stood alone in the hall, hesitating. I knew it was too early to join Gwynedd for her mid-morning break. I decided to look in on Torvan, but he wasn't in his study. Probably out in his laboratory, and probably just as happy not to be disturbed. At last, I settled for the library. I opened a book but gave it only wandering attention.

I seemed to find myself in the middle of an unexpected stillness, a stillness deeper that the usual morning quiet of the house. It didn't take much thought to figure out why. Zorn was gone. I had teased Haslen about it, but her departure had lightened the load for me as well.

I hadn't been out of her company since I had found her. During our time at Arandell and now here in the Exchanges, she had been an insistent presence. When I hadn't been wondering how she would react to things, I had been wondering how others would react to her. And the events of the last few days had put her even more squarely at the center of things I worried about. It was going to be a welcome break to put it all aside for a few days.

I had been sitting awhile over my lackadaisical reading, giving more attention to my thoughts than to my book, and had just about decided it was time to try the small parlor and see if Gwynedd was around, when the library door opened. I looked up, expecting either Gwynedd or Torvan. What I got was Lucian.

Aside from the initial staring contest the day after we arrived and silent passings by, it was our first real meeting. I assumed he was as unenthusiastic for it as I was. I stood up and said, "I was just leaving." Not markedly polite perhaps, but it was my way of saying he was welcome to have the library to himself.

But Lucian held his place in the doorway, blocking me. "Not just yet, mercenary." He threw out the words, like stones. The last he flung hardest of all. Mercenary. Zorn had called me that once at Arandell to get my attention. It meant a person who would sell anything, do anything, for a price. It was an insult. An insult Lucian had obviously come looking to deliver.

I felt an uprush of anger, but this time I was determined to master it, for Gwynedd's sake if for no other reason. "Sorry, Lucian. I'm not in the mood. I don't need another shouting match."

I started past him, but he grabbed my arm, his grip strong enough to be uncomfortable. "You listen." He shook me. "I have a message for that aristo you've sold yourself to."

"Let go of me." I pulled back from his grip but he tightened his hold. "Tell her, if she wants to accuse me, do it herself. Don't send a serv." To punctuate the last word, he shoved me away, abruptly letting go of my arm. Off balance, I stumbled backwards.

I was fighting to contain my anger, but was losing the struggle. "You could have delivered that message to her yourself. You had enough time. Before she left." I moved for the door again. I almost made it.

To my back, Lucian said, "Aristo shit and the thing that serves it."

I swung around and thrust my face close to his. "You know what I think?" My voice had gone very quiet. "I think you've come to me because you didn't want to square off with Zorn. You don't have the stomach for that."

Lucian stood absolutely rigid. His brown eyes gleamed with a yellow light and a flush mottled his fair complexion. I didn't wait for another reaction. I walked out.

In a blind fury, I headed down the corridor toward the back of the house. But I hadn't gone more than a few steps when my anger turned on myself. Against all sense I had said to Lucian the most provocative thing I could think of. I had all but challenged him to seek out a confrontation with Zorn. My words hadn't just been foolish, they'd been dangerous.

And there was no calling them back.

CHAPTER TWENTY-TWO

As I stormed down the corridor, I wasn't watching where I was going and I walked straight into Torvan, or would have, if he hadn't stepped out of the way. He took one look at me and said, "Why don't you come along with me?"

Unresisting, I let him steer me out the back of the house and across the stretch of yard that led to his laboratory.

Torvan's laboratory occupied one good-sized room, well-lit with a generous expanse of windows. It was well-ventilated too, but an astringent odor compounded of various chemicals was a permanent fixture.

Easing me through the door, Torvan pulled a stool away from a high worktable and gently pushed me toward it. "Take a minute and calm down."

"Damn. Does stupidity always have to come so easily?"

"Seems like it. What have you been up to now? Hammer and tongs with Evane again?"

"Worse," I said glumly. "Lucian."

Instead of asking me for an explanation, Torvan said, "Go on, sit down. I'll show you something."

I could tell he was humoring me, trying to break through my distress, but I probably needed humoring, so I did as he asked.

He bustled around. From a cabinet, he took a wide-mouthed glass beaker. At a sink in one corner, he filled the beaker with water, then brought it to the table.

The back wall of the laboratory held a bank of shelves filled with orderly rows of rectangular metal canisters, each one labeled with various cryptic initials. Torvan selected one. Against its dull-gray surface the letters Na stood out boldly in red. He opened it and took out a glass vial. He held it up for me to see.

The vial held small chunks of what looked like tarnished silver submerged in a clear liquid. Torvan set the vial in a wire stand and unstopped it. Reaching into it with a pair of tongs, he separated a tiny piece from one of the chunks and withdrew it. As he did so, with his other hand he immediately replaced the stopper on the vial. Without pausing, he dropped the piece, one side of which now gleamed with a brighter sheen than the rest, into the beaker of water.

"Stay there now," he said. Simultaneously with his words, the bit of matter began to fizz and skitter across the surface of the water, moving like some demented insect. It also released a trail of vapor and I caught an unpleasant whiff of a heavy pungent odor.

Torvan backed away from his own display and moved closer to where I sat near the open door. He waved his hand before his face. "The chemical reaction generates hydrogen," he said. "Not enough to cause a problem, but I still don't want a noseful."

For a few seconds, the bit of matter danced and skidded, continuing to throw off its vapor trail. Finally it used itself up, if that's the right expression. The beaker of water was quiet again. "What was it?" I asked, fascinated.

"A lesson in reactivity," he replied. "Pure sodium in water."

Torvan went to the sink and poured out the beaker, rinsing it carefully. Coming back to the table, he took up a rag and wiped it.

I leaned forward and considered with puzzlement the bright red letters on the metal canister. "Sodium, you said. So how come it says Na?"

He draped the rag over the edge of the sink. "Oh, it's part of a system of abbreviations from Veraces. Applied to elemental substances. I've been using it since I had that grant of admission to do research there. It's become standard throughout all the scola of Adveni." He smiled. "You know, scholars and researchers, they have their ways."

"Yeah," I grumped under my breath. "Mostly to make things confusing for the rest of us mere mortals."

Torvan's smile widened into a grin. He replaced the vial in its metal canister and the canister to its proper place on the shelf. Then he seated himself beside the table on another stool. Still looking amused, he said, "So what did you make of my demonstration?"

"Very impressive. And I assume you'll enlighten me about the point of the lesson."

"Bring certain substances together. You get an inevitable reaction." Torvan sounded pleased with himself.

"Is this chemistry or human relations we're talking about?"

"In this case, maybe they're not so different. You, Evane, Lucian. Under the present circumstances, like sodium in contact with water, the explosive reactions are hardly unexpected."

"Is this supposed to cheer me up?"

"No. It's just to remind you. You shouldn't be surprised by reactions that are virtually predictable."

"You left somebody off your list, you know."

Torvan leaned back and rested his elbows on the edge of the table. "Now that's a different element entirely. But equally predictable, in its own way."

I stared at him in astonishment. "Zorn? Predictable? You've got to be kidding. Her reactions aren't like anyone else's. At least not anyone I've ever known."

He shook his head. "There's a difference between the foreign and the unpredictable. A culture like the one she comes from, traditional ariston culture, values self-control over..." He stopped and thought for a minute. "Everything, I suppose. Produces a person who always wants a controlled reaction. That behavior's not difficult to predict. It's very consistent." He had assumed a professorial tone.

"What it is," I countered, "is unsettling. Sometimes I wonder, behind that ariston manner of hers, just what kind of feelings Zorn has. There must be some." I sounded like I was trying to convince myself.

"It's an interesting speculation," Torvan continued. "Both philosophically and psychologically, whether emotions can be separated from whatever expression we give them."

"Torvan, not a lecture now, please," I pleaded.

He smiled, but otherwise ignored me. "One theorist, in fact, suggested that our emotions originate in our physiological responses. We blush, so we feel embarrassed. Our tear ducts fill, so we feel sad. Rather than the other way around."

"That's a cold-blooded theory."

"Mechanistic, perhaps. But intriguing, especially if you connect it with suppressing emotion. Maybe you do that by cultivating a pattern of behavior, so that the masking itself creates the suppression. Don't act like you feel and maybe you don't. Or at least maybe you control what you feel. Then again, maybe you feel everything and all you control is your actions. Or your reactions." He paused. "My guess is, among Zorn's people, they don't concern themselves with feelings, only with acting properly. By their standards. Which, whatever its drawbacks with regard to personality development, has the advantage of forestalling the kind of frustrations you've been experiencing."

As Torvan had been speaking, his legs had stretched progressively farther in front of him, until his long body formed almost a straight line from his elbows braced on the table to his feet on the floor.

I reached over and, with a gentle kick, nudged his feet forward. He had to scramble to avoid sliding off the stool. "Thank you, professor," I said. "But I'd rather act stupidly once in a while than be Zorn of Northmarch."

He propped his feet on the bottom rung of the stool. "At least, the lesson's come to some conclusion. As long as you're willing to remember, you pay a price for that choice. Blowing up at Evane, or Lucian, even when your better judgment tells you not to. Don't browbeat yourself about it." He smiled complacently. "As for trying to understand Zorn of Northmarch, you might bear in mind, she would undoubtedly reverse the statement you've just made. I doubt she has much interest in revising who and what she is."

"You're right about that," I conceded. "But this isn't some academic exercise." On an impulse and relieved to finally confide in someone, I told him about all three of the mishaps that had occurred. After all, technically, Zorn had only cautioned me not to discuss them with Gwynedd. When I finished, I said, "I don't believe those things were accidents. The horse going down, the hay bale, and the branch falling. It was Lucian. He and Zorn are on a collision course, one I've made worse, and I don't know what to do about it."

Torvan folded his arms and let his head sink forward, a picture of contemplation. Finally he asked, "What does Zorn think?"

I shrugged. "She accepts it all seems a bit much for coincidence. But she says there's no proof Lucian is responsible. And she doesn't want me to say anything. About any of it." I sighed in frustration. "That's what I mean about Zorn. What kind of reaction is that? Who else but Lucian? Why deny the obvious?"

Torvan looked up, his long mobile face set in thoughtful lines. "Predictable reactions are one thing. But obvious assumptions. Now, those deserve to be questioned."

I looked at him dubiously but he went on, "Let's just say, for the sake of argument, that we were objective investigators trying to determine who might have a motive for injuring, maybe even attempting to kill, Zorn of Northmarch. We have the embittered former serv." He ticked Lucian off with a raised finger. "An obvious suspect, maybe too obvious. Lucian, after all, is here on important work. The insurgency's Provisional Authority needs those grain shipments. The messenger birds, too. Would he really endanger accomplishing what he's come here to do just to take some symbolic revenge?"

"You'd have to know Lucian to answer that."

"True," he acknowledged. "And neither of us really does. So, other possibilities." He raised a second finger. "What about a more concrete motive? How about someone who stood to gain from Zorn's death?"

"Gain?" I frowned. "You mean materially?"

"Yes, good trader that you are. You ought to know about that."

"There isn't anyone who stands to gain materially from her death," I said impatiently.

"There must be," he replied with irritating certainty. "If I were someone from outside this household, investigating the kinds of allegations you're making, I'd want to know who stood to inherit the ariston's property."

"That's ridiculous. I doubt Zorn has…" And then I stopped because, of course, Gwynedd would have seen to that. She would never have been so careless about dealing with the substantial estate the insignia added up to. As part of their business arrangement, she would have required Zorn to designate an heir to her considerable wealth. Torvan watched me, his eyes bright, assessing me.

It didn't take me long to realize what he was suggesting. I blurted out, "What makes you think I'm Zorn's legatee?"

"In your own words, who else?"

CHAPTER TWENTY-THREE

I froze, shocked into silence. With utter conviction, it came to me. There was entirely too good a chance that Torvan was right. Required by Gwynedd to name an heir, Zorn was just quixotic enough to have settled on me.

Smiling broadly at my obvious discomfort, Torvan walked over, put his arm around me, and gave my shoulder a friendly squeeze. "Don't mind the teasing. It has a point. If you really think someone intends harm to Zorn of Northmarch, Lucian may be the most likely suspect, but there could certainly be others. Frankly I'm pleased to see she's analytic enough to have figured that out for herself." He dropped his arm and stepped back. "And sensible enough to absent herself for a few days. So why don't you try to stop worrying? At least for now."

I got up and stood in the doorway, gazing out. Everything seemed to well up in me. I didn't think about what I was going to say, or whether I should. I just said it. "On the way here, Zorn killed someone. I saw her do it."

Torvan waited without saying anything, leaving me space to go on. So I did. I told him how Zorn had killed the bandit. "I know it was justified. Give him the slightest edge and we wouldn't have had a chance. I could see that in him. He would have raped us, killed us. Or me at least. Zorn could have eluded him, I guess, if she'd just left and struck out on her own. But she didn't give him any edge." The mingled horror and relief of that moment filled me and my voice grew hoarse. "If it had been up to me, I would have missed it. I would have given him the edge and he would have won."

Torvan came up behind me and put his hand on my back. He rubbed gently between my shoulder blades. "No wonder you're jittery." His voice was as gentle as his touch. He took me by the shoulders and turned me around to face him.

"This business with Lucian," I said despairingly. "If he attacks her directly, she will defend herself. I can't let it happen. I have to find a way to stop it. And all I've done is throw oil on the fire by provoking him."

Torvan took a step back and stood, head down, hands on his hips, elbows jutting out behind him, his weight on one leg, the other angled out in front of him. It was a quirk of posture he often adopted when he considered things. The familiarity of it was comforting.

He stood thinking for a long time. Finally he looked up and said, "Let's take the first point. If Zorn was looking for an opportunity, she could have confronted Lucian herself."

"And admit something got to her? No. That's not the way she operates."

"I'm sure you're right. So, second point, as I said, she's been sensible enough to get away for a while. Maybe let things cool."

"And when she gets back?"

"Tell me something. This outlaw she killed. So efficiently. Do you think it was done easily?"

"Not easily so much. Automatically. I think she's been trained to it, just like she's been trained to that ariston manner of hers."

Torvan looked at me intently. "You afraid of her?"

"I was. In the instant it happened. But no, I'm not."

"Why not?"

I searched for a way to explain. "I don't know. I don't believe Zorn's some kind of killing machine. That's ridiculous. It's just..."

"She's the wrong person to threaten, huh?"

"I suppose." It wasn't giving me any consolation.

"Do you think she knows when to act? And when not to?"

"She thinks she does."

"Then maybe her over-controlled behavior has its uses." Torvan stopped to think again. "One thing, if you're right about almost reflexive self-defense, and I think that's what you're talking about, presumably

Lucian understands that too. He must be more familiar with ariston behavior than we are."

"Sure," I said bleakly. "Why do you think he's been using booby traps? At least until I virtually egged him on to take a more direct approach."

"Well, with Zorn away, we have a few days. Some breathing room, hmmm?"

I nodded feebly. Torvan patted my arm reassuringly and we walked back to the house.

As we came in, Haslen intercepted us. He handed me a sheaf of invoices. "The remainder of the ariston's orders have arrived. I had them brought to your rooms. But you might want to review what's been sent, confirm that everything's as it should be."

"Thanks. I'll do that." I left Torvan and went upstairs.

Haslen had seen to it that all of Zorn's purchases were neatly put away in the large wardrobe that held both hangers and shelves. Jackets and trousers were hung precisely, shirts folded and stacked, the black dress boots carefully aligned on a bottom shelf. I looked through everything, checking materials and workmanship, and found nothing to complain about. Even on hangers, the excellent cut of the jackets was apparent. The boots were finely crafted, the leather soft and supple.

I noticed a jeweler's box on the bedside table. It held a pin, a plain bar of silver set with a rectangular onyx, appropriate for use on a neckcloth.

I glanced back at everything, the somber monotone of black and gray. There was not a spot of color in any of Zorn's dress clothing.

It occurred to me, as I surveyed Zorn's belongings, that any thoughts I had of escaping for a few days the preoccupations which centered on Zorn of Northmarch had proved illusory. She might have left the house, but her presence had not. It remained, as pervasive and insistent for me as it had ever been.

CHAPTER TWENTY-FOUR

In the days following my conversation with Torvan, I kept thinking I really owed it to Gwynedd to take her into my confidence, as well. But I didn't immediately convince myself. If anything, my revelations to Torvan had made it easier for me to put off discussing things with her. Maybe I kept hoping he would spare me that uncomfortable task by telling her himself without waiting for my OK. But if he did, she didn't broach the subject to me. I did know, however, at some point I needed to sound her out about who Zorn had named as an heir.

Gwynedd had scheduled the bidding assembly for a Friday and, as the day approached, chances for a quiet talk with her rapidly diminished. She was constantly busy. There were no more leisurely mid-morning coffee breaks. Instead there were a lot of people in and out, bidding registrations to finalize, arrangements to be made for the pre- and post-bidding receptions, accommodations to be organized for a fair number of overnight guests. All in addition to the regular business of the Securing House.

Most of the more influential traders, people like Arne and Carsten, would use an occasion like the bidding to renew contacts and pursue such other deals as presented themselves. In fact the house party on Thursday night would be more important from a business standpoint than the reception after the bidding.

I was pleased but surprised to see Rellards on the bidding register, with Patric's name as their representative. He'd be staying over the night before, too. Rellards wasn't really important enough to warrant that. I knew Gwynedd had done it in honor of Jarrell.

With all the activity, I continued to stall making a decision about what to tell Gwynedd. Arne expected his trading party back on Wednesday. But they sent a message that they'd been delayed and probably wouldn't be back till late in the day on Thursday. I said to Arne when he told me, "It'd be like Zorn to miss the bidding entirely. Just so no one would suspect her of being overly interested in the matter."

Arne chuckled. "Don't worry, my expedition chief will make sure she gets here in time. He knows he'd better."

But as the time for Zorn to get back drew nearer, my dissatisfaction with the way I'd handled things nagged at me with increasing persistence. I decided I had to be more forthright with Gwynedd. So on Thursday morning, I waited in the small parlor around the time she'd normally stop for, at least, a quick cup of coffee, but she never showed up. Haslen noticed me and told me Gwynedd had had her coffee sent to her office.

I crossed the hall, dodged a flurry of cleaning and preparations, and went down the corridor. Her office door was almost but not quite shut and I heard Carsten's voice, so I waited.

"If he wants them at the price of profitability, then he's welcome to them. He's played that game before." Carsten's voice was high with irritation. Gwynedd murmured a response I couldn't quite hear. Whatever she said must have been soothing because Carsten's voice came down in pitch. "You know I trust this House. Completely." Carsten came out of the office, nodded an absent greeting at me, and walked off.

I stuck my head around the door. "Got a minute?"

Gwynedd looked up at me. "No. But come in anyway. I figured you'd get around to it eventually."

Her tone was a giveaway. "So Torvan has talked to you," I said. I came in and sat in one of the easy chairs before her desk.

Gwynedd jotted a few notations on papers spread out before her. Then she laid her pen aside and turned her attention to me. "He gave me the highlights of the conversation you had with him. Your concerns about Lucian. And about Zorn." Gwynedd's manner seemed uncomfortably distant.

"You're mad at me, aren't you?"

"I wasn't happy not to have heard about the other two so-called accidents. Things go on in this household, I need to know about them." And then a generous smile broke through her reserve. "But, no, I'm not mad at you. I just have a lot of details to think about." She waved her hand over the litter of paper on her desk.

"I know I should have spoken with you. Only I can never figure out whether I'm making too much or too little of the things that have happened to Zorn." I sighed. "Besides, she made it very clear. She wasn't accusing anyone. And didn't want me doing it for her."

"Therefore showing more restraint than some." Gwynedd looked at me pointedly. But then she smiled again. "We can only hope that you follow her example."

With an uneasy squirm, I shifted position. "Torvan, did he tell you everything about Zorn?"

"If you mean," Gwynedd replied with a return to seriousness, "what happened to the two of you on the way here, yes, he told me about that, too."

"I'm sorry. I know I shouldn't have kept that from you. It was wrong of me."

"No. I understand what a dilemma that put you in. Choosing between what you think you owe to Zorn and what you owe to me." She paused. "But no matter what concerns I might have about Zorn's past actions, I certainly can't fault her for saving your life." Watching me, she paused again, then added, "I think neither of us is in any doubt, that's what she did."

"No," I said. "No doubt at all."

"And her conduct here has given me no cause for complaint." Gwynedd studied me. "Don't look so gloomy, Grayall. We're in the middle of this and we have to see it through. You expect Zorn back, what, later this afternoon?" I nodded. "Well, Lucian's gone all day today and won't be back until tomorrow at the earliest. Completing arrangements for the grain shipments." She smiled conspiratorially. "I sent Evane with him. You know," she said leaning back in her chair, "I think there's a good chance that young man could end up as my son-in-law. And I don't much like it. He has too much anger in him. I'm also afraid half of what Evane feels for him is pity."

I nodded. "I keep trying to remind myself that Lucian's had...well, he can't have had an easy time. Where did he serve, do you know?"

"No. He doesn't talk about it. At least not to me."

"Let's hope it was in the Domains. Not in the Marches, in one of the traditional houses."

Gwynedd smiled at my distinction. "I'm not sure that would make any great difference to how he feels."

"I suppose you're right." I knew there was one other thing I needed to tell Gwynedd, for myself, for selfish reasons. "Did Evane ever say anything more about our ruckus in the courtyard?"

"Just that you were trying to cast blame on Lucian for some, let's see, what were her words? For some stupid accident caused by the stupid aristo's bad horsemanship."

"Nothing else?"

"Well, she had a few choice words about you, most of which I'm sure she had already said to your face."

"But nothing else about Zorn?"

"No."

I allowed myself a deep breath. "I want to tell you something else, but I want you to keep it to yourself. Because I've pretty much given my word about this." Not to mention having faced Zorn's dry-ice anger over this issue before and not wanting another go. But I didn't say that.

"You shouldn't break a confidence, Grayall." Gwynedd's eyes met mine without wavering.

"Yeah, well, I've already done that. It's just that Evane didn't believe what I told her, so it didn't go any further." Then I told Gwynedd about Zorn, about her helping renegades escape from the Realm and that it was Archon Zarath who had tortured her and left her for dead, not a party of insurgents. "Of course, she refuses to say anything, or let me say anything, about any of it. Because she anticipated reactions like Evane's." I gave a disgruntled sigh. "She's probably right." I could just imagine how Lucian would react to Zorn's claims. Not to mention, the knowing skepticism which would undoubtedly come from someone like

Arne. "Anyway, I wanted you to know. And to make it clear, I believe Zorn told me the truth."

Gwynedd leaned across the desk and stretched out her hand to me. I took it. "Grayall," she said with conviction, "I'm sure she did." She managed a half smile. "If for no other reason than I think Zorn's too proud to lie, especially in the name of gaining favor for herself. From you, or from any of us." She let go of my hand and settled back in her chair. "Aiding runaway servs." She shook her head. "It's a perplexing character your friend has. But don't worry. I'll respect the confidence. As you said, Zorn's assessment is probably correct. About not making a claim like that here. Without any way of substantiating it. But I am glad you told me." She made a brushing movement with her hand. "Now clear out of here and let me get some work done."

Gwynedd returned to sorting through her stacks of paper. I knew I had kept her long enough to strain politeness but Torvan's guess about Zorn's property was still on my mind. "One more thing," I said.

Gwynedd scribbled a note on one of the documents before she looked up again. "Yes, Grayall, one more thing." She mocked me gently.

"The arrangements you set up with Zorn. You had her designate an heir, didn't you?"

Gwynedd seemed disconcerted by my question. "She hasn't discussed it with you?"

"If she had, I wouldn't be asking."

Gwynedd hesitated, then said, "I think you should talk to her about that."

"And I think that probably answers my question. Damn it, I don't want to be her legatee."

Gwynedd gave a small shrug. "She told me what she wanted done. She didn't ask my advice. As I said, Grayall, talk to her. That business is between the two of you. Now, please…" She motioned to her littered desk again.

Reluctantly I let it go at that. After all, Gwynedd was right. Arguing with her about Zorn's decision was pointless. It was Zorn I needed to talk to.

But that conversation would have to wait. It was too early in the day to look for her arrival. Fortunately I had something else to keep me occupied. I had promised Patric to stop by Rellards in the afternoon and give my opinion on a trading proposal they were considering. When we finished, he took me over to the inn for coffee.

I had suspected it wasn't just my assessment of the trading proposal he wanted. Or even my company. I was pretty sure he wanted to sound me out about the bidding as well. Which he did.

We discussed the price the insignia were likely to bring and the best markets for reselling them. He also asked for my impressions on how the bidding would go and whether there would be any serious contenders besides Arne and Carsten. I took the opportunity to satisfy a point of my own curiosity. "About the bidding. Rellards doesn't really have expectations, do they?"

"Oh, we'll just see how we go," he said vaguely. And that was all the information I got from him.

CHAPTER TWENTY-FIVE

When I got back toward the end of the afternoon, Zorn had returned. She must have just come in because she was still dressed for traveling. She was in her room sorting through the few items she had taken with her.

"How was the trip?" I asked.

"Satisfactory."

"The rest of your things were delivered. I checked them over. Everything's in order." I noticed her gun lying, cylinder open, unloaded, at the foot of the bed. "The journey was uneventful, I suppose."

Zorn picked up the gun and a case which I knew contained cleaning supplies. She walked out into the sitting room, sat down, pulled a small table in front of her and began to work. The pungent odor of cleaning oil filled the room, strong, but not unpleasant.

I tried again. "Well, was it uneventful?"

"No one tried to kill me," she said. "Life will get tedious."

I had been leaning against the door jamb between her room and the sitting room, but now I stood upright. "You know, Zorn, the only time you make a joke out of something is when it isn't funny."

"I have already conceded the deficiencies in my sense of humor." She worked on in silence. After oiling the gun, she rubbed it with a soft cloth. When she finished, she looked over at me. "And here?"

"You were gone. Why should there be a problem?" I had already decided not to mention my encounter with Lucian to Zorn. Nor that I had taken both Gwynedd and Torvan into my confidence about the three 'accidents' which had befallen her and about the killing of the bandit. And certainly not that I had also told Gwynedd about her activities in the Realm and their consequences.

Zorn re-loaded the gun and clicked the cylinder shut, a sound that still reverberated for me. "I can think of reasons there would be problems, but I'll refrain from speculation." She set the gun aside.

"By the way," I said, "Lucian's out of the house. Won't be back till tomorrow." Her expression remained unchanged. "I thought you might want to know."

She got up and carried the gun and the cleaning supplies back to her room. I went into mine and changed for the evening. When I came out again, Zorn too had cleaned up and changed, but into another set of outdoor garments, not into dress clothes.

"Aren't you coming down?" I asked her.

"Yes, but not to your commercial festivities. I will leave that for tomorrow."

We went downstairs. The hall was already prepared for the bidding the next day with semi-circles of chairs and a display table. From the sound of things, quite a few of the guests had already gathered in the large drawing room. However, Zorn turned down the nearer corridor. I walked with her to the side door.

"Before you go out, there's something I wanted to ask you," I said. I paused, but Zorn never made polite response to such conversational cues, so I continued, "Who gets your property if something happens to you?"

My abrupt question didn't disconcert her. Without hesitation, she said, "You do." But there was no mistaking the sharpening of interest in her eyes. "Why do you ask?"

All along I'd been nervous that she'd come back at me with that question. "No special reason," I said evasively. I wasn't going to admit it was my conversation with Torvan that had put it into my mind. "I got to thinking about it and I asked Gwynedd. She was noncommittal. But not so noncommittal that I couldn't draw some conclusions." Zorn met my comments with a gaze of unrelenting scrutiny. I plunged ahead, trying to ignore it. "It's not right. It's a lot of property, Zorn."

"Yes, and you should know better than I, I must dispose of it to someone." I granted that point with an unwilling nod. "Do you wish to suggest an alternative?" she asked, a little smugly, I thought.

"Well, you just can't leave a fortune to a…" I was going to say 'stranger' but, of course, Zorn was surrounded by strangers. At present, she knew me as well as she knew anyone. I tried for another possibility. "You must have some family left. Somewhere."

"Family." She spoke the word the way you might try out a foreign term. "Zarath, perhaps," she said with straight-faced solemnity. "And I have other order-kin. They survive as far as I know."

I recalled Bertel, the Presider at Arandell, consulting a record book and reading off a list of names. I dredged my memory but I could not recall them.

Zorn had evidently noticed the play of expression in my face because she added, "Zered and Zirel. I suppose you would consider them part of my family." Irony glinted off her voice like light on polished metal.

I realized again how little I knew about Zorn's former life as a member of the Alphaen order of Northmarch. Still it didn't seem the time to push her further. "All right," I said grudgingly. "I will accept you had to do something. As a formality," I emphasized. "But I want you to know, I'm not comfortable with it. And it's to be only a temporary arrangement."

"All such dispositions of property are temporary arrangements. The death of one party concludes them. But as to your original question, something turned your thoughts to the topic of inheritance." She surveyed me calmly. "You have talked with Gwynedd about the accidents."

I suppose I should have guessed Zorn would make the connection. However, to my surprise, she didn't seem angry, just very sure of herself.

Denial was obviously pointless. "I waited till this morning," I said defensively. "But finally I had to. I won't even apologize for it. With you due back," I continued to grope for words, "I owed it to her. I made it clear, *you* weren't accusing anyone. She had already figured out on her own it wasn't a bad idea to have Lucian out of the house today."

Zorn listened to my stumbling explanations without response. When I finished, maybe I didn't literally hold my breath but it felt that way. And it wasn't only her immediate reaction I was worried about, but whether I was going to get away with this partial confession, because I still didn't want to admit to what else I'd told Gwynedd or that I'd talked to Torvan as well.

From the long, steady appraisal I received, I seriously doubted Zorn was going to drop the subject easily but at last she said, "I have caused you enough conflicts in loyalty here, so I'll accept your judgment in this case. And trust Gwynedd's discretion." She stepped out the door.

I followed her. "And it is your fault," I said to her back. "That I'm especially anxious about your safety. Because now if something happens to you, I'm likely to end up one of the chief suspects."

She stopped and turned her head enough that I would hear her. "If you wish, I will add a codicil absolving you in advance of any blame."

And then she walked off, headed, I was sure, for her haven by the pond.

CHAPTER TWENTY-SIX

I was still looking after Zorn, relieved that she hadn't shown any particular displeasure with my admissions and even more relieved that she hadn't pressed matters further, when Arne showed up. His round, good-humored face was slightly flushed. "Grayall, the gathering's on the other side of the house."

"Yeah."

Coming out, he followed my gaze to where Zorn was moving out of sight around the front corner. "Her Excellency off for her daily dose of contemplative solitude?"

I tapped him on the shoulder. "Is there anything you don't know?"

He laughed. "What I don't know isn't worth knowing."

We strolled over to the opposite wing. Arne shook his head in apparent satisfaction. "I must say, she can play a crowd. With her staying out of the way, there's so much curiosity about her, they're barely keeping their minds on business."

"I don't think it's a tactic, Arne. It's just Zorn."

We walked through the side door which opened directly into the drawing room. About twenty people were clustered in small groups, filling the air with the steady drone of separate conversations. A few heads turned to see who had come in but the mutter of sound continued uninterrupted.

Arne snagged a couple of glasses of wine for us from a passing tray, then guided me to a spot near the front windows where Patric was talking to a tall, successful-looking woman I didn't recognize. "I'm not sure you know Tirze Volsted," Arne said to me. "She recently bought a major interest in Fairways Trade Route. And this," he said, turning to her, "is Grayall of Wellworth, who's brought in this splendid commission."

Although Tirze Volsted, with her amber-tinted skin and dark eyes, looked nothing like Arne, she reminded me of him. Her face, like his, was outwardly stamped with sociability and humor that didn't quite mask an underlying shrewdness. I had the feeling she had me priced from head to toe with one glance.

"Delighted," she said, extending her hand. Her voice was sleek and assured. "I can only hope this bodes well for the renewed fortunes of Wellworth."

"I'm afraid those are mostly entrusted to my brother Karel in the New Tradelands. My goals are more modest."

"And those are?" she asked. She seemed unabashed by her own inquisitiveness.

"So modest that I haven't decided yet what they are."

She laughed. Arne and Patric had drifted off and were engrossed in their own conversation. Tirze let her gaze wander over the room. "The primary player appears to be absent. Zorn of Northmarch, I mean," she added unnecessarily.

"She only arrived back today. From a trip to the Freeholds. I don't think she'll bother with all this." I gestured to the gathering.

"And tomorrow? At the bidding?"

"I assume she'll be there. I haven't actually asked her."

Tirze sipped her wine. "It must be... interesting. Associating with a traditional ariston."

"That's one word for it."

"It's quite unusual for one of them to travel this far south, isn't it? I had heard that the surviving members of the Realm's aristocracy had all fled north. To what they call the Enclaves."

Tirze directed at me an inquiring look. I returned it politely but blankly. "I've heard that too."

She smiled. "You are a model of discretion."

"No. I just prefer to let Zorn speak for herself."

"Which leaves the rest of us, Tirze, with almost no information at all." Arne rejoined us with a laugh, a loud bray that caught a temporary lull in the room. Not far from us stood Carsten and he gave Arne, if not quite a glare, at least an extremely sullen look.

Tirze noticed it too. "Carsten and Arne seem to think they have this piece of business to decide between them." She turned to Patric and said, "Shall we, lesser lights, hope they are flattering each other?"

Patric looked embarrassed. It wasn't like him to be so easily discomposed. But Arne rescued him. "We'll have to wait for the bidding to find that out, won't we?" Arne swung away from our circle and repeated, more loudly, "Won't we, Carsten?" Arne wasn't even close to drunk, but he was, shall I say, well loosened.

Carsten disengaged himself from his conversation and came over. "What's that you say, Arne?"

"Tirze was asking whether there'd be any real competition tomorrow. Will there?"

"Tomorrow, Arne, it will be the bidding that counts, not the soft soap." Carsten glanced from Arne to me as he said it.

Arne put up his hands in mock dismay. With his wine glass in one hand, it looked like he was about to raise a toast. "What will Grayall think? That I cultivate her company only for profit."

"You do everything for profit. Of one kind or another." Carsten's voice held more bite than seemed appropriate for a touch of needling between friends. Maybe he heard it too, because he laid his hand briefly on Arne's shoulder and said, "I can't blame you for making every effort. But tomorrow, we'll see."

With that Carsten walked off. Arne and Tirze started on a round of mingling. Patric and I wandered to the buffet in the dining room. Patric didn't have much to say. He seemed unusually pre-occupied. After we ate, he left me to pursue some contacts of his own.

For the rest of the evening, I enjoyed a fair amount of attention. Part of it was due to continuing curiosity about Zorn. But part of it also came from my recent change in status. I had undergone a distinct elevation from member of a once prosperous but now defunct trading enterprise to agent for the most important commission of the season. I got a lot of glad-handing and hollow assurances about the re-birth of

Wellworth trading enterprise. Most likely, none of it would outlast the week.

Toward the end of the evening, I finally had the chance for a few words with Gwynedd. She seemed satisfied that everything was going well and that Zorn's return had been uneventful. As we talked, I noticed Arne again intently in conversation with Patric. They seemed to have been in some private conversation on and off all evening. I wondered what was going on between them. And what it had to do with the bidding.

"Is Arne up to something?" I asked Gwynedd.

She gazed across the room at Arne and Patric. "I didn't expect Rellards to register for this bid."

"Did Arne have a hand in that?"

She raised her eyebrows. "It wouldn't surprise me."

"You think he has a scheme to gain an edge over Carsten?"

Gwynedd smiled. "I think your betting instincts were right. Carsten will lose this one to Arne."

I remembered what I had overheard outside her office earlier in the day. "Even if Arne has to take the bid out of the range of profit?"

"It wouldn't be the first time. You know Arne. If the goods are prestigious enough, and he decides he wants them, he won't care what it costs him to get them."

"I wonder what Carsten makes of all that."

"It frustrates him. He thinks business is business. For making a profit. Not for grand gestures." Gwynedd shook her head. "After all these years, I don't think Carsten understands it yet. Why Arne will do things like that sometime." Arne had left Patric and was making his way across the room. Still looking in his direction, she added, "But their rivalry will benefit Zorn of Northmarch. She'll get a good price for the insignia. Better, I think, than either of us expected."

Gwynedd moved off to say good night to the other guests. I suppose it was selfish on my part, but I felt a rising elation. And all my anxieties over Zorn and Lucian couldn't quite tamp it down. The bidding would be memorable and, more and more, it looked like it was going to be very successful, as well. My commercial instincts, as Zorn had once labeled them, had suddenly decided, despite everything, to take an immoderate satisfaction in the whole affair.

CHAPTER TWENTY-SEVEN

The bidding assembly would take place in the early afternoon with the reception to follow for as long as anyone cared to drag out the festivities. I slept late, getting up finally when I heard Zorn in the sitting room. From her clothing, she had just come in from riding. Evidently she had gone out earlier than usual because of the day's upcoming activities.

She had brought with her a carafe of coffee and a couple of mugs, and she appeared completely unconcerned.

"Just another typical day, is that it?" I said to her, yawning into my coffee. "Ride in the morning. Acquire fortune in the afternoon."

She cast an assessing eye over my late-rising grogginess. "A typical day for you too, I see."

"What you see is how this commission is wearing me out."

"Wise of you then to fortify yourself as you did last night with a generous measure of Gwynedd's good wine."

Both times she had topped my sarcasm with her familiar deadpan delivery, but I judged Her Excellency was in a congenial mood. And much to my satisfaction, her good humor seemed to extend far enough to pass my disclosures of yesterday without further comment because she didn't ask me anything more about them. Instead we sat and talked about the bidding. I shared Gwynedd's opinion that the rivalry between Arne and Carsten would probably drive up the price of the insignia even higher than we had originally estimated. Zorn listened without comment. Finally when she was almost through with her coffee, I decided to risk more teasing from her by asking if she knew whether Lucian and Evane were back.

"The horses they took are not in the stable," she replied. "Gwynedd appears to maneuver her difficult guests with dexterity."

"It does help that one of them was smart enough to clear out on her own. At least for a while. Although undoubtedly with additional motives, as yet unexplained." I buried my nose in my mug, waiting for a comeback, but Zorn, with uncommon forbearance, merely finished her coffee.

As she stood up to leave, I said, "You will make it to the bidding?"

"Is my presence required?" She almost got me with that until I caught the calculated blandness of her tone. I raised my mug in a pretense of throwing it at her. "Unwarranted violence," she said smoothly. "The last resort of a feeble wit." Then she started out the door.

"Zorn." I stopped her. "If Lucian does show up today, be careful."

"That is my custom. Even without him to inspire me."

After Zorn left, I lounged around drinking coffee, stalling until it was a reasonable time to dress for the bidding. I had given some thought to my appearance, influenced by my lingering pride in the trading enterprise of Wellworth and personal pride as well, I suppose. I knew there would be displays of finery at the bidding assembly, elegant and expensive clothing marking status and success, either actual or apparent. And I intended to match myself to the event.

I had decided to wear the wine-colored trousers Gwynedd had given me and the matching boots, polished to a high sheen. Going through the things I had left with her, I chose a shirt of heavy cream silk, with a high collar and imposing cuffs. To all this I added the richly-hued blue jacket, Zorn's gift, with its impeccable line and equally impeccable fit. I also had a brooch, a circlet of garnets set in gold, the only valuable piece of jewelry I still owned. It had been a gift from Jarrell and I had kept it when I sold off most of what I had of value. I might have to sell it sometime, but I would wait until necessity demanded it.

One of the household staff, a pleasant quiet person named Larit, stopped in to offer assistance. She laid out my clothes while I washed and then helped me dress. She draped my neckcloth into elegant folds, secured it with the garnet brooch, then held my jacket for me as I slipped it on. She stood back and considered me.

"Will I do?" I asked, trying not to preen excessively.

"Very well indeed. You will hold your own with all of them."

"Well, I can at least look the part." I tried to sound unassuming, but it felt good to be impressively dressed.

As Larit prepared to go, I said, "You might keep an eye out for Zorn. She should be back again soon." I laughed. "At least I assume she's planning to change into something suited to the occasion."

"If you wish."

Maybe I imagined the hint of reluctance in Larit's tone. "After all," I added, "she's the one who's really brought this commission to the House."

I walked over to the head of the stairs and stopped to survey things below. The hall was already filling with people. Serious bidders, interested second parties, and curious onlookers. As I expected, everyone present was dressed for display and their shifting movements made the room a kaleidoscope of bright and fashionable color.

I picked out Arne, in red trimmed with cream. Not the best choice for his florid coloring, but a good match for his outgoing personality. Carsten wore a regal shade of purple. Patric, wearing a light-tan jacket and brown trousers, was more subdued. Tirze wore bronze contrasting with gold, the colors of marigolds. And Gwynedd had outdone herself. Over a shirt and trousers of pale spring-green, she wore a sleeveless robe of shimmering iridescence. It all beautifully set off the rich, deep color of her skin.

I smiled to myself. It was a world I used to take very much for granted. I was surprised at how much that was no longer true. But I was going to enjoy this day because I suspected it was going to be my last in the full flush of this world for a long time. And that was not so much because it had to be so but, because deep within me, I wanted it to be so. I didn't know what I was going to choose as an alternative, but I didn't think I was going back to this, despite the opinions of Patric, Arne, and probably Gwynedd herself.

Chapter Twenty-eight

When I came downstairs, I was quickly swept up by Arne. "It's going to be a good thing, Grayall," he said expansively. He looked over my shoulder. "Where is Zorn of Northmarch?"

"Got me," I said with deliberate flipness. "Contemplating the ducks at the pond for all I know."

Arne looked stricken. After all what was the point of cultivating favor with Zorn these past weeks if he couldn't show off the acquaintance at the proper moment. I relented. "Don't worry. She'll be here."

Arne broke into a wide grin. "Grayall, you shouldn't tease like that." He tapped me good-naturedly on the arm and then started off on a round of mingling.

Patric came over. He was keyed up too. He held a glass of wine which I didn't think was his first. We chatted for a few minutes but his eyes kept flicking toward Arne, which only tended to confirm my suspicions that they had some scheme between them.

After Patric left me, I circulated until it was almost time to begin. People began taking their seats in the semi-circle of chairs arranged around the bottom of the staircase. I was about to do the same when I heard a perceptible change in the noise level of the room. I didn't need to look up to see what had caused it but I did anyway.

Zorn was descending the stairs. Her posture upright but not stiff, she kept to the middle of the staircase. She didn't touch the banister on either side. She didn't glance down to check her footing. If her knees were troubling her, you'd never know it from the steady confidence with which she moved.

And she had dressed to proclaim her identity. She wore black. With her jacket and trousers of flawless cut, she looked like a grave, elegant raven bestowing her presence on a flock of brightly colored, but far more frivolous, birds.

Slivers of silver gray from the collar and cuffs of her shirt showed beneath her jacket but they seemed to emphasize, not alleviate, the somber dignity of her appearance. Her pale-gray neckcloth, tied stock fashion, was secured with the new silver and onyx pin she had purchased.

Around me I could sense people were staring while trying to appear not to. But Zorn, entirely self-contained, seemed oblivious to the attention she drew.

When she reached the bottom of the stairs, she walked straight across to the back row of chairs. As she passed me, she favored me with her usual unrevealing stare, but perhaps her gaze held a message for me. Maybe a lot of messages.

I didn't have time to reflect on the matter because, as soon as Zorn seated herself, Gwynedd went to the stairway and climbed up a few steps. The noise in the room subsided and the heads which had been craning to follow Zorn turned back to the front.

"If you would all take your places," Gwynedd said firmly but with a smile, "we are ready to proceed with the business which has gathered us here." When everyone had settled down, Gwynedd continued, "As you know, today a unique opportunity presents itself to the Exchanges and to us. We are about to commence bidding on items of great rarity. None such, in fact, have ever been put up for sale before. We offer for your consideration insignia from that territory formerly known as Regeren or, more familiarly among us, as the Realm. Insignia that were attached to the Alphaen order of Northmarch and the Wardership of Farnorth."

With a raise of her hand, she signaled. Household employees came forward, carrying the boxes which held the insignia. They slowly advanced through the assembly presenting the contents for inspection. They were followed by others who distributed printed cards giving descriptions of each piece of the insignia and detailing their actual weight in gold and composition in stones. Of course, that information had been available previously, but this was the first time the bidders were seeing the insignia for themselves. However, it was not the intrinsic value of the pieces that aroused everyone's interest. As I had noted and as Gwynedd had reminded everyone, it was their rarity which was their attraction and which would bring the price.

Murmurs of appreciation had followed the insignia. I wondered what Zorn thought of it all. I didn't look back at her to see because I knew her face wouldn't show a thing.

When the insignia had been placed on the display table and all the cards distributed, Gwynedd said, "Before we begin I would like to ask Grayall of Wellworth to stand. Many of you, in years past, traded profitably with Wellworth and Grayall's family. You will be pleased to know it was Grayall who brought this outstanding commission to us."

I stood to a round of polite applause, feeling equally proud and embarrassed. As I sat down again, this time I couldn't resist a glance at Zorn. She had turned her head slightly to watch me. Her face was impassive but I was sure she was amused. I was becoming quite expert at reading the nuances of her varying degrees of non-expression. Or so I fancied.

Needless to say, Gwynedd did not single out Zorn for similar attention as the seller of the insignia. And without further delay, the bidding began.

Tirze Volsted opened with a formality bid of five hundred argen. Carsten promptly raised that to five-fifty. Others joined in, but Arne kept silent. Carsten looked at him uncertainly a couple of times as the bidding climbed to eight-hundred. The rest of the bidders dropped out and it became a contest between Carsten and Tirze. I felt that Carsten was sure he could outlast her. Still, his gaze kept darting to Arne but Arne offered no bid. Carsten seemed unsure whether to be perplexed or pleased.

When Carsten bid a thousand, Tirze sighed slightly and went up another hundred, but it was obvious she had reached her limit. Undoubtedly Carsten was sure his bid of twelve-hundred was going to win. Watching him, I thought he was trying hard not to bounce on his toes in anticipation of victory. Only once he called out his bid, Patric, of all people, entered with a bid of twelve-fifty.

Carsten responded with an audible grunt of exasperation. No one expected Rellards to handle that kind of price. Patric, for his part appearing nervous but determined, stayed with Carsten as the bid continued to rise. Thirteen. Thirteen-fifty. Fourteen. Fourteen-fifty. Finally Carsten, his face rigid with frustration, called out fifteen-hundred.

That was awfully close to the limit of any expectation of a reasonable return on investment. The insignia should bring eighteen-hundred, but not much more, in the coastal ports. Allowing for fees paid to Gwynedd and other expenses, at the current bid Carsten could still turn a profit, not a generous one, but adequate. However, if he went any higher, he'd be lucky to break even.

Patric held silent and Gwynedd began a three count. Carsten leaned forward. His head and shoulders rocked back and forth as though to urge her along. On the second count, Arne finally spoke. He bid two-thousand. An exorbitant amount. Surely more than he could hope to recoup.

A rash of murmurs broke out and rippled through the assembly. Carsten, head drooping, shoulders now slumping, actually seemed to deflate physically. Twice he had been sure he had the bid, and by his calculations should have had it. Gwynedd looked at him. He shook his head in disgust and Arne took the insignia with his one and only bid.

When Gwynedd officially named Arne as the successful bidder, applause broke out and he stood to receive it. He was rapidly surrounded by well-wishers and back-slappers. They'd be talking about this bidding for a long time. A lot of them would fault Arne for his extravagance but they'd be impressed nonetheless. That he could be so heedless of the demands of profit. And he'd always be known as the trader who scooped up with one bid the first traditional ariston insignia ever offered for sale.

CHAPTER TWENTY-NINE

I watched Arne move to the front of the gathering to sign the purchase verification which one of Gwynedd's clerks offered him. I noted the bleak anger in Carsten and I knew Gwynedd had been right. Arne's actions had very little to do with ordinary trading. It wasn't the insignia Arne had purchased. It was the demonstration of his ability to win, specifically to win over Carsten. He had shown his acumen in sizing up the limits, both financial and personal, of his chief rival. And poor Carsten, who didn't think in terms of symbolic victories, surely couldn't understand it. It must have seemed to him simply a willful and foolish undercutting of his attempts to conduct sensible business.

But if over the years there was any reason why Arne was perceived as the most influential trader in the Exchanges, it was because he was willing to pursue victories for their own sake, for the status they conferred, even if it cost him to win them.

I made my way against the flow of the crowd back to Zorn who stood temporarily forgotten, it seemed, in the excitement of the bidding.

"Congratulations," I said, trying to moderate my own excitement. It had gone even better that I expected. "As Gwynedd said, nothing like a little friendly rivalry to produce a good result."

Zorn didn't bother to remark on the acquisition of a substantial fortune. Instead she stared past me to where Arne stood amid well-wishers and then to where Carsten stood alone. "The rivalry appears to be more costly than friendly." Shifting her gaze back to Arne, she asked, "Will he make any profit? Bennetson."

I laughed. "You worried about him?"

"Answer my question."

"If you mean monetary profit, almost certainly he will not."

"I was not aware they recognized any other kind of profit here."

I followed Zorn's gaze and watched Arne beaming at the center of a cluster of admirers. I said, "There is such a thing as investing in prestige, in reputation. With an eye toward future profits."

Another voice spoke over my shoulder. "If that's what he bid on, he seems to be getting his money's worth." It was Tirze who joined us, clearly expecting an introduction, so I obliged.

"Zorn, this is Tirze Volsted. A major shareholder in Fairways Trade Route. Tirze, Zorn of Northmarch."

Tirze started to extend her hand, reconsidered, and then inclined her head instead. "I'm honored, Your Excellency. And may I also extend my congratulations. An excellent price, even if too rich for me."

Zorn was spared the effort of a response because just behind us Carsten had come up to Patric and was whispering fiercely to him. I couldn't make out what he was saying, but Carsten looked furious and Patric looked defiant. After a minute, Patric shook his head, turned away, raised his eyebrows at me, and then walked off. Carsten went in the opposite direction, still seething if I was any judge.

"What did you make of that?" Tirze said to me. Another curiosity had sidetracked her from Zorn.

"I'm not sure I should say."

With a smile, Tirze provided an answer to her own inquiry. "Arne played it well. And he's willing to pay for what he wants." She turned back to Zorn. "Does this all seem very silly to you, Your Excellency?"

"As my agent, Grayall insists that I treat all financial matters with the utmost seriousness," Zorn said gravely.

Tirze bubbled with laughter. "I imagine she does. Although, with no disrespect to Grayall, I also imagine such insistence comes only with your permission. But I do congratulate you both." She patted my shoulder. "Nice commission, Grayall. Very nice. Perhaps we can discuss business sometime."

She floated back to the rest of the crowd.

"Did you understand any of that?" I said to Zorn.

"I understood she was indirectly offering you employment." An attendant came by with glasses of wine. I took one and handed one to Zorn. "Also that she suspects some collusion between Bennetson and Patric." Zorn frowned slightly. "Does it make sense to encourage an ally to raise the bidding?"

I shook my head. "Patric was just a proxy. My guess is that Arne assumed Carsten would go as high as he did in a straight head-to-head between the two of them anyway, so he used Patric to take up the bidding in his place. In part because he knew it would throw Carsten off stride, make him more likely to buckle when Arne wanted him to. But mostly because it would make his own win more impressive. Which it did. Of course he could have simply opened with that final bid, but…"

Zorn finished for me. "That method would have lacked sufficient drama." Her voice held a faint note of distaste.

"You got it." I looked back at the people still gathered around Arne. "They'll talk about this for a long time. How Bennetson jumped in and took the ariston's insignia with one bid. Arne'll love it."

Zorn paused to consider. "What if Carsten had dropped out sooner than Bennetson expected?"

"Arne knew there wasn't much risk of that. But if he'd figured wrong, he would've covered Rellards' bid, buying the insignia back from them at that price. Not as impressive, but still a loss for Carsten. Only Arne didn't figure wrong."

"And Patric's employer receives a fee. For his cooperation."

"Sure. Patric gets his percentage too. And Arne's good will, which is even better."

Zorn's gaze slid back to Arne and his well-wishers. "Is Bennetson's maneuver considered ethical here?"

Her question surprised me. "It's considered sharp practice. And it'll be suspected, but there won't be any proof because nobody's going to be talking."

"And the suspicion will not hurt Bennetson's reputation."

I confirmed Zorn's judgment with a twist of my head. The group around Arne was beginning to spread out. "You planning to stick around?" I gestured toward the dispersing crowd. "They'll be after you next."

"Should I consider that a daunting prospect?"

"They were curious enough when you were just exotic. Now you're rich and exotic."

A glimmer of amusement shone in Zorn's eyes. "Fortunately I have papers to sign," she said.

I was about to lead the way back to Gwynedd when I saw an awkward movement at the edge of the cluster of people, as if they had been jostled. Evane's voice, pitched high with emotion, rang out. "Lucian," she called shrilly. Simultaneously the small sea of people parted to make way for the disturbance in their midst. Lucian, having moved ahead of Evane, was standing there like a suddenly risen island, and standing rock firm despite the fact that he was obviously drunk.

CHAPTER THIRTY

Like a rolling wave, heads, one after another, swiveled toward Lucian. On faces, a variety of expressions played. On some, amusement. Disdain on others. On many, gratified fascination.

But Lucian wasn't noticing any of it. He was staring straight at Zorn. "Aristo shit. Aristo garbage." He didn't shout it. He spoke almost conversationally, his voice slurring only a little. Evane moved quickly to his side but, when she put her hand up to his arm, he shook himself free and stalked forward.

I wanted to tell Zorn to give way, but she had already stepped aside from me, her attention focused on Lucian. Her expression betrayed neither anger nor apprehension. She simply looked observant.

Lucian advanced with a steady, if stiff-legged, gait. And when he was close enough, his right arm shot forward. With the heel of his hand, he shoved Zorn hard, striking her on the left shoulder. He punctuated the blow with, "Aristo shit," again. Lucian's range of insults was unimaginative.

The force of his strike staggered Zorn backwards a couple of steps. The wine glass in her right hand tilted and the wine spilled, its deep red staining her pale gray cuff. She released the glass and let it fall. The crystal broke melodically on the stone-tiled floor.

"Zorn." I tried to intervene but Lucian pushed me and I slipped on the wine and broken glass. Zorn paid me no attention whatever. I had seen a look like hers before. I have watched a cat become totally absorbed by some movement which might signal potential prey. Zorn looked like that. Her face was fixed in concentration, the rest of her surroundings might as well not have existed. There was only Lucian. She would kill him, I thought.

Even as I thought it, Lucian stepped forward and shoved her hard again. She gave with that blow, too, although less sharply. She had been ready for it.

I couldn't see Lucian's face, so I couldn't tell what, if any, satisfaction he was getting, nor what level of escalation he might be intending. Needless to say, this was one of those times when things happened much more quickly than it takes to tell. By now some people had come to their senses and were moving toward Lucian. Whether he noticed them, I didn't know, but his arm thrust out a third time. "Aristo shit," he repeated convulsively. This time his voice rasped, almost tearfully I thought.

And this time Zorn reacted with one fluid movement. As Lucian's arm drove forward, she turned sideways so that his arm passed in front of her. His blow meeting no resistance, the force of it carried him forward, off-balance. His arms jerked to the side, his fingers splayed out, the last two on his left hand awkwardly askew. Zorn hooked her leg around his and he went sprawling. As he fell, she took a quick step away but it was an unnecessary precaution. He hit hard. I could hear the crack of his chin on the floor and the whoosh of breath knocked out of him.

Zorn's actions had temporarily halted the movement toward them. And now, before anyone else regained their composure, Evane rushed forward. I was sure she was going after Zorn. I grabbed for her, and missed. But instead she went down on her knees beside Lucian, who was slowly trying to push himself up to his hands and knees.

A couple of the men came forward and eased him to a sitting position. His chin was bleeding and his cheeks were streaked with moisture.

Gwynedd was there too. She stared down at Lucian, her face frozen in disgust. She made no commiserating move as the others helped him to his feet. Evane looked at her mother, trying, I thought, to come up with something to say, but evidently not finding any words. Lucian, too, appeared to have used up his meager store. Supported by the two men, he slowly headed toward the back of the house. Evane followed them.

Gwynedd turned to Zorn who was standing by in apparently unruffled composure. "Are you all right?" she asked her.

I burst into a sputter of nervous laughter. "Of course, she's all right," I said. "It was Lucian who ended up flat on the floor."

Gwynedd gave me a silencing look, then turned back to Zorn. "I apologize for this. I only wish an apology had more worth."

"You have nothing to apologize for." Zorn's tone was neither petulant nor challenging. She spoke as a simple matter of fact. But Gwynedd did not seem reassured. Seeing her discomfort, Zorn added coolly, "It was bound to happen. Eventually." Zorn's gaze flicked to the entranced faces of the people gathered around. "We should conclude our business."

With apparent relief, Gwynedd collected Arne and led them both from the hall and down the corridor to her office.

CHAPTER THIRTY-ONE

Once it was clear that the impromptu entertainments were over, people began to drift in the direction of the ample buffet spread in the dining room. I was tempted to follow the principal players into the seclusion of Gwynedd's office, but I decided that, despite all the excitement, I was hungry. So instead, I went off to the dining room, too.

I filled a plate and staked out a reasonably quiet corner of the small parlor. But I couldn't avoid the steady stream of congratulations on the splendid commission, almost all of which were followed by some version of how much we look forward to meeting Her Excellency. I assumed that was an indirect way of asking if Zorn planned to reappear. At least when it came to direct inquiries about the altercation with Lucian, most people showed some tactful restraint. To all the congratulations and the inquiries, I offered polite, but evasive, comments.

When I finished eating, I strolled back into the hall where Arne was again at the center of a buzz of people. While I watched, he detached himself from the crowd and moved over for a few words with Carsten who had come back and was standing with a group of friends. Arne motioned him aside and they spent a couple of moments in close conversation. Then Arne turned and gestured toward the others. He said something I couldn't hear. Whatever it was drew their approval, but the smile of reconciliation from Carsten was obviously forced.

Gwynedd had returned also and was circulating gracefully. I looked around for Zorn, but saw no bit of sober black in the mosaic of colors.

Eventually Gwynedd worked her way over to me. I saluted her with my wine glass. "Can we say, we did well?"

"We can. Although the real credit goes to our old friends." She glanced over at Arne and Carsten. "Arne was always gracious. In victory," she added wryly.

"And Carsten's choking on it." I sipped my wine. "What did you do with Lucian?"

"They took him upstairs. He needs to go to bed and sleep it off."

"I'm not sure what's bothering him can be slept off." I looked around the room again. "Zorn didn't come back?"

"She took some papers into the library. Something to do with the Freehold trip, I think."

Gwynedd was interrupted by other guests claiming her attention. I started across the hall, figuring to see what Zorn was up to, but a hand on my elbow stopped me. It was Patric. He clinked his glass against mine, a little unsteadily. "A good show. Both acts."

"Since when does one of the actors give the review?"

"I just followed my employer's instructions." He grinned at me.

"Sure, and Rellards could really have managed a bid of fourteen-hundred or so. How much did Arne give them?"

Patric raised his eyebrows. "Grayall, how suspicious." Then the corners of his mouth turned up slyly and he said, "Two hundred."

"What's your share?" I asked.

"Ten percent."

"Twenty argen," I said. "Not bad for a few minutes work."

"Not as good as you." Patric drained his glass. "Let's get some more wine." As we walked to the dining room, he continued, "Gwynedd took in, what? About five-hundred in bidding registration fees. That comes out to at least fifty argen for you by my reckoning." I didn't want any more wine, but he refilled his glass. "So your ariston has been good business for both of us. Which is more than you can say for what's-his-name."

"Lucian. He was drunk," I said, my eyes shifting toward Patric's glass.

Noticing, he lifted it to the light. "I've had a bit of Gwynedd's excellent wine. But *I'm* not drunk."

"I think you could get there without too much trouble."

"You're probably right." He set his glass down. "How about a walk? Clear my head." I glanced around. The assembly of bidders and guests had thinned and I was ready for some quiet anyway.

Patric and I went out the back. Without any particular intention, we wandered down to the dock. Part of the shipment which Lucian had arranged, including the things from Arne's, was stacked waiting to be loaded. A welcome reminder that Lucian would be leaving soon.

We stood gazing at the river. We'd had some more rain on and off the last few days and its current was running strong. I got the same feeling I'd had the day Patric and I had lunch. That he had something on his mind, but I didn't prod him. After a while he said, "What are you going to do now?"

"I don't know. I have some breathing room, thanks to my agent's percentage from the sale."

"You're really not going to head south to join your brother, are you?"

I shook my head vaguely. "I don't think so. I told you, I don't have much enthusiasm for giving the next twenty years of my life to rebuilding Wellworth."

Patric bent down, picked up a few stones, and idly began to throw them in the river. I took a couple of the stones from him and tossed them in as well. We both picked up some more and began trying to hit a piece of wood that was drifting by. I did better than Patric, but then again, I'd had less wine.

He let his handful of stones fall and looked at me seriously. "I know Jarrell's death has...well, what has it taken out of you, Grayall?"

I shrugged. "I used to know what I wanted. Right now, I don't. I loved him, you know. We would have had a good life together." I flung the rest of the pebbles I held into the river. Some of them chunked on the floating log. "But he's dead. And I'm going to make a life. I'm just going to give myself a little time before I decide what it will be."

"Will you marry? Someone else?"

"I wasn't planning to advertise," I said brusquely. Patric looked crestfallen. I summoned up an apologetic tone. "I didn't mean to be short with you. I would have married Jarrell. But understand, marriage in the abstract is not what I had in mind. Maybe it's one of the reasons I'm not anxious to rejoin the family endeavors. Pressure to help re-build the dynasty, give it heirs, I mean."

"I don't suppose you'd consider me?" He said it so quietly I almost missed it. "Listen, I know I'm not Jarrell," he went on before I could react, "and I know it wouldn't be between us the way it was between you and him but…we both have to re-make something. We come from similar backgrounds. I have money saved. Between us, we have enough to make a new start. Build something of our own."

I almost blurted out, but, Patric, I don't even like you. Fortunately I caught myself. I turned away from him, searching for a way to answer, a way to tell him I had no interest in him and no interest in founding the new enterprise he aspired to. It would have been easier if I had some idea what I did want.

My continued silence must have told him a lot. "Grayall," he started to say but that was as far as he got because from somewhere beyond us, to the side, came a whoosh of sound, and then a series of quavering shrieks which rode on the air like some tortured, demonic chant.

Chapter Thirty-two

Patric and I both turned in the direction of the sound. It came from beyond a stand of trees which blocked our view. All we could see was a column of smoke rising over them, growing thicker as we watched.

"What the hell is that?" I heard Patric exclaim, but I was already running. I knew what was on the other side of those trees. The pond.

My dash toward the pond caught Patric off guard. "Grayall. Wait." But his protest ended abruptly. A swirl of wind had blown across to us an odor that stuck in the throat. I didn't look back but I could hear Patric hurrying behind me.

As I threaded my way through the trees that separated the dock area from the other side of the grounds, the smell intensified. It seized me and made me gag. Before I was through the trees, the shrieks had stopped.

By the time I broke into the open, Patric had caught up to me. The pond was now in view. Beside it, a roaring fire blazed. Peaks of flame, snapping wildly, engulfed the pile of logs where Zorn had so often sat. We tried to advance, but fierce heat pressed us back. The throat-clogging odor closed around us. At last we staggered, choking and retching, to a halt.

Stupefied, I was dimly aware of a growing confusion of noise and movement behind us. Others had seen the blaze and come rushing from the house and stable. But like us, they too had stopped and we all stood, dazed, unable to grapple with the vision that confronted us.

Because at its center, the fire raged around a dark, distorted mass, not yet formless enough to disguise that it had once been a person.

Someone had died a writhing, agonized death in those flames. Someone. Even then my mind rejected what was certainly true. Not someone. "Zorn." My cry was involuntary, as futile as it was anguished.

Then I ignited with rage. Rage was a refuge from the horror of that appalling death. And it grew as hot within me as that inferno without. I raged at Zorn's arrogance and pride which had brought her to the unspeakable heart of that conflagration. Somehow, Zorn, finally the right trap has been set. Is that evidence enough for you now? Are you satisfied? "Are you satisfied?" I shouted.

Someone pulled me back a few steps. Patric, I supposed. Gwynedd appeared and soon a ragged line of people stretched toward the near end of the pond and began to pass buckets of water as close to the fire as possible. But no sooner had the first arc of water descended than the heart of the fire flared again, the water seeming to feed it, instead of quieting it.

And then Torvan was there, ordering everyone away. He yelled, "No. No water. Not yet." Which made no sense to me. I heard disconnected fragments about gas and reactivity and danger. The fire continued to roar, and everyone drew further back, away from its suffocating fumes. It burned unhindered, reducing the thing within it to a lump of shapeless matter. Somewhere behind me I heard Gwynedd's voice. "Find Lucian. And stay with him." I felt an arm around my shoulder. "Grayall." It was Gwynedd again. "Come away. There's nothing you can do."

I think she said something to Torvan and to Patric. And then, with gentle pressure, she tugged me away. As we turned from the heat and stench, more people, members of the household, flowed past us. I was vaguely aware of Gwynedd issuing orders as we went. Some part of me wanted to stop, to go back, but Gwynedd, her hand on my back, firmly urged me forward. And I guess a greater part of me wanted to leave because I did not resist.

Chapter Thirty-Three

I don't remember walking back to the house, or crossing the hall, or saying anything. It was just that after a time I found myself seated in the small parlor, Gwynedd hovering over me, insisting that I drink the brandy she was holding out to me. When I had gulped it down, she poured a little more. I drank that too and then sat staring sightlessly at the glass that dangled limply in my hand.

Gwynedd reached down, took the glass away, and placed it on the table next to me. "Let me help you upstairs. You need to lie down."

I shook my head. "I'll just sit here," I said in a disconnected voice. "You have things to do."

There was a bustle of noise in the hall, the sound of people and unintelligible voices. "The officer from the district watch," Gwynedd murmured under her breath. I heard her cross to the door but her footfalls stopped abruptly. She uttered a wordless exclamation and I looked up. Zorn of Northmarch was standing in the doorway.

I suppose at enough distance it will become funny to me. For an instant I knew what it was like to see a ghost. My mind knew Zorn was dead. And I couldn't reconcile the contradiction that stood before my eyes. Dumbfounded, I stared at her like the apparition she was.

As for Zorn, her face registered no surprise at the confusion before her, but her eyes rapidly assessed the scene. With her usual observant appraisal, she looked at me, at the glass beside me, at Gwynedd, then back at me. "Are you all right?" she asked. Her voice, like her expression appeared unmoved, but somewhere within that question lurked a note of genuine concern.

I was too stunned to do more than gaze at her open-mouthed, but Gwynedd blurted out, "We thought you were dead. In the fire."

"Why would you think that?" Zorn's voice was composed, although perhaps a trace of wonderment passed over her face.

I stood up to meet her. "The fire. At the pond. The fire. And someone's there. Dead. In the middle of it." My words came out in ragged bursts. And I tottered.

"Grayall," Gwynedd said gently. She took my elbow and eased me back into my chair.

I put my head in my hands and said with a muffled voice, "Damn you, Zorn." Anger and relief battled within me.

Someone came to the doorway and called Gwynedd out. I heard her say, "I have to meet the district watch officer. Will you stay with her?" She wasn't talking to me. "I think Grayall's right. Whatever happened out there was intended for you." Gwynedd's voice was bleak.

After she left, I seemed to be sitting in a pool of stillness, even though in the background I could hear the sounds of voices, footsteps, doors opening and shutting. The sounds seemed to come from a distance and to have nothing to do with me.

There was a clink of glass next to me. It sounded very loud. The brandy glass, refilled, appeared under my nose, my field of vision contained in the pale-tea color of its contents and bounded by the scarred fingers that held it.

"Drink it." The familiar, flat, uninflected voice.

I took the glass, sipped from it, and then tried to put it aside, but my hand shook and the glass rattled against the tabletop. Zorn reached over, steadied my hand, and slid the glass away.

"I was upstairs," she said. "Besides it's early. Earlier than the time I usually go out there."

I shook my head. "I thought it was you." I felt numb, as groggy as if I'd been punched.

Zorn picked up my glass and offered it to me again. "Finish your brandy."

I pushed her hand away. "Don't patronize me."

Zorn set my glass on the table and reached for the brandy decanter. She took another glass and poured herself a small measure. She pulled a chair over and sat opposite me. "I am sorry. For your distress."

"Distress. That's a word for it." My anger, the shelter from the turmoil I'd gone through, seemed to have curdled into a kind of sullen resentment.

Zorn studied me with her dark appraising eyes. "It's hardly reasonable of you to be displeased with me for not being dead."

I finally reached for my glass and drank off the brandy in one gulp. "What I'm displeased about," I dragged out the words, "is that all along you've refused to take seriously enough the things that have been happening. Someone *is* trying to kill you, Zorn. And getting better at it. And you're too stubborn or too proud, or maybe too afraid to face any more vulnerability, to admit it."

She sipped her brandy. "An interesting and plausible analysis. Although it happens to be inaccurate. It also misses the central point."

"Which is what?"

"I'm not the one who died in the fire. But someone did." She looked past me. Her thoughts had turned inward.

"Yes," I said. "Someone died. Someone died in your place."

Zorn didn't pay any attention to me. "Now the questions are, who was it? And why?" She seemed to be talking to herself.

"Why?" I all but shouted at her. "Didn't you hear me? Someone walked into a trap set for you. That's why!"

I don't know if she intended to respond but she didn't get the chance. I had been so intent on my conversation with her that I hadn't noticed Gwynedd reappear in the doorway. Her elegant clothing was stained with soot and sweat. Her face was drawn into lines of strain. "We think it may be Carsten," she said dully.

"Carsten," I repeated, unbelieving.

Gwynedd came into the room, dropped wearily into a chair, and took the brandy Zorn held out to her. "We can't find him. His belongings are still upstairs. But no one knows where he is."

As it turned out, of course, we did know where he was. They were right. It was Carsten who had died in the fire, died evidently for being in the wrong place at the wrong time. For visiting the spot that Zorn of Northmarch had appropriated for her own. I was convinced Carsten had died the death undoubtedly intended for Zorn herself.

Chapter Thirty-four

The rest of that awful day was devoted to the constabulary sorting out as many facts about the fire and Carsten's death as they could. The local watch officer Gwynedd had sent for had taken one look at the situation and had called in the District Constable. Within the hour, he had taken charge of the investigation. The DC's name was Daniel Oletto. He was a tall, thin, brown-skinned man with an angular face whose nervous mannerisms masked an inner assurance. He brought with him two Under Constables to assist in compiling statements and a physician who aided in the removal of what could loosely be called, the body.

They worked with unhurried efficiency, thorough but scrupulously polite. After all, it was a board composed of the proprietors of major enterprises, such as Gwynedd's, that paid their salaries. They directed their attention first to the assumption that it was Carsten who had been killed. And confirmed it, not only by the fact that he was missing, but also by fishing out of the remains of the fire a ring which had belonged to him. It was bent and misshapen but still identifiable. What had brought Carsten to the pond, they were unable to determine. But a couple of the grooms had seen him walking past the stable shortly before the fire, heading toward the gardens and the path which led back there. According to their report, he had been alone at the time.

The constables asked those of us who knew Carsten well enough to have an opinion, if we could think of any reason for him to go out to the pond. I told them he might have been walking off his anger at losing the bid for the insignia to Arne. Later Gwynedd told me she had offered the same possibility.

They also confirmed very quickly that the fire in which Carsten had died had been no accident. As I feared would be the case, he had walked into a purposeful and terrible contrivance. He had been caught in one of the spring-traps that had been among the supplies Lucian had purchased.

The trap had been placed, undoubtedly concealed under leaves and grass, on the path in front of the logs Zorn had often used as a bench. Placed so that anyone approaching the spot would step on the trap, trip its mechanism, and bring its jaws slamming shut. As had happened to Carsten. With his leg pinned, he had been unable to escape the fire when it ignited.

However the cause of the fire was a puzzle. It seemed to have erupted spontaneously, too hot and too intense for any normal explanation. If Carsten himself had thrown a match down at his feet, not even the driest scraps of tinder would have burst into such a conflagration. And in fact, the remaining debris of vegetation that ringed the spot had not been dry, but sodden from the recent rains.

Fortunately for the District Constable and his people, Torvan had a solution to this problem. Summoning Gwynedd and me to join him, he presented it to DC Oletto. I'll never forget the expression on his face when he laid before us two metal canisters and explained that he had recognized in the fire's stench something other than the horror of burning human flesh.

The canisters, the kind he used for storage in his laboratory, carried labels with noticeable red letters. One read Na, the other K. The former I recognized. Torvan extracted from it the glass vial I had seen before, with its bits of material that looked like tarnished silver submerged in clear liquid. "This contains pieces of pure sodium," he told Oletto. "This other," he nodded to the canister marked K, "held a similar vial of potassium."

"Held?" Oletto questioned.

Replacing the vial of sodium, Torvan removed the lid from the second canister. From it, he pulled protective wadding but nothing else. "That vial's gone now." He took a breath. "Sodium and potassium. Alkali metals. In their pure state, they're highly reactive." He laid a finger on the rim of the empty canister. "The potassium that was in here started that fire. I'm sure of it. I don't know how it got there. But I do know the fire reeked of burning hydrogen. Released in the chemical reaction." Torvan's normally animated voice had collapsed into a dull monotone.

DC Oletto dabbed his brow with a neatly folded handkerchief. "When you say, highly reactive, what exactly does that mean?"

"The alkali metals ignite in water or air. Sodium will burn in water." Torvan glanced at me and I understood why he had asked me to be present at this explanation. I didn't leave it to him to tell the DC about the demonstration with sodium he had given me. I spoke up myself and described what Torvan had shown me. I concluded by saying, trying not to sound defensive, "But I didn't know about the potassium."

Torvan patted my arm and said, "That's right. You didn't." He turned to Oletto. "Potassium is even more reactive than sodium. It needs only the slightest trace of moisture to burn in air, explosively. To be more precise," he continued, the scholar in him taking over despite his distress, "it's the hydrogen that burns. The alkali metals react with air and water, generating hydrogen gas. The reaction generates heat which ignites the gas." He tapped the vial of sodium. "You store them in an inert substance. Mineral oil. Or in this case, kerosene."

The DC was following. "You're saying, if you smashed one of these vials and exposed the material within it just to the air, it would start a fire."

Torvan nodded. "The sodium probably would, the potassium certainly would. Especially in damp conditions."

"So if the missing vial had been attached to the jaws of the trap which was near the pond and probably covered in wet leaves, and then the vial had been broken when the trap snapped shut…?" Oletto let his voice trail off into a question.

"The potassium would surely have ignited." Torvan shook his head despairingly. "As I'm convinced it did. Setting off everything else. The kerosene, the clothing, and…" He didn't need to finish the sentence.

The DC dabbed his brow again with precise little pats, then gestured to the canisters. "May I ask why you had these…materials…on hand?" In his pause you could all but hear the word 'hazardous' he had refrained from voicing.

Torvan met Oletto's question with assurance. "I would have such things for study, generally. But in this particular case, I was preparing a talk for our local research institute."

"And they were kept where?"

"On shelves in my laboratory. A small detached building behind the house."

"Locked?"

"For the night. After I quit work in the evening. Not usually during the day."

Oletto made clucking sounds of disapproval.

"We are not accustomed to worry about thievery in this house," Gwynedd interjected.

The DC glumly surveyed the canisters. "No," he said, "although there seems to be nothing customary about this matter." He turned his attention back to Torvan. "These containers, you found them today in their normal places?" Torvan confirmed that he had. "The empty container. Had the lid been put back on?"

"Yes."

Oletto nodded and then instructed Torvan to return the canisters to the laboratory. "But keep its door locked."

"Yeah," Torvan agreed bitterly. "Only, in this case, late is as bad as never."

CHAPTER THIRTY-FIVE

The weekend that followed lingers in my memory as existing in some kind of half-life. Normal activities resumed, but they seemed a minor counterpoint to the persistent presence of District Constable Oletto and his underlings. With Gwynedd's consent, they more or less took over the house with their observations and interrogations.

They questioned and re-questioned everyone in the household and everyone who had attended the bidding about their actions that day. They asked how many people knew that such volatile substances as sodium and potassium were kept on the premises. Torvan acknowledged that it was hardly a secret. He was in the habit of discussing his research with friends and acquaintances. He had never had a reason not to. Had he ever talked about the alkali metals specifically with Lucian? Yes, he had. But certainly with many others as well. And no, he could not tell how many people knew that Na and K were symbols for sodium and potassium. He had probably mentioned it but couldn't remember exactly to whom.

As their tiresome rounds of interviews continued, the constables learned nothing about why anyone would want to kill Carsten of Wrightwork but plenty about the ariston and the former serv. They learned about Lucian's anger at Zorn's presence in the house. They learned about the previous mishaps. The branch, the hay bale, the horse going down. And they learned about Zorn's habit of sitting by the pond by herself every afternoon.

In view of it all, they paid particular attention to what Lucian had done following his confrontation with Zorn after the bidding. They determined that, once he had been taken upstairs, no one had seen him until he was found, not in his room, but walking back to the house from the general direction of the dock. Asked for an explanation, he said he had decided he needed some air and walked out to check over his shipment of supplies. That he had noticed the commotion on the other side of the trees and was coming back to the house to inquire what was wrong. However, if he had been near the dock before the fire, Patric and I hadn't seen him while we were out there.

Evane had desperately wanted to provide Lucian with an alibi by supporting his story but she could not. Upset over the spectacle he had made of himself in his scuffle with Zorn, she had sought out her father and they had been together until the fire broke out.

Of course, I found all this out after the fact, in bits and pieces, since we were all interviewed separately. By the end of the weekend, the constabulary had reached what seemed the inevitable conclusion. Carsten's death had been an accident and not an accident. An accident in that it was he who had died, not an accident in that the fire was a deliberate attempt at murder. And in view of recent events in the household, that attempt had been aimed at Zorn of Northmarch. They had also, to no one's surprise, selected their chief suspect.

When most of us were reeling with weariness, DC Oletto informed Lucian that they were taking him into custody until a hearing could be convened to determine whether a formal charge would be lodged. Under the law in the Exchanges, they could detain any suspect that way for seven days. Usually in such cases, you could post a bond of appearance, but they didn't grant that option to Lucian.

Lucian submitted to it quietly enough, although his face was pale and stiff, whether more with anger or fear I could not tell.

The hearing was scheduled for Monday morning and we were all required to be present to attest to the statements we had given. That was going to be a long day because Carsten's commemoration had been arranged for the afternoon.

The assisting physician had released the remains for burial, reporting there were no indications to contradict the assumption that Carsten of Wrightwork had in fact died because of the fire. No indications. I wasn't exactly sure what that meant. What did they expect to find? A bullet hole in the head, a stab wound to the back? I wondered whether there was enough of Carsten left to find even things as obvious as that. I suspected the physician's conclusion simply accepted the obvious. Then again, there was no reason not to.

Anyway, as was customary, fortunately in the present circumstances, Carsten would be buried privately. The gathering of friends and acquaintances who would meet to honor his memory would be held separately. Gwynedd, Arne, and a few others would speak. And Carsten's loss would be finalized. And for most of us, his tragic death would be put to rest. But not for Lucian, and probably not for Evane.

As for Zorn, through all of this I hadn't had much chance to speak with her. On Saturday after giving her statement, she had been gone most of the day. Some business to do with her trip to the Freeholds, although I didn't know what that was all about and I had neither the time nor the inclination to inquire.

The only thing I remember was, during one of our fragmentary conversations that weekend, she asked who I had spoken to about the three earlier incidents. "Like I said," I'd answered, "I told Gwynedd." Then I finally admitted, I had told Torvan as well.

"So I had assumed," Zorn said with a touch of impatience. "Anyone else?" she persisted.

Her questioning reminded me how stupidly nonchalant we had all been. I shrugged. "I didn't exactly keep it a secret that I thought the horse falling was no accident." She waited as if expecting something more from me. "Especially with Evane and Lucian," I added. "But that's all, I think."

But it wasn't just that Zorn and I didn't have much chance to talk. All weekend she seemed unusually preoccupied and distant, unapproachable even when she was present. Any of my attempts to discuss what had happened, she turned aside.

At the time I assumed her persistent avoidance of the subject was a natural response to the horror of Carsten's death and her own escape. And maybe also the result of contemplating the role her stubbornness had played in writing the scenario we were being forced to enact. I kept thinking, if Zorn had been willing to explain herself more, all of this might have been forestalled. Lucian might not have believed her claim of helping the insurgent cause, but it might at least have given him second thoughts.

On Sunday afternoon when the constables were finishing up, I'd had another long session with the DC during which he had me go over for the third time the altercation between Zorn and Lucian. He also had me review what I knew about the other apparent booby traps. One of the Under Constables diligently scratched away with pen and paper as I talked. When we had finished, Oletto thanked me, tapped his chin with his fingers and, with a polite nod, told me I could go.

"Is that all you need from me?" I couldn't resist asking.

Oletto's fingers had moved from his chin and were now tracing his jaw line. "Except for your presence at the hearing tomorrow to affirm the accuracy of your statements, yes. Thank you."

I hesitated, debating the wisdom of putting the question which was really on my mind, but decided I couldn't let it rest. In the course of my first interrogation, I had told Oletto that I stood to inherit Zorn's considerable property but he had not referred to that admission again. Reminding him of it, I said, "You don't seem to attach much importance to the fact that I would gain substantially from Zorn of Northmarch's death. I was wondering why not."

He smiled condescendingly. "You think I am giving insufficient attention to motive."

I shrugged. "I just thought you'd make more of it."

"We do not consider you a suspect, Grayall of Wellworth." He picked up a pencil and idly twirled it between his fingers. "But if it makes you feel better, we did make inquiries. We find no basis for entertaining the idea that you could have acted on such a motive."

I couldn't suppress a large sigh. "Gwynedd must have given me an impressive testimonial."

"That's true. But not only her." He tapped the pencil against the edge of his hand. I think he was trying to decide whether to elaborate. I waited. "We discussed the matter with Zorn of Northmarch herself." His smile turned rueful at the memory. "She granted that we had to pursue our investigations as seemed appropriate to us but, for her part, she trusted you with her life and had good reason to do so." He watched for my reaction, then set the pencil aside in a gesture of finality. "No. Despite your knowledge of the properties of sodium and your prospects as the ariston's legatee, we don't consider you a feasible suspect."

I should have felt relieved, but it was strange, what I mostly felt was that I somehow had an unfair advantage. In discussing the mishaps which had befallen Zorn, Torvan had teased that, since I stood to gain if anything happened to her, I might have been viewed as a logical suspect. Only just as he had then, the constables now were not taking that possibility seriously. The truth was, I occupied a privileged position, insulated from what might be considered reasonable suspicion by friendship, confidence, and trust, while Lucian had no such buffers between him and the cold accumulation of evidence and accusation. Of course, I knew my own innocence and, like everyone else by this point, believed in Lucian's guilt. I was just very glad not to be a stranger here, like he was.

As I left the small office at the back of the house where the interviews were being conducted, Evane was waiting to go in. They were not immediately ready for her which left us with an uncomfortable meeting.

I couldn't just walk by her without saying something but, when I paused, she spoke before I could. "I don't want to talk to you." Her voice was dead, without spirit.

I knew whatever I offered would be futile, but I said it anyway. "I am sorry about all this."

"Sorry." The word dropped from her like a stone down a well. She seemed more resigned than angry. "You brought the aristo to this house. None of this would have happened if it weren't for that. And now none of it can be undone."

The door to the office opened and an Under Constable called her in. I stared at the door after it shut upon her. And realized what the worst of it was for Evane. She too believed in Lucian's guilt. That must have been intolerable for her.

It didn't leave me feeling any too great either, because I knew Evane was right. Lucian's conviction for murder would change things as unalterably as Carsten's death had. I wasn't sure how much she had come to care for him, but my role in the brutal ending of whatever relationship they might have had would stand between us for the rest of our lives.

CHAPTER THIRTY-SIX

The hearing Monday morning was held in the Exchange's Civic Hall in a plain, unimposing room. It was long and narrow with tall uncurtained windows overlooking a narrow walkway that separated the Civic Hall from the Civic Archives. The floor of polished wooden planks was bare of carpet.

The magistrate, a strong-featured woman as unpretentious as the room, sat behind a simple table at the front. Rows of straight-backed chairs had been arranged for the participants and spectators. Lucian was led in by two Under Constables, but otherwise unrestrained. The three of them sat in the front row on the left. District Constable Oletto and the assisting physician also sat in the front row but across the aisle from them. Directly behind Lucian sat Evane. She had left earlier than the rest of us to see him before the hearing began.

Gwynedd and Torvan had arrived with Zorn and me. They went up and joined Evane. Zorn motioned to seats near the back and I followed her lead. It was strange to see everyone, Patric, Arne, other familiar faces, even Tirze Volsted, with the one outstanding absence of Carsten himself. I realized just how much of a change his death would bring to all the scenes in which he would have played a role.

I had never attended a legal proceeding in a criminal case in the Exchanges before. But then criminal proceedings were rare. The legal apparatus in the Exchanges more commonly ran to civil cases, disputed financial transactions, and other such litigation. I had sat in on a couple of lawsuits in the past and those had been heated enough, but in this case the magistrate conducted the hearing with a dispassion worthy of Zorn herself.

First DC Oletto rose and, reading from a prepared report, presented the details of the method by which Carsten had died. He described the fire, the position of the spring-trap and the body, and he recounted the facts about the properties of alkali metals. When he had finished, he handed the report to the magistrate. She set it to one side and pronounced, "It is my ruling that the death of Carsten of Wrightwork was caused by deliberate and willful human action employing the method laid out in District Constable Oletto's report." This ruling was pro forma. It was obvious she had reviewed all this material before. Still, now Carsten's death was officially a murder.

Next Oletto produced lists of all the residents, employees, and guests present at Gwynedd's on the day of the bidding. He read summaries of the accounts people had given of where they had been and who they had been with up to the time the fire was discovered. Again, upon completion, he gave them to the magistrate who laid them beside the first report. Then she signaled to a clerk who came forward with a sheaf of papers. "We will now hear the statements of testimony which District Constable Oletto has submitted as pertinent to a possible charge in this case."

The clerk, not Oletto, read the statements. He began with the accounts that had been gathered about the accidents which had occurred prior to the fire. As his voice droned on, branch, hay bale, and horse began to sound like some ritualistic formula. Not just to me, I suspected. By the time he reached the end of it, Zorn stirred beside me. I assumed she was finding her patience tried.

Next the clerk moved on to the statements from those who had witnessed Lucian's attack on Zorn after the bidding. Each of these asserted that Lucian had obviously been drinking, that he had been gratuitously abusive, and that he had ended up humiliated. Despite the dryness of the clerk's reading, a distinct note of fascinated titillation rippled through the room at the various accounts of how Zorn had bested Lucian. I noticed that Lucian sat stony faced through it all, but it seemed to take an effort on his part.

When all the testimony statements had been read, the magistrate directed those of us who had made them to rise. "If any of you wish to amend what has been read here today, come forward." No one did. Then each of us was required individually "to attest and affirm" that our statements were truthful and that their presentation had been accurate.

It had all been very workmanlike, even boring. And then the magistrate called Lucian up to the front. One of his escorts whispered to him and he positioned himself alongside the magistrate's table, facing the whole assembly. He stood with his arms behind him, his face set and strained.

The magistrate began a brief, straightforward series of questions. "You have heard the description of the fire-trap which caused the death of Carsten of Wrightwork. Did you devise and set that trap?"

"No." The word was out almost before the question was finished.

"Do you know or suspect any reason for the murder of Carsten of Wrightwork?"

"No."

"Did you set the trap which killed Carsten of Wrightwork with the intention of killing Zorn of Northmarch?"

"No." This answer was even more impatient than the first two.

"Did you know that Zorn of Northmarch customarily visited the location where the fire-trap was placed, those visits normally occurring in the late afternoon?"

Lucian licked his lips. "It was generally known in the household."

"Did *you* know?" the magistrate insisted.

"Yes." Lucian drew the word into an emphatic hiss.

"Did you know that previous incidents had occurred, the broken branch, the hay bale, the horse brought down?" The magistrate listed them without consulting her notes.

Lucian turned toward the magistrate. "I knew she had a fall from a horse." He hesitated, then corrected himself. "I knew a horse had gone down with her."

"Face forward, please." The magistrate's formal politeness did nothing to lessen Lucian's discomfort. "How did you know?"

"Evane told me."

"Is that all you knew?"

"I knew about the hay bale. I heard them talking about it, joking about it, in the stable."

"Joking about it?"

"They were laughing anyway." Lucian looked directly at Zorn. He flushed, then suddenly brought his arms from behind his back and placed his hands at his sides. But he held his fingers stiffly.

I took a sideways glance at Zorn. She appeared attentive, nothing more.

The magistrate continued, "When you say, they were laughing, does that include you?"

Lucian hesitated again. "Yes." He looked down and then quickly back up, like he was ashamed that his gaze had faltered.

"Did you arrange those earlier apparent accidents?"

"No."

"Did you arrange them with the intention of causing harm to Zorn of Northmarch?"

"No. I told you. No." His repetition sounded more nervous than convincing.

"Do you contest the accuracy of any of the testimony you have heard today?"

"No." His voice had dropped so low I barely heard him.

Finally the magistrate invited Lucian to make a concluding statement. "Have you anything else you wish to say at this time?"

He looked around. He stared for a moment at Zorn and then looked at Evane. We were sitting diagonally to her and I could see her profile. Lucian didn't seem to find much consolation in her rigid face.

He began, "You know that I come from the serving class of the Realm. I hate those who have oppressed us. And I have good reason to do so." He stared at Zorn again and she stared back at him. "But I have not murdered anyone, nor tried to." His statement had so far been dignified and impressively restrained, but the faces before him must have seemed terrifyingly unconvinced. "I came here because we, our Provisional Authority that is, need supplies and grain. Do you think I'd risk that endeavor for the satisfaction of killing one aristo? Her life isn't worth that much." The last words were steeped in contempt.

And although it was a reasonable assertion from his point of view, one that Torvan had raised with me, unfortunately for Lucian the venom with which he delivered it overshadowed its substance. Abstract hatred of Realm ariston as a class was one thing but it was clear, for Lucian, his hatred had localized very particularly on Zorn.

It struck me the psychology of the proceedings was pretty well considered. Each of us in the room certainly had a good opportunity to observe Lucian's answers and his demeanor. To weigh for ourselves whether we believed him. Through it all, he had seemed to me nervous and defiant at the same time. And I suppose I didn't believe him, in part because his hatred was so evident and maybe in part because I had already made up my mind.

When Lucian had re-taken his seat, the magistrate began her summation. "By his own admission, Lucian, here present, formerly in service in the polity known as Regeren, also designated the Realm, hates and holds in despite Zorn of Northmarch, as Warder of Farnorth formerly a governing ariston of Regeren. This hatred constitutes motive in any action presumed to have been taken with the intention of causing injury to Zorn of Northmarch. Further, undisputed testimony of witnesses establishes that Lucian has acted upon this hatred following the recent bidding assembly at Gwynedd's Securing House. In this attempted assault, he acted with no direct provocation and with inhibitions undoubtedly diminished by the use of intoxicating drink. It should be noted that, as a result of this incident, Lucian suffered public humiliation.

"In evaluating the grounds for a charge against Lucian in this matter, the probable intent of the fire-trap that killed Carsten of Wrightwork must be considered. This trap was laid in a location frequented regularly by Zorn of Northmarch and, according to uncontradicted testimony, only by Zorn of Northmarch. In the absence of testimony or evidence indicating a motive for the murder of Carsten of Wrightwork, it is reasonable to presume that the trap which killed him was in fact set for Zorn of Northmarch. In support of this conclusion, the earlier mishaps aimed at her appear significant in that they establish a pattern of action leading to the final, and fatal, trap.

"Finally in consideration of opportunity, Lucian does not deny the testimony which asserts that he knew of the properties and presence of the volatile substances known as the alkali metals. And that he knew where and under what conditions they were stored in the household. In addition he had in his possession a shipment of animal traps, one of which was used as part of the mechanism of the lethal fire-trap.

"Undisputed testimony confirms that, following the altercation with Zorn of Northmarch, Lucian was left unattended for a period of time sufficient for him to have gathered the necessary materials used to set up the fire-trap. The laboratory was vacant and unlocked during this period. By his own admission, Lucian had by then recovered sufficient sobriety to wander the grounds.

"In retrospect, we can all regret that Lucian was left alone in his unsettled frame of mind and that potentially dangerous materials were not stored more securely. We can also regret that the earlier non-fatal incidents were not given more serious attention. However, these lapses of judgment fall within the range of normal human fallibility and are not found to constitute culpable negligence.

"It is my ruling that Lucian possessed sufficient motive, means, and opportunity to warrant the bringing of a formal charge against him in the murder of Carsten of Wrightwork and the attempted murder of Zorn of Northmarch. By the authority granted to me as magistrate, I do so charge Lucian, here present and identified, and order that he remain in custody, bond of appearance denied, until such time as he shall be tried and found guilty or acquitted of this charge. A date for trial will be set after consultation with District Constable Oletto and the accused. Since Lucian is a non-resident, we will extend any aid he requires in securing and selecting an advocate."

With that she rose, the clerk gathered up all the documents and statements, and they left by a side door. Lucian's escorts, or more precisely his guards, motioned him to his feet and started to lead him out the same way. He made what seemed to be an involuntary gesture toward Evane, but one of his guards stopped his arm and he let it drop without protest. Evane simply stood there, without moving, as they led Lucian away.

People filed out of the room to the accompaniment of a steady mumble of voices. I was probably imagining things, but I thought I heard relief in that indistinguishable sound. That whatever the horror of Carsten's death, it was a stranger who was almost certainly responsible, not one of their own.

Torvan, guiding Evane, came past Zorn and me but Gwynedd stopped before us. Her face was stiff and I had a pretty good idea of the burden of guilt she felt because I felt it too. "I should feel fortunate, I suppose," she said, "that our legal proceedings limit themselves primarily to facts when they assign blame. Which lets some of us off with only a mild reprimand for extremely bad judgment." She sighed heavily. "I should have prevented this, Grayall."

I put a consoling hand on her shoulder. "If there's any blame in the matter, it's certainly not yours alone. All of us underestimated Lucian." I included Zorn in my gaze, but she was standing aside, seemingly aloof to any suggestion that her own behavior might have contributed to what had happened. Her attitude rankled me, but I tamped down my irritation.

Gwynedd, with a disconsolate shake of her head, walked out slowly. We followed her. Once outside, I assumed Zorn would return to the house. But she surprised me by saying she was going to accompany me to Carsten's commemoration. I couldn't decide whether the circumstances of Carsten's death made Zorn's presence there appropriate or awkward.

Chapter Thirty-seven

The commemoration would take place in a piece of parkland behind the Civic Hall. It was often used for such public-private occasions. As Zorn and I walked up, almost everyone had already gathered in a central grove of trees. The weather had cleared and it was a beautiful day, one that mixed the crispness of fall with the lingering warmth of summer. Most of the trees in the grove still had their leaves which had turned a golden yellow.

Zorn and I joined the gathering but we stayed on the outer edge. Gwynedd spoke first. She praised Carsten for his honesty and expertise, and described him as someone who could be trusted in all his dealings. "His loss will be with us for a long time to come," she concluded.

Arne followed, looking as pale and reserved as his ruddy complexion would permit. Everyone knew, after all, that he had beat Carsten out in the bidding for the insignia and that Carsten had wanted that victory very badly. So Arne began by reminding everyone that Carsten had been his best and most respected rival. "A fair and worthy opponent is the best measure for one's own achievements. In losing Carsten, I have lost my measure." His voice broke slightly as he said it. I saw heads nodding. Arne had struck the right note for his audience. Other speakers followed, citing Carsten's accomplishments and reiterating how much he would be missed.

It lasted about an hour in all. As the gathering began to disperse, Patric worked his way around the fringes of the crowd, obviously looking for me. Between us was our unfinished conversation at the dock. But when he saw Zorn, he drew up short. I realized they had never actually met, and I wasn't sure if his theoretical approval of my business dealings with her would extend to practical courtesy. However, he quickly recovered his composure, walked up to us and nodded a polite, if somewhat stilted, greeting. "Grayall, Zorn of Northmarch. But for the circumstances, I would congratulate you both." It was a particularly Patric-like thing to say. And in Zorn's case, he could just as well have meant her survival as the successful outcome of the bidding.

Zorn chose not to ignore the ambivalence. "The consensus seems to be that I am doubly fortunate," she answered coolly. "Just as Carsten was twice unfortunate."

"It's hard to imagine things without him," I said, mainly to fill the awkward pause that followed and in which the two of them seemed to be sizing each other up. "He's been part of all this for so long."

"And yet," Patric said, "eventually someone will take his place."

"Not for a while," I countered. I wondered if Patric saw Carsten's death primarily in terms of its impact on the commercial scene, and its opportunities. Probably he did. Another strained silence seemed about to fall, so I added, "It's been a long three days. I think we'll head back."

As Zorn and I turned to go, Patric touched my elbow and motioned me aside. "I guess I know your answer," he said quietly. "Unless when all this is over, you want to think about it."

"No, Patric." I wanted to offer something. "With you, I'd never be able to forget Jarrell. And that wouldn't be fair, to either of us." What I said was true. It just wasn't the reason I wouldn't marry Patric, but it was enough of a reason to give him.

I followed Zorn to the horses. She handed my reins to me and said, "Did he presume when he offered himself as a substitute?"

"I don't know about presuming. More like showing how little he knows me." I had answered automatically, but then I was struck by Zorn's perception because I certainly hadn't told her about Patric's proposal and I doubted she had overheard us just now. "Anyway how did you know about that?"

"Lucky guess." Since Zorn was equally skeptical of luck and guesses, I knew she had picked the unlikely phrase on purpose.

"Lucky guess," I mimicked. "You're too damn observant, Zorn."

She stood for a moment, her face grave, almost troubled, then she swung up onto her horse. "Not quite observant enough." Whatever inspired that, she wasn't thinking about me or Patric any longer. The hearing had obviously not dispelled the preoccupations which had been evident in her all weekend.

"I know self-control is something of an obsession with you," I said after I had mounted as well, "but you might give in enough to admit how much all this bothers you. After all, it was supposed to be you who got killed. On top of that, knowing that Carsten…well, that he took your place." She remained unmoved which provoked me to add, "Not to mention that Gwynedd is right. We should have been able to stop this. And you bear part of the responsibility that we didn't."

Her eyes seemed to darken with sudden intensity but just as quickly she shut off whatever emotion had stirred in her and we rode the short distance to Gwynedd's in silence.

It was apparent that Zorn's mood of brooding contemplation had returned completely. I was confident in my longstanding assumption that she was bedeviled by thoughts of a singularly narrow escape, of someone dying in her place, and of the errors in judgment which had led to those events, but she showed no willingness to admit to any of it. When we arrived at the house, Haslen greeted us and asked whether we wanted anything. We both declined and Zorn went off to the library. I headed upstairs to try for a nap.

I was so tired I thought I would sleep immediately. But when I lay down, all I got was a restless churning in my mind as thoughts and images tumbled over each other. A keening shriek kept ringing in my ears and a noisome smell filled not just my nose but my entire head. Images of faces passed before me. Lucian's, Evane's, Gwynedd's, all strained with fear, or shock, or sorrow. And then came the calm, droning voice of Oletto, his questions, confirming, clarifying. But out of all that turmoil there was always a return to that pitiless fire with the blackened object at its heart. After tossing and turning for an hour or so, I gave it up. I came back downstairs. The house was quiet. Trays of food were set out in the dining room but it was otherwise empty. I didn't stop. Even I had no appetite.

Besides I was too restless and unsettled to stay in one place. I wandered outside. The wind had come up and a few high clouds had moved in to oppose the day's earlier sunshine. Apparently the weather wasn't going to give us a respite for long.

Without much thought, I walked toward the front gate. As I approached, Caled came over to me, and said with a tone of voice just short of a sneer, "Looking for Her Excellency?" Before I could say, no, he jerked his head toward the rear of the house. "You know where to find her," he said unpleasantly.

I found myself at a loss for a response. Not even Zorn could be detached enough to go back to that scene of horror as though nothing had happened. At least I hoped she couldn't. But there was no mistaking the spitefulness in Caled. He watched for my reaction. Maybe he wanted the satisfaction of an argument or an evasion, something to show that I found his information unsettling. Instead of giving him any of that, I nodded curtly, thanked him, and walked off.

CHAPTER THIRTY-EIGHT

With little enthusiasm, I started down the path through the gardens. When I got to the base of the small rise that led to the pond, I could smell the acrid aftermath of the fire in the burned vegetation and the charred, soot-covered logs. Suddenly it seemed ridiculous to have expected Zorn to be perched there like some carrion bird. And much to my relief, she wasn't. Without going any closer, I turned to leave and then Zorn spoke my name quietly.

She was there all right, but standing to the side. I hadn't seen her because she was partially hidden by the trees. She wasn't facing the pond, but rather the black, burned spot a few feet in front of her.

A jumble of emotions stirred in me and I called out sharply, "Zorn, what's the matter with you? Come away from there."

Her head came up, like a dog sniffing the wind, but otherwise she didn't move. I had no intention of going up to join her. After a few moments, she stepped out of the shelter of the trees and came down to where I stood. Without saying anything, she walked past me down the path to the gardens and seated herself on the nearest bench. I followed her. She stretched her legs out and let her head sink forward in contemplation.

I waited for her to say something, maybe to unburden herself. It seemed about time. But she continued to sit, silent and unmoving.

I came over and sat beside her. "You want to talk?" I asked. "You could have just let me walk away." She raised her head, but didn't turn toward me. She was clearly still immersed in her own introspection. "Look," I said, "you made a bad judgment call. Ignoring Lucian. But then again, so did we all." I paused to consider how to say more directly what I had tried to say on the way back from the commemoration, but I never achieved whatever tact I was aiming for. Instead I blurted out, "Damn it, Zorn, maybe if you'd been willing to give some explanation of yourself. Even at the risk of not being believed, it would have been worth it."

At last, Zorn turned toward me. Her eyes were dark and expressionless. "You think I could have prevented Carsten's death." It was a statement, not a question.

"Maybe. Mostly I think we all handled the situation here badly. And it's natural to be upset about that."

"As you are." She looked away again. After a while, she said calmly, "I am bothered by something, but not by what you surmise." She fell silent, then finally said, "This case they are making against Lucian. You find it convincing?"

It was hardly what I was expecting and I answered impatiently, "Of course I find it convincing. And so does everyone else." My voice sounded more confrontational than I intended. I added more quietly, "Even Evane thinks he's guilty. Which is sad."

"I didn't ask whether you thought he was guilty. I asked whether you found the case against him convincing."

I gave a long histrionic sigh. Then ticked off the points pedantically. "Number one, he had access to the spring-traps. Number two, he could certainly have learned about the potassium and he would have had access to it as well. Number three, he had time to set the trap. Number four, he knew you always came out here. And number five," I swung around to face her, "he detests you and everything he thinks you stand for."

I studied her unrelenting profile. I could readily believe Zorn would distance herself from any second-guessing of her judgments, but something was eating at her, and suddenly I thought I understood what it was. "That's it, isn't it?" I said. "The insurgents. All those former servs. You still feel you owe them something. That's why you're so reluctant to accept an accusation against Lucian. It seems to me, you've paid your debt, whatever you think it is." I took her by the wrist and held her scarred hand up before her face. "Remember?" She didn't resist my grasp but turned her head and gave me one of her full-bore stares. Sheepishly, I released her.

"You are in no position to judge the debts incurred in Regeren," she said icily. She allowed a pause for the reprimand to sink in but then added, her voice thawing a degree or two, "However, my doubts about Lucian are not based on feelings of guilt, past or present."

"What are they based on then?" I asked, trying not to sound belligerent.

"Gwynedd was wrong," Zorn said. "The legal proceedings here do not limit themselves to facts. They are generous with inference as well. What is lacking is evidence."

"No evidence," I exclaimed. "That's what you said about the other mishaps. And look what happened."

Zorn disregarded my protest and continued, "In the time we have been here, have you ever seen anyone but me out there?" She gestured toward the pond by lifting her chin. She didn't wait for my obvious answer. "I have seen no one else but you, Grayall. And then only when you were looking for me. But Carsten presents himself conveniently at the right time to suffer a death intended for me. That strains credibility."

"Coincidences do happen."

"That's a change of argument for you," she said quickly.

"Even you don't believe those earlier occurrences were coincidental. As for Carsten, I think he just wanted to walk off some frustration and ended up out here."

"It is possible," she allowed. "The premise on which the accusation against Lucian rests and all that follows are also possible. But so are other assumptions and other conclusions."

"Such as?" I felt like I was humoring her.

"That Carsten came to the pond because someone arranged for him to do so. And that the fire-trap was set for him, not for me."

"But no one had a reason to kill Carsten."

"You don't know that. The point has not been seriously examined."

"No, because Lucian's motive is obvious. And because he tried it before. Nobody tried to kill Carsten by bringing down your horse, Zorn. Or by dropping a branch and a hay bale on your head."

"Those other incidents. They do not trouble you at all?" Her dark eyes gleamed with challenge.

I shrugged my perplexity. "Trouble me? How?"

She drew a breath as if gathering her patience. "The working premise is that Lucian has made repeated attempts on my life. And that he finally succeeded. Only he caught the wrong prey in his trap. That does not make sense to me." I started to interrupt but she overrode me. "Consider, the branch, the hay bale, the horse. All simple, but more notably, none of them effective methods for killing someone, none of them a reliable threat for that."

My first thought in response was that not many people had Zorn's particularly high standards of lethal action, but I managed not to give voice to that observation. Instead I said, "I'd say bringing down a galloping horse constitutes a pretty reliable threat."

"Not even at a racing pace," she said dismissively. "You have to be unlucky to get seriously injured in a fall like that, much less killed. Those earlier mishaps," she continued, "I acknowledge they are unlikely coincidences. And that someone has attempted to inconvenience me, perhaps even injure me, but kill me? No. Even if it were Lucian, which I doubt, it was a matter more of spite, like his performance after the bidding, than of true homicidal intent."

"That distinction gets a little fine for me," I said. "A broken neck is a broken neck, no matter what the original intention was. Besides, I think I suggested before, maybe Lucian just got better at it."

Zorn moved her head slightly, an economical gesture of dissent. "He may be undisciplined. But he doesn't appear to be stupid. You think he made three ineffectual trial runs just to ensure suspicion focused on him when he finally made a serious attempt?" She exhaled a scornful breath. "Because that fire-trap was as serious as it was successful."

"Glad you're willing to grant that, at least."

She ignored me. "It was complex, carefully planned, and close to certain in its result. Therefore different in method from the other incidents. Sufficiently different to raise a doubt of whether it was done by the same person. Or for the same reason."

Through all this, Zorn's voice and demeanor maintained their usual neutrality, but as I listened to her, I realized she wasn't idly theorizing. Despite her outward detachment, this mattered to her. A lot.

Keeping my voice level, I said, "Maybe you should share these opinions with Oletto." Zorn conferred on me a frosty look. "Oh," I concluded lamely.

"Yes. He listened politely." She thought for a moment. "I suspect he judged I was being both self-important and officious."

"Well, without a reason for someone wanting to kill Carsten, it's hard to blame him for preferring the obvious to the subtle."

"Not only the obvious but the expedient. Guilt attributed to the stranger rather than to one of their own."

"That seems a little harsh," I said, despite the fact that earlier my own thoughts hadn't been far from the same point.

"Does it? It reminds me of the situation Brandon, the physician's ward, found himself in at Arandell." That took me aback. Noting my reaction, Zorn went on, "I am not questioning Oletto's integrity. But Lucian as an outsider must make both the accusation and the presumption of guilt easier. Consider how you would feel if this same case were being made against Evane."

"Impossible. Evane's no murderer." My words rushed out.

"Why don't you match her against your list? Access to the traps and the potassium, opportunity to set the trap, knowledge of my habits, and motive of hatred." Zorn watched my expression as she re-stated what I had said. "Before you lose your temper," she said equably, "I use Evane only as an example. However, your reaction illustrates my point. You tolerate the thought of Lucian's guilt more easily than you would the guilt of anyone closer to you. The rest of them here feel the same."

I leaned my elbow on the arm of the bench and looked at her doubtfully. "You're really putting forward the idea that Lucian is innocent?"

"I cannot speak for his innocence. I only suggest he may be guiltless in this particular instance."

I shook my head. "If I didn't know you better, I'd think you were playing a hunch, indulging in intuition. Whether for the reasons I suggested earlier or not, I don't know."

"Intuition, like other modes of thought, has its proper place."

"Tell me," I said, irritated by her complacency, "does your intuition suggest an alternate suspect?"

"Yes." I had asked my question flippantly, but Zorn's one word answer fell upon me like a weight. I waited, but she didn't continue.

"You don't intend to give me a name, do you?" All the lightness had gone from my voice.

"Not yet. Not until I have settled some things in my mind." She gazed at me speculatively. "I need your assistance."

I made a disgruntled face. "Without telling me anything more?" Her expression didn't waver. I shrugged. "All right. What do you want?"

Instead of answering, she asked me what seemed a completely irrelevant question. "Are public records kept on most of the business transactions that take place here?"

I frowned but, catching the resolve in Zorn's eyes, I changed my mind about demanding to know what that had to do with anything. "It depends." I wasn't sure what she was after. "A lot of deals are struck quietly."

"Transactions like the bidding on the insignia?"

"Oh, major public bids like that. Yes, those are recorded. Files are kept in the Archives."

Zorn nodded. "I want your help examining those records tomorrow."

"Whatever you say," I replied too easily.

She heard the glibness in my voice. "I caution you, if I am correct, you will not like the outcome." She sounded very somber and very certain and it made me uncomfortable. But if I had a choice in the matter, I couldn't see it.

"Have you ever heard a saying about not looking a gift horse in the mouth?" I said. "If you have doubts about Lucian's guilt, I'll help any way I can. I don't want him to suffer for something he didn't do. No matter how obnoxious he is."

"Lucian is not so much obnoxious as defensive," Zorn said coolly.

I sighed. "You know, I think I'd like you better if you just simply hated his guts."

Her lips curved upward, the shadow, not the substance, of a smile. "What makes you think I'd give him that satisfaction?" She took a moment to savor my reaction, then added, "Besides, we seem to be oversupplied with hatred of late."

CHAPTER THIRTY-NINE

Despite my doubts and confusions, by mid-morning the next day I had spent almost three hours up to my eyebrows in the dust of the Civic Archives, sorting through old bidding records at Zorn's direction.

We worked our way through tedious lists that gave the outcomes of major bids over the past few years. None of it was very well organized. The information was entered in a variety of different hands and there was no standard format. What Zorn wanted was the commodity at bid, the price it went for, who achieved the bid, and the non-winning bidders, if their names were included. I helped her dig all that out, but she also wanted something else from me. She wanted an estimate of the profit value of each item at bid. In other words, she wanted to know whether the bidding had come in at a price reasonably sure to guarantee a decent return on investment. What all this had to do with the fire, Carsten's death, and the accusation against Lucian was beyond me. And when I asked her what she expected to get from all this, she only said, "The means to progress from intuition to evidence." Which made no sense to me, as I supposed she well knew. But she offered no further explanation.

As we plodded through the records, Zorn was meticulous and indefatigable. When I had finished my estimates of profit values, it was well past the time I would have stopped for lunch. I insisted that I was hungry and suggested we adjourn to the inn. Zorn told me to go ahead, that she would join me shortly. I left her sitting at a large table, the records we had been examining piled around her.

At the door, I glanced back. She was already bent over her work again, her face obscured beneath the glossy black hair that hung over her forehead. "Why don't you come and eat? Finish whatever you're searching for after." But she didn't look up. I doubted she even heard me.

When she finally joined me, an hour and a half later, carrying a few sheets of paper and a small parcel, I was through with my late and leisurely lunch, including dessert, and was sipping coffee sweetened with a liqueur.

"I figured if I didn't go back, you'd get here eventually," I said. "What do you want to eat?"

She waved off my question. She laid the parcel, which bore the label of one of the larger general merchandise vendors, on the table. Pushing aside my coffee cup, she set before me one sheet from the papers she carried. "Give me your assessment of these transactions."

She had given me a list of twenty major public bids. They were spread out over the last ten years, but according to the dates, they got closer together as time went by. While I reviewed the list, Zorn broke off some bread from a loaf that remained on the table and nibbled at it. I stopped my perusal long enough to signal the waiter and order some cheese and fruit, as well as fresh coffee.

Zorn reached over, tapped the sheet of paper she had placed in front of me and said, "Pay attention."

On the list, she had provided a detailed description of the commodities at bid, their selling price, and their estimated profit. It was apparent, if her catalog was accurate, which I didn't doubt for a minute, that these transactions had a couple of things in common. First they were all classy, the kinds of items, like Zorn's insignia, which, by the way, was the last one on the list, that attracted attention, not just for their monetary worth, but for their prestige as well. The other thing was they had all been bid to a price which seemed overvalued, a price you might pay if you wanted the things for yourself, but not a business price, not one which guaranteed an acceptable return.

"This is a pretty good compilation," I said, looking up from the list. "You could set up as an information broker." The waiter had arrived and set out the food I had ordered.

Zorn deftly quartered an apple and took a slice of cheese. "Is that the extent of your analysis?"

"No." I summarized for her the two characteristics I had noted.

She put aside the unfinished apple, took the sheet of paper back, and studied it. She nodded over it.

"You going to tell me why you're so interested in all these old bids?" I sampled a bit of the inn's fine old cheddar which Zorn was neglecting.

She set the paper down and placed her hand upon it. "They are all bids that Carsten of Wrightwork lost."

"I'm not surprised. Like I said, they were all overpriced."

"He lost them all to Arne Bennetson."

"No kidding." I reached over and took the sheet of paper back. I looked at the items on the list again. "Maybe that's not so surprising either. Arne goes after the showy bids and he likes to win."

Zorn slid another piece of paper over to me. It listed all the transactions on the first sheet, which were ticked with neat check marks, plus quite a few more. "Here is a good sampling of Bennetson's major bids over the same period of time," she said. "He does not make a habit of overbidding. But he has overbid consistently against Carsten."

I read over the second list and she was right. "Well, it makes sense. They always were each other's keenest rival."

Zorn took the last piece of apple. It had begun to brown. She ate it absently, watching me. She seemed to be expecting something more from me, but what it was, I didn't know. After all, the competition between Arne and Carsten was no secret. We didn't need to spend half a day in the archives to discover what everyone already knew.

I scanned both lists again. "I'm sorry. I don't see the point to any of this."

"If Bennetson had been killed, would you see a point to it?"

Zorn's question seemed completely irrelevant to me and I answered without giving it any consideration. "No. It'd be the same. I would think he'd been caught in something intended for you."

Impatience crossed over Zorn's face like a fast-moving cloud. "It wouldn't have occurred to you that Carsten of Wrightwork might have had a motive to kill Bennetson?"

"That's a hell of a question," I said, startled. "No…" But then I remembered how angry and frustrated Carsten had been at losing the bid on the insignia. From the information on Zorn's lists, Carsten must have felt that way before, on lots of bids, and Zorn's question no longer seemed quite so outlandish. I looked up into her steady, noncommittal stare. "I suppose it would have been a possibility," I amended. "But I still don't see the point. After all, it was Carsten who was killed, not Arne."

"Yes, it was," Zorn replied impassively.

"Then what in the world does it matter that Carsten might have had a backlog of resentment against Arne? Unless…" A possibility occurred to me. "You're not suggesting Carsten was setting up something to kill Arne and got caught himself?"

"It is the kind of supposition Lucian is entitled to have considered. Although as it happens, it is not what I am suggesting." I expected some further comment from her, but instead she gathered up the papers and the parcel she had brought and stood up.

"That's it. That's all you're going to say?" My voice rose in frustration and a couple of heads turned in our direction.

"Whatever else I might have to say, this is not the place. And before I speculate further, I need to question Torvan."

"Torvan," I exclaimed.

"Yes. I have an idea, although not much confidence in it."

When I asked for an explanation, all Zorn would add was that a demonstration, if it worked, would be more convincing. I shook my head irritably, but I was tired of asking questions to which I would not get answers. "I hope you're enjoying yourself," I said. "Because you're being a real pain in the…. Well, some people would say, neck, but there is an alternative."

Zorn ignored my jibe completely and answered with dead seriousness, "No, I am not enjoying myself." There was an undercurrent in her voice that made me uneasy. It was the same tone she had used when she warned me I wouldn't like the outcome of whatever it was she was up to. Worse, by now I had a very unpleasant notion of where her suspicions were tending. I hoped I was wrong. More important I hoped she was wrong.

CHAPTER FORTY

We settled our bill and headed back to Gwynedd's. Yesterday's promise of a return to stormy weather was being kept. The clouds had become heavier and the wind which blew at our backs was stronger. It seemed to push us along, hurrying us to a result I wasn't sure I wanted. But it seemed to match Zorn's mood of unhesitating action very well. When we reached the house, she led the way straight back to Torvan's laboratory. Torvan was sitting at his high worktable, his long back hunched over a microscope. With his free hand he was making entries in a notebook. He looked up when we came in, started to smile at me, and then his expression turned to surprise when he saw Zorn.

He slid off his stool and cocked his head inquisitively. I knew that anything in the way of preliminary courtesies would rest with me, so I said, "Sorry to bother you. But Zorn wants to ask you something."

Torvan's long flexible mouth curved upward. "I would have thought we'd used up all the questions and answers this past weekend." The humor in his tone couldn't disguise that it was also a serious observation.

Zorn set the parcel and the papers she was carrying on the worktable and walked over to the storage shelves on the back wall. Torvan motioned as if to stop her, but then changed his mind. He waited to see what she would do. When Zorn had located the canisters marked Na and K, she turned back to us. They were on a shelf just above her eye level.

"Have you handled these since you showed them to Oletto?" She didn't reach for them or gesture toward them, but there was no mistaking which canisters she was referring to.

With admirable restraint Torvan didn't ask how it was any of her business. "No, I haven't," he answered. "I'm more than a little put off by the alkali metals right now." He said it with some intensity of feeling and without apology for that.

"And, as instructed, since then you have kept this room locked in your absence?"

"That's right."

"So we can presume no one else has handled them either?"

"Yes, we can." Torvan frowned in perplexity. "Why does it matter?" He was being polite but he was obviously taken aback by Zorn's abrupt interrogation.

"Not even Oletto during his investigation?" Zorn asked. I smiled. The first lesson in Zornian conversation. Her questions were pertinent. Yours were expendable.

Torvan's jaw dropped a notch. He shot a glance in my direction which I met with wide-eyed blankness. He looked back at Zorn. "No. Not unless it was that first day I brought them to him. I'm not sure I remember." She waited, obviously giving him time to furnish a more satisfactory answer. But instead he turned to me. "You were there, Grayall."

I visualized what I remembered of that scene. "You came in with the canisters," I said. "You set them on the table. You removed the lids, took out the vial of sodium from one of them. You took the wadding from the other, the one that had held the potassium." I thought some more. "I don't think anyone else touched the canisters again until you left with them."

Torvan agreed. "That sounds right to me."

I think he was about to ask again why this inquiry when Zorn reached up and lifted down the canister that held the sodium. "Careful with that," Torvan warned. She set it on the table, then slid forward one of the small stands Torvan kept handy. She opened the canister, took out the vial of sodium, and placed it securely in the stand. She laid the now empty canister on its side in front of her. She seemed as comfortable handling all these items as Torvan himself. His own nervousness seemed to subside in the face of her competence and he eased back to watch her with bemused interest.

Zorn picked up the parcel she'd brought from the inn. She undid the wrapping to reveal a soft-bristled brush and a small round tin. She opened the tin and I could see it contained a fine dark-gray powder.

She selected a narrow spatula from a jar of utensils which sat on the table. With the spatula she lifted a pinch of the powder and deposited it on the sodium canister. Next she took the brush. With delicate flicks, she spread the powder over the canister. I had no idea what she was doing but, when I glanced over at Torvan, he seemed fascinated.

After a while she dabbed out a little more of the gray powder and brushed it on just as lightly as the first batch. As she worked, she bent forward, her face only inches from the canister. She kept her breathing shallow. "What are you doing?" I exclaimed, but Torvan motioned me to silence. Zorn worked on with her brush. Eventually she put it aside, blew lightly across the surface of the canister a couple of times, then stood back.

I craned forward to see and almost bumped heads with Torvan. He too had leaned forward and was staring fixedly at the canister. In places the gray powder had adhered to it and formed intricate patterns of whorls and curves. The elegant designs were faint but clearly visible.

After a moment or two, Torvan drew back and stared at Zorn, his face a mixture of doubt and recognition. "Those are fingerprints, aren't they?" he said in amazement.

"Fingerprints?" I echoed.

I peered more closely at the canister. Most of its smooth surface appeared unmarked but, where the powder clung, the islands of swirling lines appeared like fine etching. I brought my hand up close enough to see the lines of interlocked arches on the tips of my own fingers. "But how can that be?" It seemed incredible to me that the markings could emerge from the apparently clean surface of the canister.

"The patterns are transferred by perspiration as well as by slight traces of oil on the ridges of the skin," Zorn answered.

Dubiously I asked, "And they're still there? It's been, what? Four days since Torvan handled this canister."

"The prints will remain longer than that. Sometimes indefinitely, if not disturbed." Zorn offered her pronouncements as simply as if they were commonplace knowledge.

Torvan meanwhile had settled on one of the stools, his elbow propped on the tabletop, his chin resting on the heel of his hand. "You know, I think I've actually heard about this technique. Or rather, read something, somewhere." He clucked his tongue in mild self-reproach. "Although I certainly wouldn't have recalled it without this demonstration."

He picked up the tin and touched the gray powder lightly. It stuck to his fingertips like a film. "It's graphite, isn't it?" he asked.

Zorn nodded. With his other hand, Torvan reached for his notebook and pressed his fingertips to a blank page. The impressions he left were a little blurred but they showed up well enough. "The theory is," he said to me, "that everyone's patterns are unique." He looked at Zorn. She nodded again. "So these," he touched the page, "would match any I had left on the sodium canister. And," he had moved into his lecturer's voice, "should be distinguishable from those Zorn has just left on it as well."

"You can't be serious," I exclaimed. I peered again at the swirling patterns that the graphite had revealed on the canister. "You really think it would be possible to match the patterns you've just deposited on the paper with yours on the canister?"

"We'd have to get a better set of my fingerprints than the ones I created with the graphite." Torvan made that sound like a minor detail. "Ink would work, wouldn't it?" he asked Zorn.

She thought for a moment. "If I recall, printer's ink works reasonably well. It is drier than writing ink and gives a sharper impression."

They both seemed to share an easy complicity of knowledge but I still couldn't quite make sense of it. It seemed to me Zorn was continuing the pursuit of things which were already well-established.

I voiced my frustration. "Of course we know Torvan's fingerprints are on the sodium canister. So what if we can see them?"

It was Torvan who gave me a look of patient tolerance, like a teacher dealing with a well-meaning but inept student. "The point, Grayall, is whether we can find anyone else's fingerprints on *that* one." He pointed to the canister labeled K for potassium that still sat on the shelf. He turned back to Zorn. "Do you think it's likely?" he asked her.

"I don't know." Zorn's tone was devoid of enthusiasm. "You handled the potassium canister when you brought it to Oletto. You may have obscured any other prints left before that. If there were any useful earlier prints."

"What do you mean, if there were?" I objected. "Either you leave these…" I managed not to say 'so-called', "fingerprints when you touch something or you don't." My general skepticism sounded clearly in my voice.

Torvan said, slightly under his breath, as if he was thinking aloud rather than answering me. "Lucian could have been wearing gloves when he took the potassium. Or even wiped the canister for some reason."

"Those possibilities aside, it is still uncertain," Zorn added. "The clarity of the prints varies greatly. If the hand moved, some will be blurred. Depending on the contact pressure, others will be too faint. Most will be partial." She bent over again. "Although the surface of these canisters appears receptive."

Getting up, Torvan leaned over her shoulder. "It just might work," he said. "And if we can verify that Lucian's fingerprints are on the potassium canister, at least we'll know for sure, which will be a relief for all of us." His long mouth twitched. "I haven't quite been comfortable with this case. After all, given my familiarity with the alkali metals, if you left aside the question of motive, even I should have been a suspect. As for the accusation against Lucian, it's built only on probable conclusions and no real evidence."

"You sound just like Zorn," I blurted out. "Only she doesn't think it was Lucian."

Torvan's face contracted into an expression of perplexity. "Why not?" he asked.

Zorn didn't answer. Instead she replaced the lid on the tin of graphite and blew the excess powder from the brush. She crossed to the sink, moistened a cloth, and wiped the tabletop. Handling the now empty sodium canister, with its sample fingerprints, gingerly by its edges, she set it aside. She re-wrapped the tin and the brush and put them into a pocket.

Torvan rummaged in a cupboard and brought out another canister. He labeled it with the letters Na and put in it the vial of sodium which had remained in the stand. When all the tidying up was finished, I said to Zorn, "All right. Now, answer Torvan's question."

She seemed to consider for a moment and then did as I asked. She outlined what she had shared with me about the ineffectiveness of the earlier booby traps and the lethal certainty of the fire. As she spoke, Torvan's long face grew longer with deliberation. When she had finished, he tilted his head back thoughtfully. "I've been a bit bothered by that discrepancy myself." He shook his head. "I didn't think I had any company."

"Especially from this quarter," I said, indicating Zorn. I still had my own notions about why she was pursuing this attempt to exonerate Lucian, but in order to clear him she had to offer someone in his place. I had an idea about that too, and it was making me increasingly anxious. As far as I was concerned, the time for confronting Zorn and her suspicions was long overdue. "You think you know whose fingerprints are on the potassium canister, don't you?"

CHAPTER FORTY-ONE

My question hung in the air between us. Zorn's expression didn't change but, despite the impassive angles of her face, I sensed reluctance in her. Torvan watched us, his eyes alert with interest.

"All right, Zorn, I'm not stupid," I said. "All this business about the bidding history between Carsten and Arne." The papers containing the information from the archives still sat on a corner of the worktable. I grabbed them and held them up, crumpling their edges. "It's Arne you suspect, isn't it?" I heard a breath from Torvan. "Which is absolutely crazy." My voice frayed. I turned to Torvan for support but he maintained a disconcerting silence. "Tell her," I demanded of him. "Tell her it's impossible. Trying to blame this on Arne." Torvan licked his lips but still offered no comment. I looked back at Zorn. "He couldn't have done it." The ragged edge of my voice beat helplessly against Zorn's unyielding expression.

Torvan spoke very quietly. "Is Grayall right? You think it was Arne who set the fire-trap?"

Zorn gazed from me to Torvan and back again. Her dark eyes shone like polished stone. "This rivalry between Carsten of Wrightwork and Arne Bennetson," she began, "all of you here take it for granted. Yet when one of them is murdered, you do not inquire into the possible motives of the other." Zorn reached for the papers. I gave them to her and she smoothed them out. "As the records show, Bennetson has been sacrificing profit for years to win against Wrightwork. The pattern is so consistent that even you, Grayall, can imagine it could cause a murderous anger in Carsten. An anger directed against Bennetson."

"It wasn't Arne who was killed," I protested.

"No, it was the other party in the rivalry." Zorn paused, her thoughtfulness forming into the trace of a frown. "The one over whom Bennetson has always wanted to maintain primacy." She tapped the papers lightly against the table. "Bid after bid, overpriced, unprofitable, purchasing only Bennetson's status of superiority over Wrightwork. And all of you, if you notice it at all, shrug off this behavior as 'just Arne'. Arne who likes to win, who is willing to pay a price for his prestige. An almost amusing quirk of character.

"What you do not see is the depth of emotion driving his actions. You do not recognize Bennetson's obsession for what it is because it is too familiar to you. You do not observe that he has locked himself into a pattern of behavior from which there is no easy escape, not without diminishing his prestige and the identity that goes with it. And you do not ask what price he has paid over the years. Not simply the monetary price, the sacrifice of profit and sensible business, but also the price in anxiety, in compulsion.

"And therefore, you do not ask what Bennetson might do if, weary of it all, he found himself with an unusual opportunity to rid himself of the burdens of his obsession. An opportunity provided by the arrival of another conflict, another set of motives. An opportunity to kill Carsten of Wrightwork under circumstances in which the obvious suspect would be Lucian the insurgent and former servitor, and the obvious assumption would be that a plan to murder Zorn the ariston had miscarried."

Zorn's voice had pressed on, passionless, devoid of feeling. She might as well have been speaking about some abstract problem, unconnected to anybody or anything that might touch us.

"Arne is my friend." I choked out the words. My throat was so tight it hurt to speak.

"I warned you. That you wouldn't like it." Zorn folded the papers from the archives and slipped them into her jacket.

I could feel the heat rise in my face. "Evidence. You're always talking about evidence. You don't have any, for this. Not really." My voice shook with emotion.

Zorn looked at me intently. "I asked you once. Who else you told about the earlier mishaps. Because not very many people knew about all three of them. The perpetrator, of course. The two of us. I told only you about the branch. You told Torvan and Gwynedd. Did you tell Bennetson, as well?"

I thought back. I shook my head in frustration. "I don't think so. Why would I?" Then a recollection came to me and I said, "Maybe I did. The day I went with you to his place to see you off for the Freeholds." I struggled to reconstruct that conversation. "I asked Arne if he knew why you were making the trip. He was examining the rest of the shipment of spring-traps, thinking they'd interest Lucian." And then something nudged in my memory, Arne satisfied with himself because, as usual, he knew more than most. "He suggested you were leaving to get away from trouble at Gwynedd's. He knew about the horse going down. There'd been enough talk about that."

"And the other incidents?" Torvan urged.

Then I remembered. I had decided that taking Arne into my confidence would be the best way to ensure his discretion. I nodded wearily. "Yeah, I did tell him. About the three accidents. I had the impression he'd already heard about the hay bale and I thought I could forestall his gossip. Play up to his sense of insider's knowledge." I looked at Zorn imploringly. "But it doesn't mean anything, that he knew about the branch as well as the other two things that happened."

"It means he knew the fire would be perceived, not as an individual event, but as the fourth in a series of incidents. And that suspicion would fall on Lucian because the other three had been directed at me. He also had access to the spring-traps. He had as much, if not more, unaccounted time than Lucian on the day of the bidding. And he knew about the alkali metals."

She looked at Torvan. He nodded. "Yeah, I'd talked to him about them. You know Arne." His voice sounded apologetic. "Always has to know everything."

I felt deflated. "You're wrong," I said to Zorn. "You have to be." I tried to recover some strength of response against her speculations. "You just don't want it to be Lucian. You have your own frustrations about the Realm. So you spin out these theories. That's all they are. Just theories."

"You are correct," Zorn said. "What I offer is just a theory. But then, the case against Lucian is also theoretical. If you weigh the theories fairly, Bennetson is, at least, as likely a suspect as Lucian."

Torvan sighed heavily. "She's right, you know," he said to me. Zorn acknowledged his agreement with a minor nod of her head. "Although…" he began and then stopped, perhaps unsure how to continue.

Zorn completed his statement for him. "Although bringing such an accusation against Arne Bennetson will not be popular."

I tried to swallow away the lump in my throat. "What are you planning to do?" I asked thickly.

Torvan raised his eyebrows at Zorn and said, "Try to get Oletto interested in the possibility of fingerprint evidence. Wouldn't you agree?"

Zorn's gaze turned toward the potassium canister. "Assuming there is any fingerprint evidence." Outwardly she appeared as calm as ever, but it seemed to me beneath her unbroken composure lurked the strain of weariness or vexation. After all, she might be confident of her suspicions about Arne, but convincing Oletto was going to be something else altogether.

"And if there isn't any?" My question sounded more defiant than inquiring. More evenly I said, "I mean, Zorn, you did say it's not a sure thing, being able to raise these fingerprint patterns."

"I suggest we deal with that problem if and when it arises," Torvan said. "First we demonstrate this technique to Oletto. Once he understands how it works, we can apply it to the potassium canister. If that doesn't yield useful results, then, Zorn, you'll just have to try your theory on him even without evidence." He looked at her but all he got back was one of her searching stares.

To fill the silence, I said, "That should prove interesting."

Torvan made a face. "Let's just hope we get some fingerprints where we expect them to be." Listening to him, I realized how fully he had accepted Zorn's argument. It depressed me. "We'll ask Oletto to come here tonight," Torvan concluded.

"Rather, you will." Zorn spoke with that tone of unquestioned command I had heard often enough. But then she added, "He might listen to you." She dropped a wry emphasis on the last word.

Torvan pursed his lips, acknowledging the implication. "I'll do my best," he said. He hunted up another unused canister and handed it to her. "For the demonstration. With Oletto."

She took it and we filed out of the laboratory. Torvan locked the door behind us. But I carried away with me the image of that other smooth metallic canister we had carefully left behind, the one emblazoned with a bright red K, the one which was a token of past death and present menace. I didn't want that canister to prove that Arne had murdered Carsten. I didn't want that at all. Yet if Zorn was right, and everything I knew about her told me in all likelihood she was, that was exactly what I should want. Without it, there was, at best, uncertainty. At worst, Lucian convicted for a crime he didn't commit.

With unwilling steps, I followed Zorn and Torvan back to the house. I felt I was learning in full measure the accuracy of the old phrase, heavy of heart. Mine felt like a weight of stone.

CHAPTER FORTY-TWO

Torvan stopped at the house long enough to grab a coat. I handed him a hat as well and saw him off under a sky that had grown noticeably darker in the hour or so since Zorn and I had got back. The weather was now playing into my mood, which had grown darker as well. I went back into the house. Zorn was waiting for me in the hall. Without saying anything, she walked off to the small parlor. I joined her.

"You think Oletto will come?" I asked.

With her usual economy of motion, Zorn set the empty canister Torvan had given her on a side table. She took the parcel containing the tin of graphite and the brush out of her pocket and placed it beside the canister. "I think he will accommodate Torvan." She drew up a straight-backed armchair and sat. She put her hand on her right knee and kneaded it.

Going over to the sideboard, I poured two glasses of wine. I handed one to her and said, "You want something? For that." I gestured toward her knee.

"This will do," she said, sipping the wine.

I sank wearily into a comfortable chair across from her. Through the window behind her, I could see the clouds heavy with the threat of rain. The silence lengthened between us as I thought about Zorn's case against Arne. Finally I said, "You could be wrong."

Zorn scrutinized me with her dark unwavering gaze. "I do not think I am wrong."

The strain and weariness in her I had noticed earlier seemed stronger now, but I couldn't muster much sympathy for her. I said, "All you're really worried about is not being able to prove your suspicions, aren't you? You want to get Lucian off, even if it means sacrificing Arne." Zorn didn't answer. "It must have been a lot easier for you, when your word was law."

Zorn's chin came up. "There are times, Grayall, when you sound either astoundingly naïve or astoundingly ignorant." She drank off the rest of her wine. "Usually when you speculate about what you call the Realm." She stood up and went to the sideboard.

"Maybe that's so." My ongoing discontents with the way Zorn had handled herself all along rose to the surface, spurred on, I suppose, by my anxieties over Arne. "But you don't help matters any. Heaven forbid you should ever explain anything about Regeren, as you prefer to call it, or about yourself." I took a gulp of wine. "And why not? Pride, that's all. You'd rather be misjudged than suspected of courting favor. I think you even like it. Watching everyone make the wrong assumptions about you. That's a more superior position, isn't it? Than telling the others what you told me. That your sympathies aren't completely with the Realm and its traditions, no matter how you present yourself. I still say if you'd told people here about what you did to help the insurgency, this mess might have been avoided. And maybe you know that too. If you'd be willing to admit it, if only to yourself."

I had been flirting with versions of this complaint repeatedly, and it had finally all come spilling out, heedlessly, without any attention to its timing or its effect on Zorn. After all, I had criticized her often enough, and sometimes even goaded her, but even as I had prodded at her self-possession, I had come to take it for granted, assuming I would provoke at most a brief chill of disapproval.

Throughout my tirade, Zorn had been standing at the sideboard, holding the wine glass she had not yet refilled. When I finally ground to a halt, she turned toward me. Her face had gone rigid and her eyes glittered. I had finally succeeded, if that's what it deserved to be called, in stirring up, not the usual self-contained iciness, but raw, hot anger.

"Damn it, Grayall." Her voice rasped. "Enough." She was gripping the glass so tightly her scars shone white. With a muted crack, the stem broke and the base of the glass fell to her feet where it landed softly on the carpet. Zorn stared down at the bowl of the glass which she still held. Then with a sweep of her arm, she flung it into the fireplace. The burst of sound as it shattered punctuated her words. "Leave it be. Damn it all, leave it be." I sat transfixed. In a blazing voice, she went on, "I have borne with enough of your self-righteous certainties, your glib assumptions about my motives."

I should have anticipated that Zorn was overdue for a speech of her own, one which I unquestionably had earned, and I braced myself for it, but she stopped abruptly. Voices murmured outside the door.

I looked up at her, trying for a wordless appeasement, but she gave back to me an unreadable expression. She bent down, picked up the broken-off base of the glass by its stem, and set it on the sideboard.

What a great moment for Torvan to arrive with Oletto, I thought. Only when the door opened it wasn't them. It was Gwynedd and Patric. And Arne. Zorn gazed at them calmly. She had capped her anger like someone snuffing a candle. With a steady hand she took a fresh glass, poured herself some wine, and re-seated herself.

"We're glad to find you here," Gwynedd said cheerfully. "I was afraid you'd miss them." She nodded toward Arne and Patric.

"Miss them?" My voice sounded a bit strangled but no one seemed to notice.

Arne answered for Gwynedd. "Maybe it's awkward, with everything that's happened." He spoke solemnly but then added in an easier tone, "Still, there's really nothing more I can do here. So I've decided not to postpone the southern trip." He paused for consideration. "Carsten would approve, I think."

I looked at him blankly. Patric joined in. "You remember, Grayall. We're going to the ports in the Tradelands. Among other things, to arrange the re-sale of the insignia. We'll be gone a few weeks." Teaming up with Arne was part of Patric's reward for helping with the bidding and he sounded happy about it.

"We're leaving early tomorrow," Arne added. "Just in time to catch some more rotten weather, it seems. But we won't let that stop us, will we, Patric? Not for a trip this important." He walked over to the sideboard. He set his fingers on the base of the broken glass and pushed it aside without commenting on it. He poured out three glasses of wine, took one for himself and handed the others to Gwynedd and Patric. He looked expansive and self-satisfied. I tried to find in him a hint of uneasiness or guilt, but I couldn't. He was just Arne. Eyes crinkled with good humor, round face, florid and hearty.

The three of them pulled chairs over and we sat in what should have been a companionable grouping. The first spatter of rain played against the windows.

"Of course we'll have to do some sharp trading. To keep up with Her Excellency. A fine price you achieved." Arne raised his glass to Zorn in salute.

"It was hardly my achievement," Zorn said. "Yours, perhaps. And Carsten's."

Arne ducked his head. He seemed unsure how to take Zorn's remark. Finally he said almost shyly, "True enough." He peered into his wine glass, tipped it again in a gesture of recognition, and added, "He always gave me a good fight."

"A sad business," Patric interposed. "But life goes on. Anyway in this case, it seems we would have had another death if not Carsten's." He looked at Zorn.

She met his gaze evenly. "Mine would have been the death of a comparative stranger. Certainly an easier circumstance. Much like the accusation against Lucian."

As I listened to them, I seemed to be getting air only about every third breath. In part because I was sure, beneath Zorn's outward calm, a complex of emotions smoldered. And also because I worried how she was going to react to the news of Arne's intended departure. I was waiting for some kind of explosion. Alkali metals, indeed. Volatile substances, needing only air or water to ignite them. I took a deep breath.

Gwynedd noticed my distress but misinterpreted it. She said sympathetically, "These last days have been difficult. Tragic about Carsten. For Lucian, pathetic." She shook her head. "But it's done and we all need a break." She got up and offered around the wine. Patric and

Arne accepted, but I had had enough. I noticed that Zorn too set her glass aside.

"Not quite…done," Zorn corrected imperiously. They all looked at her in surprise.

Patric recovered first. "I don't think there's going to be much doubt about the outcome of the trial." He studied Zorn over the edge of his glass. "If that's what you're concerned about."

"No, no." Arne picked up on Patric's lead. "You can be sure Lucian will be dealt with."

"You assume they will find him guilty then," Zorn said.

Arne's features shifted with an expression I couldn't quite identify. But it was Patric who said offhandedly, "Yes, of course."

On the heel of his words, as if on cue, the parlor door opened and Torvan walked in with Oletto. They brought with them the damp smell of rain and, for me at least, the sense that something had started rolling downhill that wasn't going to stop until it reached bottom.

CHAPTER FORTY-THREE

Torvan, seeing Arne and Patric, exchanged a glance with Zorn. His face asked a question. I wasn't quick enough to tell whether he got an answer from her.

Gwynedd rose, smiled at Torvan and greeted Oletto but her surprise at his presence was obvious. "Do you have further inquiries to make, District Constable?" she asked politely but without enthusiasm. "Something important enough to bring you out in the rain?"

It was Oletto's turn to look surprised. "Torvan came to get me." Glancing around uncertainly, he took out a neatly folded handkerchief and patted his fingers. "Something about..." He hesitated. "Something you wished to tell me about the case against Lucian." He spoke directly to Zorn.

A spasm of dissatisfaction crossed over Torvan's face, but Zorn appeared unperturbed. "We were just discussing that," she said.

Arne broke in. "We were assuring Her Excellency that she need have no fear. Our court will hold him to account." I thought, at last, I heard a hint of disquiet in him, but maybe I only heard what I expected.

Torvan hesitated at the door but, when Zorn showed no willingness to leave and go off with him and Oletto, he drew forward a couple more chairs. He and the DC took their places. With their addition, we now formed a semi-circle around Zorn.

She sat very erect, her shoulders square beneath a dark-gray jacket. Her arms rested along the arms of her chair. Her hands lay relaxed, her fingers curling lightly. An onyx ring, the one item of the insignia she had retained, gleamed in the light from lamp and fireplace. Her entire demeanor suggested authority, long accustomed and easily carried. She looked more like a judge than the workmanlike magistrate we had appeared before yesterday. Watching her, I was distressingly sure she had decided to play her hand.

"Nonetheless," she said, "your case, as presented at the hearing, remains circumstantial." Without any particular inflection, Zorn had managed to make her voice sound arrogant, even contemptuous.

"Still, we believe it to be adequate." Oletto fumbled with his handkerchief, slipping it back into a pocket. "Although I'm certainly willing to hear anything you care to add."

"What your case lacks is evidence," Zorn said. "However, that deficiency can be remedied."

"I would be more than happy to hear how." Oletto's handkerchief was out again.

From the side table, Zorn picked up the sample canister we had brought from Torvan's laboratory. "The canister, similar to this one, that held the potassium, the killer handled it." She paused and Oletto gave a minimal nod. I couldn't help looking at Arne. His eyes were sharp with interest and his face was flushed.

Abruptly Zorn stood up. She reached out her hand toward the handkerchief. Oletto, frowning, gave it to her. She wiped the surface of the canister and, without saying a word, thrust it at Arne. Taking it, he held it up and said, "What am I supposed to do with this?"

"You have already done it," Zorn replied. Grasping the canister at its top and bottom, she took it from him and placed it back on the table. She swung her chair around to face the table and sat. Unwrapping the parcel she had also left lying there, she repeated the demonstration she had given to Torvan and me. She tapped out a little of the graphite and, with the brush, carefully dusted it over the surface of the canister. When she finished, she moved her chair out of the way, sat again, and nodded at her work. We all crowded forward to see. Just as had happened in the laboratory, the fine whorls and lines appeared. I let out a long breath, whether of relief or resignation, I wasn't sure.

"The fingerprint pattern revealed here is unique to each person," Zorn intoned. "When Arne Bennetson handled this canister just now, he left a sample of his pattern. It will remain until it is wiped away. The same is true for the canister in the laboratory from which the vial of potassium was removed. The fingerprints left on it can also be made visible."

Zorn had chosen her words carefully. Without accusing Arne, she had focused them on him. She was also giving her explanation differently than she had given it to Torvan and me. She had omitted all the practical difficulties she had mentioned to us. Instead she spoke with relentless assurance.

"We know that Torvan's fingerprints are on the potassium canister," she continued. "Once we eliminate the patterns that match his, we will be able to determine who else handled that canister. We will know who set the fire-trap that killed Carsten of Wrightwork." She looked straight at Arne. "Then we will be done with this."

All I saw was a blur of motion as Arne lunged forward. His arms outstretched, he flung himself at Zorn. He reached for her neck but she brought her knee up. I heard a slight oof of pain from her and a louder groan from him as she caught his weight on her knee. Zorn's chair overbalanced and they tumbled backwards. As they landed, Arne rolled sideways, clutching his groin. Zorn had also rolled clear. She ended up sitting on the ground, one knee drawn up, her other leg crooked beneath her. Her left elbow rested on her knee, her left arm giving support to her right. In her right hand was her revolver, aimed steadily at Arne.

"No." "For heaven's sake." "Don't shoot." "Arne." The shouts rang out in unison like some raucous chord. Oletto rushed to place himself between Zorn and Arne, but I knew she wouldn't shoot. Not then anyway, with Arne momentarily helpless on the floor.

Arne, his face contorted with pain and rage, clambered to his knees. But Torvan and Patric were already beside him. They took hold of his arms. Oletto, still standing between Arne and Zorn, said, "They have him. Put the gun away."

"Zorn, please, do as he says," Gwynedd added urgently.

Zorn did not comply immediately but, after a long, considered moment, she broke her aim and slid the revolver into the holster at her back. She put her arm up to me. I reached down. Bracing herself against me, she staggered to her feet.

Torvan and Patric helped Arne up as well. Arne stood between them, swaying slightly. "Damn you, Zorn of Northmarch. May you rot in hell." His voice was thick with despair. "And damn the rest of you for your part in this." I assumed he thought we had all conspired in setting him up.

Oletto turned to face Arne. "You have incriminated yourself." The DC sounded disbelieving. "I have to take you into custody," he said, with a touch of apology.

"Go to hell," Arne muttered. He hung his head in apparent defeat. Torvan and Patric seemed unsure what to do. Perhaps they relaxed their grip slightly. If so, it was what Arne was waiting for. With a violent sideways twist, he lurched free. Patric, on his left, was thrown off balance. Before he could recover his footing, Arne had flung the door open. It crashed against the wall and he ran. Ran through the dining room and on toward the back of the house with Patric, Oletto, and Torvan pounding after him. I could hear the series of doors banging.

Gwynedd and I started to follow them but, when I looked back at Zorn, she hadn't moved.

Gwynedd came back and stood before her. "How did you know?" she asked, her eyes glistening with unfallen tears. But she didn't wait for an answer. She left to rouse the house and send for reinforcements from the district watch.

I put my own interpretation on Zorn's failure to react. "You expected that. That he'd seize any chance to break free."

"Didn't you?"

"Why'd you put the gun away then?"

"They asked me to," Zorn said as if it was as simple as that. Maybe I imagined the hint of sarcasm in her reply. She walked over and joined me in the doorway. She was limping. "Besides, the gun would not have stopped him. Bennetson has shown a willingness to gamble. And he knew it would have been a risky shot. With the others in the way." She paused. "I might have achieved it. That shot. But if I had been so eager to act as both judge and executioner in this matter, what would you have made of that?"

Stepping past me, she moved out into the hall. I stood there numbly for a moment, then hurried after her. I caught up with her at the base of the stairs. Grabbing her arm, I said shrilly, "Arne willing to gamble! He gambled whether Carsten would beat you to the pond that day."

Zorn shrugged as though dismissing a matter of small consequence. "I assume he arranged a meeting. He would have had no difficulty persuading Carsten. Not if it involved some offer about the insignia."

"But Arne must have known it could all so easily have miscarried. A slip of timing and it would probably have been you who walked into that fire-trap." My voice was shaking.

"Another reasonable gamble from his point of view." The hall was dimly lit and the angles of Zorn's face were edged in shadow. "Had he killed me, suspicion would still have fallen on Lucian. And in that event," her voice took on a tone I could not define, "at least you could have written my epitaph as it suited you." She turned away and slowly made her way up the stairs.

CHAPTER FORTY-FOUR

It was the beginning of a long, weary night. Whether Zorn managed to get any sleep, I didn't know. The rest of us didn't get much. Additional officers, even some from out of district, arrived. They organized a search of the house and grounds, but they didn't expect any useful results from that. According to a statement from Patric, it appeared that Arne had taken his chances with the river.

Patric explained that, as he, Torvan, and Oletto had run in pursuit, he had outdistanced the other two. Reaching the dock ahead of them, he was sure he had heard the sound of a loud splash. Although with the rain and the dark, if Arne had jumped, he had not been able to see him.

There wasn't much the constabulary could do about searching the river that night. But at daybreak, they were out in force along its banks. Fortunately sometime overnight the rain had stopped. But although they kept at it all the next day, they found no sign of Arne.

They had no real difficulty, however, verifying the fingerprint evidence. Despite Zorn's cautions about the possible problems in obtaining and matching fingerprints, cautions which she repeated to Oletto, the potassium canister proved very cooperative. It yielded two sets of impressions, both clear and distinctly different from each other. At Zorn's suggestion they also brought up prints from the base of the broken wine glass that Arne had touched.

Actually, as Torvan later made clear to Gwynedd and myself, it was Zorn to whom they had entrusted the delicate operation of dusting for the prints. Then she and Oletto, with Torvan's help, had worked over them for a considerable time with a magnifying glass. The three of them had been closeted in the laboratory most of the day. At the end of it they were satisfied they had matched both sets of prints, the ones Arne had left on the canister Zorn had maneuvered him into handling and the ones on the base of the wine glass, to the second set on the potassium canister, the ones which were not Torvan's.

By the time they had assembled their evidence, I'm not sure it was necessary any longer, but they spent the next morning presenting it anyway. They met privately with the magistrate. Torvan said she questioned Zorn extensively, making intelligent inquiries about the reliability of fingerprint identification. However, in view of Arne's panic-stricken flight, no one seemed to have any doubts about his guilt.

The magistrate promptly ordered the convening of another hearing. Oletto, supported by testimony from Zorn and Torvan, presented the new evidence. The magistrate issued a warrant for Arne and an order for his trial, but those were formalities. The presumption was that Arne had drowned in the river. It had been high and flowing fast the night he disappeared. And, of course, Lucian was released, cleared of all charges, with expressions of regret for the inconvenience to him, but with no other apology.

There were some things that, lacking an account from Arne, they would never know for sure. They couldn't be certain how he had lured Carsten to the pond, although Zorn's theory about him having arranged a meeting with his intended victim, with some offer about the insignia, seemed reasonable. Nor could they be sure exactly when Arne had set the fire-trap. He was a familiar presence at Gwynedd's and no one would have taken much notice of him puttering around, especially as busy as everybody had been on the day of the bidding. He would also have been familiar enough with Torvan's movements to pick a time to slip into the laboratory unobserved and remove the vial of potassium.

The more I thought about it, the more it chilled me to fully grasp how long that lethal apparatus must have waited for its intended victim and how easily it might have claimed Zorn, or someone else in the household.

When the hearing was finally adjourned, Gwynedd, Torvan, and I traveled back to the house before the others. Evane had stayed behind with Lucian to complete the details of his release. Zorn, Torvan explained, had gone off with Oletto. Once home, we headed, as we would normally have done, for the coziness of the small parlor. Gwynedd and Torvan settled into comfortable chairs but the taint of the confrontation with Arne lingered for me in that room and I stood restlessly at one of the windows. Gwynedd watched me for a while, then said, "Soon there won't be a spot on the place without unpleasant memories."

I stared out the window as if you could see the dock from there, which you couldn't. "You think Arne is dead?" I turned and braced myself against the window sill.

They both looked at me solemnly but it was Torvan who answered. "Yes, Grayall, I do."

"Arne and Carsten," Gwynedd said. "It's hard to believe. That we've lost them both." Her elegant face was drawn into lines of sadness. The rich brown of her skin was dulled with pallor.

Seeing her distress, I said, "I can't help thinking none of this would have happened, except for a particular opportunity. One I helped provide." I looked away.

"Grayall," Gwynedd said firmly, "the guilt was Arne's, not yours. Or any of ours."

"Gwynedd's right," Torvan added. "You can't take responsibility for Arne's choices and you can't be presumptuous enough to blame yourself for them."

"That sounds like something Zorn would say."

"Your friend generally makes good sense." He smiled. "In fact, I've come to have considerable admiration for her."

"You'd admire the devil if he brought you some knowledge you didn't already have." I pushed myself away from the window and dropped into an easy chair. Torvan laughed. "What did Oletto want with her anyway?" I asked.

"It seems I'm not the only one hungry for knowledge. He wants to be certain he has all his notes straight. About fingerprints. We haven't seen the last of that technique around here, you can be sure of that." Torvan grew thoughtful. "Interesting how Zorn knew all that. Not the kind of knowledge you'd expect from the Realm. And that reminds me,

I'm sure I have a reference somewhere." He unwound himself from his chair.

Gwynedd and I exchanged tolerant looks. She reached out her hand to him as he passed. He stopped and bent over to receive an affectionate kiss. "Nothing interferes with the pursuit of knowledge," she said to me over his shoulder.

Torvan grinned sheepishly and continued to the door. As an afterthought, I called to him, "Where *would* you learn about identifying fingerprints?"

"At a guess? Veraces. Although I can't decide what's more unlikely. That a traditional ariston would travel there or that they'd grant her a visitor's research permit if she did." He drifted out the door.

"Veraces," I grumbled. "They who speak the truth. Aloof, alone, and damn proud of it."

"Your prejudices are showing, Grayall," Gwynedd said.

"My prejudices? What about the Veracians? They're the ones who hold themselves apart. Restrict access, stand guard over their learning and their library like a miser over his gold."

"Each to their own methods. And they do offer their services to the outer world, and occasionally grant access. As Torvan's experience with them has shown."

I kept following my own line of thought, however. "It is kind of funny though. The image of Zorn confronting the Veracians, seeking to qualify for visitor's admission. In such an encounter, I wonder whose pride would suffer the greater denting."

"An interesting, but presumably idle, speculation," said a voice from the doorway. Gwynedd and I both turned to see Zorn standing there.

I was acutely conscious that Zorn and I had barely spoken since I had provoked her anger on the night of Arne's flight. Of course, she had been pretty fully occupied assisting Oletto and submitting testimony about fingerprints to the magistrate, but I couldn't help wondering whether she had been purposely avoiding me.

"You still speaking to me?" I asked. I wasn't sure my flippancy quite covered my nervousness. Gwynedd looked quizzical. I said to her, "The last time Zorn and I spoke, she almost threw a decanter at me."

Zorn walked into the room. "It was a wine glass," she said matter-of-factly. "And I threw it at the fireplace." She turned specifically to Gwynedd. "My apologies. To you," she said with particular emphasis. "That makes the second glass I owe you."

"No apologies needed. No debt either. We have glassware to spare." Gwynedd glanced at me. "Besides, I've had the urge to throw things at Grayall a time or two myself. Mostly when she won't give up pestering about something."

Still looking at Gwynedd, Zorn said, "In decadent times, any test of one's equanimity has its value." Her delivery was deadpan and it took Gwynedd a count or two to catch the teasing that lurked in her words. Meanwhile, Zorn shifted her attention to me. "To answer your question. Since I have matters to discuss with you, I must be." I frowned at her in confusion. "Still speaking to you," she added.

Gwynedd prepared tactfully to excuse herself, but Zorn asked me to accompany her to the library instead. I raised my eyebrows at Gwynedd to indicate I had no idea what this was all about, then followed Zorn into the hall.

Before we had taken more than a step or two, we heard the commotion of arrival in the entry. "Oh, hell," I said under my breath. It was Lucian and Evane, returning at last from seeing to his release. Considering that Lucian had been exonerated, they both looked pretty solemn as they came into the hall. Their expressions grew even more somber when they saw Zorn. In fact Lucian looked downright grim.

He took a step toward us, his arms behind his back. Then he stopped. Just as I had noticed in him at the first hearing, as soon as he became aware of his posture, he abruptly let them fall to his sides. He faced Zorn stiffly. "And now I suppose, I am obligated to feel grateful to you." It was clear that for him even those ungracious words were like a dose of extremely unpleasant medicine.

Zorn surveyed him impassively. "Your obligations are your own concern." She moved to walk past him.

He wavered as if intending to take another step toward her, a step that never quite materialized. Instead he said, "The other things that happened, Your Ex…" I thought he'd choke himself biting the word off.

He cleared his throat. "I didn't arrange them." The effort of getting the words out had overlaid his fair skin with a deep blush of color.

"I never suspected you did." Zorn's tone was neutral, neither arrogant nor consoling. Without further remark, she continued across the hall.

Lucian stared after her. If there was any emotion in his face, it was resentment. "You might have tried a simple thank you," I said to him. He turned back to me, but Evane forestalled anything he might have said by placing an anxious hand on his arm. She looked displeased but whether with Zorn, or me, or Lucian, or maybe even with herself, I couldn't tell. Probably with us all. But she didn't say anything. She only tugged at Lucian and he let himself be pulled away.

CHAPTER FORTY-FIVE

I followed Zorn into the library. As I closed the door behind us, I said, "He can't stand it. Owing his freedom to you." Zorn had taken a place on the long side of one of the library tables. Before her was a document of some pages, on heavy, legal-weight paper.

"That is hardly surprising," she said. She motioned to a chair across from her and I sat down.

I almost made some quip about her indifference to Lucian's surliness but, as I looked at her, I changed my mind. She looked weary. The planes of her face stood out in sharp relief and smudges of darkness lurked beneath her eyes. "I guess you're right," I murmured.

A gleam of suspicion narrowed Zorn's eyes. "You've turned unusually docile," she said with a touch of acidity.

I ignored the bait. "What's all this?" I said, waving my hand at the document.

She reached across and handed me it to me. "I recorded this last Saturday, but have had no suitable opportunity to present it to you. Perhaps the time is still not opportune, but it is overdue."

I began to glance through the pages. They consisted of deeds and titles to a freehold with the picturesque name of Wendenwood, a property of three-hundred and fifty-six acres, well situated in the southeast corner of the Freeholds, with frontage on the Seaward River. The legal descriptions affirmed that most of the acreage was in wheat and produced a moderate but consistent profit. There were also about forty acres of woodland and thirty in pasture. Structures included a residence, a stable complex, storage buildings, and housing for employees. All in all, a pretty complete set-up. The price had been seven-hundred and fifty argen. Good value, as far as I could tell.

The purchase had been finalized, so I figured Zorn wasn't really asking for my professional opinion, but I gave it anyway, out of politeness. "I think you've done well. It looks a fair price, and it should prove a good investment, in case that's what you were thinking. And it still leaves you plenty of capital as well."

I flipped idly to the last page. It was the certification of ownership decked out with all the proper seals and attestments. At the bottom, in acceptance of purchase and deed, was a precise signature, Zorn Northmarch. Just that, with the 'of' omitted. Above the signature, in the recording clerk's neat printing, was the name of the legally designated owner. Zorn's name was there of course, but it did not stand alone. My name was there, too. She had named me co-owner of Wendenwood Freehold.

As I stared at the sheet of paper, I scarcely heard what Zorn was saying. "I plan to live at the holding. If you still intend to establish a trading route through the borderland villages, it might be convenient for you as well. If you have other plans, your share of the income … "

Zorn broke off because I had let the document fall from my hand. The heavy pages glided halfway across the table. "I can't accept this." My words tumbled out in emphatic protest.

"The deed is already recorded," Zorn said, as if that settled the matter.

"I don't care. You can't just give away half-ownership in a freehold."

"As you are apt to remind me, I can do what I want." Zorn rearranged the pages on the table. "Besides, according to your own assessment, it does not impoverish me."

"That's not the point and you know it."

"What is?"

I sighed my frustration. I had lost the earlier battle about being named in Zorn's will as her legatee. I had given in on that mostly because I knew at the time she'd had to name someone as her heir. But this was different. This was a real transfer of real property. And it was too much. Too much to give away so casually. Certainly too much to accept.

I latched onto what seemed to me the most obvious objection. "I've told you before. You don't owe me anything. Stop trying to pay off a debt you don't have. Or do you choose to forget, if I saved your life, you returned that with payment in kind."

Zorn took a moment to consider her reply. Then she said, "I would have neither life nor property but for you, Grayall. Nonetheless, whatever you may think of this," she pushed the document toward me, "it is not repayment. It could not be." She stopped, her face closed into thoughtfulness. At last she added, "I can only say. It seems appropriate to me. That you have a share of this property. If you want an explanation beyond that, I cannot give it to you."

The last thing I expected from Zorn was an appeal to emotion over reason. Uncertain how to respond, I grumbled, "You're not much good at explanations in general, are you?" I think she caught the implication in my words before I did. The introspection in her face sharpened into alertness. I hadn't really meant to resurrect our quarrel of the other night, so I quickly added, "Look, I can't let you do this. That's all there is to it."

I didn't want to give Zorn a chance to argue. I stood up, ready to leave but, before I reached the door, she said, "You can't leave it alone." It was an observation, not a rebuff. And I knew exactly what she meant.

I turned around. "I am sorry about the other night. Truly I am. You might joke about it with Gwynedd, but you were furious. Because of me. I'm not proud of myself for that."

"I don't know why not," Zorn said, her voice as level as a measuring stick. "You have been after a reaction like that from me since our first encounter."

I came back and sat across from her again. "All right. I admit, that's true enough." I allowed myself a good, long, thoughtful examination of her. The strong, tan-skinned, angular face set in the familiar lines of judicious calm, the black-brown eyes that gazed back at me steadily. It was time to have my say, once and for all. "This front you feel compelled to maintain, this ariston manner." I tried to keep my voice as neutral as her expression. "Sometimes I think it's just silly. As I've said before, the result of stupid pride. Or maybe I try to convince myself of that. So I won't have to admit that it's worse. Scary, maybe even dangerous." I was onto forbidden territory again, but I was determined to finish. "I meant it when I said I wasn't proud of making you lose your temper, but I haven't changed my mind. I think about the way events played out here and I still think you were wrong not to admit how you aided renegade servs, assisted the insurgency. Wrong, not to explain yourself, even at the risk of appearing to be self-serving. I think you let your pride get in the way of your common sense. And I still think, to some degree, that contributed to what happened here."

I held myself ready, waiting for Zorn's anger to flare again, but she listened to it all with no visible sign of displeasure. Instead she said, "You may be right. I should not claim to be objective on this topic. Then again, neither should you. My reputation touches yours. As long as we are … associates."

"As long as we're friends, Zorn. Because I do consider you my friend. And I have thought about what you've said. That I worry about what people think of you because it affects me. I've even tried to compensate for it, I think. Bending over backwards not to be defensive about you. But with all that, I still don't understand why you couldn't have unbent a little yourself, on this point."

When I had finished, Zorn's silence lasted a long time, so long I assumed the discussion was over, although nothing seemed to have been resolved. Then with apparent irrelevance, Zorn said, "An interesting characteristic of rigidly structured societies is that the positions within them are fixed. They will be filled. By someone."

Despite what seemed an abrupt change of subject, for once I had the good sense not to interrupt.

Zorn went on, "I told you I had spent some time away from Regeren. In fact, I had not intended to return. However, when the wardership of Farnorth fell vacant, due to Zered's abdication," her lips twisted into a humorless smile, "Archon Zarath sent word. She offered the wardership to me." Zorn's expression turned inward as if she was reconstructing the memory. "I could have refused. Had I done so, that position and with it rule over Farnorth would have passed to the only other remaining member of my cadre of Alphaen order-kin. Zirel." She paused. Whatever was passing through her mind was obviously not pleasant. But her voice remained dispassionate. "I could not permit that. I would not consign anyone to live under Zirel's governance. He is...well, someone not fitted even to have command over the land and household allowed to each of us when we reached our majority. Much less to have the greater power and authority the wardership would have conferred. Not even for the relatively short time Regeren was then likely to last. So I returned. I became the Warder of Farnorth. I took on the responsibilities that come with rule and governance."

Zorn had been speaking in a lecturer's tone, but abruptly her voice changed. It got harder edged, mocking, but the mockery was for herself. "Helping those insurgents to flee, those third-rate heroics on my part you find so admirable, that you wish me to stand upon here. For that escapade," she cut the word in pieces like she'd taken a knife to it, "Zarath, if she'd learned of my activities soon enough, would have called me up before an assembly of Archons and Dominors to answer for my treason." She must have seen a flicker of expression pass over my face because she said, "No. Such an assembly would not have ordered my execution. Punishing a ruling ariston like a servitor. That would have been considered inappropriate. A bad example to the serving class. But they would have dispossessed and banished me. Then Farnorth would have gone to Zirel anyway. Thanks to me." It wasn't mockery anymore that resonated in her voice, but scorn. "Fortunately by the time Zarath discovered my offenses, it was too late. Regeren was on the verge of dissolution and she had to settle for a private resolution with me."

"Yeah," I muttered. "And Archon Zarath was after something a touch more severe than banishment."

Zorn waved off my interruption. "By aiding a few renegades, I put the entire province of Farnorth at risk. And for what? To ease my own discontents? To reassure myself of my nobility of character?" She gave a contemptuous nod. "What I did was reckless and self-indulgent. And I will not trade in it. Do you understand what I say? I will not trade in it." She put full weight on each of the words. "If that makes me prideful and arrogant, so be it." Zorn stood up. She gathered up the deed and title document. "The ownership of Wendenwood Freehold will remain recorded as it is. You must accept that or not, as you see fit." She walked out of the room before I could say another word.

And in truth, I wouldn't have known what to say. I was shaken by the unexpected intensity which Zorn had so abruptly revealed. And it was awhile before I thought of things I might have said. Things like, being torn between two calls of conscience, whatever else it was, was hardly a matter to be dismissed as selfishness or recklessness. Or that the people whose lives she had undoubtedly saved by assisting in their flight from the Realm might have taken a different view of the matter than the one she had put forward. Or that if her actions were self-indulgent and foolish, she had paid a substantial price for her pleasure and her folly. Archon Zarath had seen to that.

But later when I did think of those things, they didn't inspire me to open a debate with her again. In part because, strictly speaking, the judgment Zorn had passed on herself was correct. She had risked the greater interest for the lesser. I had to respect her rigorous integrity in acknowledging that. Especially since I had no way of determining what the real consequences would have been for Farnorth, and its people, if Zirel had replaced her as Warder of Farnorth.

But mostly I think I didn't argue with her because I finally felt reconciled to my friendship with her. I could finally like Zorn. I liked her for what she did. I liked her for giving, in defiance of the demands of pragmatism, immediate aid to the insignificant few, even at a potential cost to the abstract many. I admired Zorn for what she condemned in herself as failure and weakness. Whether that says something about failure and weakness in my own character, I'm not sure.

I thought about all those things for most of the evening and a good part of the night. And somewhere in all of that, I reached a decision, or I should say it reached me, because I knew I would accept co-ownership of Wendenwood Freehold.

Zorn's generosity would give me a place, a physical place, from which to build whatever life I finally decided on. And there was no denying the commonality between Zorn and me. We had both lost all the grounds on which our lives had previously rested, and we both had to discover new ones. The freehold would provide real ground on which to stand while the details of our lives rearranged themselves. Or so it seemed to me, as maybe it had to Zorn as well. I dropped off to sleep, more at ease, more settled in mind and spirit, than I had been at any time since I had gone in search of Jarrell.

My mind became so full of my decision about Wendenwood that I failed to give sufficient attention to everything Zorn had told me about how she had come to be Warder of Farnorth. Particularly about her having spent time out of the Realm. As she had reminded me, she had mentioned that before. That had been on the ferry as we had crossed into the Exchanges. Only this time, she had added, "I had not intended to return." That statement really should have weighed more heavily with me. But, it would be a long while before I fully learned that part of Zorn's history and its significance to my understanding of her.

Chapter Forty-six

When I awoke the next morning, very late and with a start out of heavy sleep, it wasn't Zorn's confidences or Wendenwood Freehold that filled my thoughts. While I had slept, some part of me must have been busy, prodding away at my new-found complacency and replacing it with the disquieting realization that one loose end from recent events still dangled, tantalizingly free.

I yanked myself out of bed, dressed quickly, went into the sitting room and knocked on Zorn's door. Getting no answer, I opened it. The room was empty, the bed was made. Zorn, as I could have expected, was evidently up and gone some time ago. I hurried downstairs. Haslen was crossing the hall and, noticing my rush, asked if anything was wrong. Despite his well-schooled politeness, his tone of voice did not quite manage to suppress a note of frustration. Enough trouble was more than enough, it seemed to say.

Hearing his discontent, I slowed myself down. My urgency was, after all, self-invented. "No," I said. "Nothing's wrong. Have you seen Zorn this morning?"

"No. I haven't." He checked his watch. "If she's not in the library, she's probably out riding."

"You didn't see her though?"

"She does not check with me before she goes out." He frowned. "Are you sure everything's all right?"

I sidestepped his question. "Gwynedd in her office?"

He nodded. "She has a lot of work to catch up with."

I knew that was a hint not to bother her, but I ignored it. As I headed down the corridor, I felt Haslen staring after me. I took a quick look in the library. Zorn was not there.

"Go away, Grayall," Gwynedd said when I walked in on her. "It's past coffee time." Several large account books lay open in front of her.

"The branch, the hay bale, the horse," I blurted out. "We never figured out who was responsible for them. Assuming we believe Lucian's denials, which I do."

Gwynedd's head snapped up. "Damn. How stupid of me! With everything else, those things went completely from my mind."

I hadn't meant it as an accusation against her. "All of our minds," I corrected. "Even Zorn's."

Gwynedd's eyes turned stormy. "The difference is, it must have been someone in my employ. Thus I consider myself accountable." She stiffened. "Has something else happened?"

"Everything's fine." I shrugged. "As far as I know."

"And Zorn?"

"Haslen says she's out riding. That makes sense. Her usual routine."

Gwynedd still looked troubled, but abruptly her face cleared. She was gazing past me to a side window. She crossed the room and peered out. I joined her just in time to glimpse a horse being led toward the stable. It was a tall roan. "That's her horse, isn't it?" Gwynedd asked.

"Yeah." We glanced at each other and with unspoken agreement headed out the door.

We stopped for a moment, not knowing which way to go, but Haslen who was coming down the corridor said to me, "I came to tell you, since you seemed concerned, Zorn of Northmarch has returned and has gone into the dining room."

Zorn was sitting down to a cup of coffee and a frugal meal when we descended on her. "Are you all right?" we called out in unison. Only of course, it was obvious she was. Gwynedd and I exchanged glances again and then, with studied nonchalance, we poured ourselves some coffee. We joined Zorn at the table.

Zorn noted it all. After we sat down, she asked Gwynedd, "Haven't you had a sufficiency of trouble?" The way she posed the question told me I had been wrong. I should have known better than to think Zorn would have overlooked anything. She had not for one moment forgotten, if we discounted Lucian, with regard to those earlier mishaps the culprit was still unidentified.

Gwynedd must have read the same meaning in Zorn's question that I did because she said, "Trouble. We don't always get a choice of how much. But such trouble as comes must be dealt with." She took a sip of coffee. "Do you know who in this household made those attempts to injure you?"

"No. I do not know." Zorn's answer was prompt and suspiciously placid.

Gwynedd caught Zorn's literalness immediately. "If you don't *know*, could you make a good guess?"

"I could guess. How good it would be is another matter." Zorn went back to her food, as though putting aside an unwelcome interruption.

A sparring match between Zorn and Gwynedd had its points of interest, I decided. It was difficult for Gwynedd to push the matter without seeming rude. She drank her coffee thoughtfully, then she stood up and said to Zorn, "When you've finished eating, I'd appreciate a few moments of your time in the library. If you wouldn't mind."

When Gwynedd had left the room, Zorn, with a sharp glance at me, murmured, "And even if I would."

I didn't comment. The aromas from the warming trays of fresh bread and baked ham seemed more worthy of my attention, especially since recent events had tended to discourage anything in the way of regular meals. I went to the sideboard and with a generous hand loaded a plate, for what was either a very late breakfast or an early lunch.

Zorn and I ate in amiable silence. When she was done, she took a second cup of coffee and waited for me. When I had speared the last morsel of ham, I said casually, "I suppose Gwynedd's right, you must have thought about who set up those earlier mishaps."

"I have thought about it," Zorn said with no particular emphasis.

"Gwynedd's going to want to find out."

"That is her affair. It is her household." Zorn pushed back her chair. "Have you finished?"

"In case you haven't noticed, my eating's been a little thin lately. Not that you would notice, I suppose. You never have done justice to the food here. Which reminds me, at Wendenwood, I'll take charge of the provisioning, if it's all the same to you."

Zorn's head lifted, a barely discernible movement. I glanced away self-consciously. What was it I'd told Lucian? A simple thank you. I took my own advice and said it. With admirable fortitude, Zorn managed to contain any display of satisfaction, as well as any surprise she might have felt at my decision. She nodded once and said, "I cede to you all authority over the kitchen and the larder."

"I will hold you to that." And she actually allowed me to have the last word.

CHAPTER FORTY-SEVEN

We left the dining room and Zorn headed for the library, with me tagging along. Gwynedd was waiting for us, seated at the same table and in the same place Zorn had occupied yesterday. With a pass of her hand, she indicated a chair next to her and Zorn took it. I retreated to an easy chair off to one side.

"What are you doing here, Grayall?" Gwynedd asked.

I angled my head toward her. "Being nosey."

I was spared Gwynedd's comeback because the door opened and Haslen walked in. He looked ill-at-ease. "You wanted to see me," he said to Gwynedd, but his eyes kept shifting to Zorn.

"Sit down," Gwynedd directed. Haslen picked up a chair. Being careful not to drag it across the floor, he set it before the table. Another tribunal, I thought.

Gwynedd folded her hands before her. "Someone employed by this House attempted to injure not only a client, but a guest." She nodded in Zorn's direction. "I want to know who."

It was clear Haslen wasn't comfortable, but he wasn't easily intimidated either. "You know, we all thought it was Lucian." It was a polite but firm evasion.

"Well, think again," Gwynedd shot back. "You're house chamberlain. You must have some idea."

Haslen rubbed the palms of his hands together, then interlaced his fingers. His thumbs fidgeted. But he stood his ground. "You're asking me to put forward an accusation. But I have no evidence. I'd be guessing, and I'd rather not do that."

Gwynedd's irritation burst out. "You prefer not to guess. Zorn would prefer not to guess. But I need to start somewhere and your guesses," she included both of them, "appear to be all I have."

Haslen seemed surprised. Maybe he had thought this interrogation was more Zorn's idea than Gwynedd's. For her part, Zorn offered nothing, although it seemed to me she watched Haslen with interest.

I swung forward in my chair. "Granted no one has asked me, but I'll give you a guess." They all looked at me, Gwynedd and Haslen with inquisitive frowns, Zorn with no change of expression. "Caled. I think it was Caled."

Gwynedd leaned across the table. "The gatekeeper? Why him?"

I had spent the last few minutes sifting through recollections and I had my answer ready. "Remember the day the hay bale fell out of the loft. Caled wasn't at the gate when we came in. We took our horses to the stable ourselves." I turned to Zorn for confirmation, but she only waited for me to go on. "And again, the morning the horse went down, Caled wasn't around then either." This time I turned to Gwynedd.

"Yes, I remember," she said.

Haslen shifted position restlessly. "That doesn't mean anything. It's not unusual for the gatekeeper to be off the gate for short periods of time."

"He seems to have made a habit of it," I said. "At least I noticed he wasn't there a lot." I remembered an impression I'd had. "I think you noticed it too," I said to Haslen. "There were times it seemed to me you were checking on him."

"Is that right?" Gwynedd asked him.

Haslen's answer came unwillingly. "Yes, I suppose it is. Caled had fallen into a pattern of being neglectful. And I did mention it to him. I would have spoken to you about it. Except for everything that's happened. But still I...I'm sure it wasn't Caled who arranged those other incidents." Haslen unclasped his hands and rested one on each knee, bracing himself against his arms. "If it really wasn't Lucian, then," he hesitated, "they must have been accidents after all." The last sentence seemed to be directed specifically at Zorn.

"You can't seriously believe that," I said derisively.

"Do you have any other reason to suspect Caled?" Gwynedd asked me.

"Ever since we got here, he's barely been civil. And it's more than a guess he doesn't like you," I said to Zorn.

Gwynedd looked inquiringly at Haslen. "Surely *you* know his attitudes." Haslen's face turned stubborn. Gwynedd pressed him. "I can ask others. It would be better for you to tell me."

Haslen slid his hands off his knees. "All right," he said with sullen concession. "From the time they arrived," he gestured to include Zorn and me, "Caled never missed an opportunity, insults like Lucian's, only Caled would laugh about it. He'd say things like, aristos, so high and mighty, they don't even shit, but it's OK, because they are shit. And then he'd laugh again and say, even high and mighty shit can be shoveled out with the rest of the dirt." Surprisingly Haslen's voice had grown easier as he went on, as if reporting Caled's insolence had released some tension in him.

When he finished, he glared defiantly at Gwynedd and Zorn. He didn't have to say, you asked for it, now see how you like it, but surely that's what he was thinking. A smear of anger spread over Gwynedd's face, but as I could have told them, none of it provoked the slightest reaction from Zorn.

"And you permitted this to go on?" Gwynedd's voice was harsh.

Haslen met her emotion without faltering. "You've always made it clear that in this household people are entitled to their own lives. And their own opinions. As long as they do their work. Besides Caled wasn't alone in his attitude. Only more outspoken about it. If you suspect everyone who..." He stopped and stared at Zorn. "Who hates the ariston and everything she stands for, you'd have to include half the staff." His own neutrality had fallen away, replaced by clear hostility.

Gwynedd seemed to be holding herself in, with effort, but she said quietly, "I doubt anyone here is really in a position to know what Zorn of Northmarch stands for."

She waited, giving an opening to us both. I knew I wasn't going to take it, but I looked at Zorn. It seemed the right time to hear from her. She let a few moments pass, then she said to Haslen, "You are correct.

Caled is not the person responsible for those apparent accidents."
Having delivered that assertion, she lapsed into silence again but she
continued to scrutinize Haslen.

CHAPTER FORTY-EIGHT

I started to tell Zorn to quit stalling and say what was on her mind, but then I noticed that Haslen had stiffened, his whole body tensed like he was avoiding a blow.

"You know, don't you?" he said to Zorn. His jaw was so tight the words were a whisper.

"Yes," Zorn answered. Then she went on, steadily, implacably. "I know who holds the keys in this household, who has access to everything and whose presence anywhere causes no comment. I know whose work requires a familiarity with schedules, those of employees and clients alike. I know who has had experience trading with Regeren, whose aversion to 'aristos' comes from observation rather than from conjecture."

As Zorn had been speaking, Gwynedd had slowly risen to her feet. Astonishment and outrage contended in her face. "Haslen?" she breathed.

Something in Haslen collapsed but, when he finally spoke he sounded calm, like he was simply giving Gwynedd a report. "The first was almost an accident. It had been a bad night and I checked around the next morning, as I normally would. I saw the branch. It looked like it was about to come down and I planned to have it seen to. Then I thought about how the aristo had the habit of sitting on the logs by the pond, and I just let it go. Left it to chance. Later I knew the branch had fallen, but she never said anything, so I assumed it happened when she wasn't there. Pushing the hay bale out of the loft, well, I suppose I felt cheated. About the branch. I don't know, it was easy. The bales were piled awkwardly."

"And the horse going down?" Gwynedd's voice was deadly.

Haslen glanced away. He rubbed one hand restlessly across the other. "I shouldn't have done that." His voice had sunk with the first hint of shame.

"Yeah, you might have injured the horse," I said scornfully.

"I had no right to risk household property," he said. It was an automatic response.

Gwynedd burst out, "No right to risk household property. No right! What about your duty." Her words trembled with disgust. "The duty to protect anyone who comes under this roof." Haslen's head came up but he sat silent in the face of Gwynedd's fury. "You betrayed that. And then, rather than own up to it, you let them arrest Lucian."

"I really believed he was guilty." Haslen's voice was barely audible. "That he had gotten the idea from what I'd done, the other close calls. Only he took it further. He wanted a more certain result." He opened his mouth as if to say something more, but then stopped.

I had never thought to see Gwynedd so enraged. She could hardly choke out her words. "Get out. Get out of this house. Take your things and go." Gwynedd turned to Zorn. "I'm not sure how the law will view this, but I will support any action you choose to take."

Zorn got up, but instead of acknowledging what Gwynedd had said, she came around to the other side of the table and stood in front of Haslen. "And now?" she asked with almost no rise in inflection.

He looked at her uncertainly. "What do you want? You want me to say I'm sorry?" He sounded defiant, but also apprehensive.

"Are you?" Zorn's voice continued smooth as glass.

"I haven't offered any excuses."

"Do you have any?"

Haslen scrambled to his feet. The chair clattered behind him. Zorn didn't react, which I thought was lucky for Haslen. "When I thought Lucian had tried to murder you," he said, "and got Carsten instead, I hated what I'd done. Because I thought I had instigated it. And got an innocent person killed. When I found out about Arne and Carsten, that it wasn't you and Lucian at all, I still hated what I'd done. Because it made me something I didn't want to be. Gwynedd's right. I don't know what you are. I don't why you helped save Lucian or helped condemn Arne Bennetson. But if I had it to do over, I wouldn't lift a hand against you. Not for your sake, but for myself. And for this household."

From where I sat, I could see Zorn's face, its absolute impassivity. And I knew very well how that detached calmness must appear to Haslen. It smacked of prerogative and authority and of an arrogant pride which wouldn't even deign to show anger. I knew because I had attributed those same qualities to Zorn often enough. I also knew she would not relent in the slightest about the way she presented herself.

Very deliberately she turned her back on Haslen to face Gwynedd who was still standing on the other side of the table. "I have no interest in taking this matter to your constabulary. But I will presume to offer a suggestion to you. Reconsider your decision. I would prefer that you do not dismiss your chamberlain because of the actions he took with regard to me."

Haslen stirred behind her. Zorn pivoted sideways, so that she faced them both.

"That's a generous position to take," Gwynedd said. "Perhaps more generous than I can be."

"It is your household and your choice. However, you might bear in mind, I intend to maintain my accounts with this House. Dismiss him," Zorn indicated Haslen, "and I may have to go through this again. With whoever replaces him. Whereas this house chamberlain, by his own admission, has at last accommodated himself to my unwelcome presence." Zorn walked halfway to the door, then turned back. "Grayall led me to believe that in the Exchanges monetary considerations prevailed over everything. She misrepresented you." Then she left.

Gwynedd sank slowly back into her chair. Haslen sat without moving. I stood up, leaned over the table, and said to Gwynedd. "You might remember Zorn's a pretty good client, even if a touch bothersome. You might humor her in this matter." Gwynedd gave me a sour grin and a twitch of her shoulders which I took for resigned acquiescence. I turned to face Haslen. "And if I were you," I said to him, "I'd count myself lucky. You ought to watch Zorn take target practice sometime. One thing about her, she aims at something, she hits it. Fortunately she's pretty selective in her choice of targets."

Maybe it wasn't the most devastating of exit lines, but I liked it.

CHAPTER FORTY-NINE

Our last days at Gwynedd's continued to be busy, but pleasantly so. They were filled with making arrangements for our journey to Wendenwood and for taking up residency there. Our immediate plans for the latter were simple enough. We would maintain the current operation in wheat which ran well under a farm manager and with long-lease tenants. In addition, Zorn intended to raise horses, using the colt she was going to purchase from Traina as a founding stud. I guess that made sense. Although I couldn't help wondering whether the whole idea of purchasing a freehold had been inspired by the colt in the first place.

For myself, I abandoned any plan of taking on a trading route through the borderland villages. There would be ample work at the freehold to keep me busy.

Patric didn't think much of my decision. He urged me again to join him in building an enterprise in the New Tradelands. "Trading's in your blood, Grayall," he told me. "And don't worry, ours would be only a business partnership. I wouldn't press you for anything else." But I declined and he didn't have much chance to argue. Acting as representative for Arne's estate, he was off for the southern ports to complete the re-sale of the insignia. The executors were going ahead with that even though the final settlement of Arne's property would be delayed since his body had not been found.

In some ways, Arne ends up with almost the last word in all this. It was the day before Zorn and I were to leave and I was hunting for her to consult about some last minute details. I couldn't help recalling that I had spent part of our first day at Gwynedd's tracking her down as well. I walked to the pond even though, as far as I knew, she no longer went there. I noticed the burned spot had been covered with new soil and carefully raked into obscurity. The remnants of the charred logs had been hauled away as well.

I crossed through the stand of trees back toward the dock, conscious of the way I had made that trip in reverse the day Carsten had died. The dock was empty. The last of Lucian's shipments had departed on schedule and he along with them. But, because of Evane, he was not gone for good, of that I was sure.

I took a moment and perched against one of the stout posts that came up through the dock. I stared down at the river. It was flowing swift and strong. Ripples of current shone in the sun, but iron-gray clouds, scattered through the blue sky, foretold more rain soon.

As I watched the swollen water tumble past me, suddenly my eyes brimmed full and tears trickled down my face. The tears were for Arne. It seemed strange to be weeping for him, a murderer, and a particularly ruthless one at that. But the Arne I had known for so long kept separating in my mind from the Arne I had recently discovered. And the old Arne, just Arne, remained a lot more real to me than the new one.

Behind my tears was an irrepressible hope that he was not dead. If Patric was right and Arne had jumped, taking his chances with the river, he might have made it. Across or down stream. He was a strong swimmer. But if he had, it was at the cost of everything he'd killed Carsten for. His trading enterprise, his primacy of place in the Exchanges, his final triumph over his rival.

Maybe it was kinder after all to wish him dead, to hope he had paid for his crime with a self-inflicted execution.

My reverie was interrupted by a shadow falling across my face. "Gwynedd said you were looking for me." I turned aside but Zorn had surely noticed my tears. She stepped past me to half lean, half sit against one of the other dock posts. Without saying anything, she too directed her gaze toward the river.

Zorn was better at prolonged silences than I was, so after a while I said, "You know, Arne guessed you'd buy a freehold. The day you left. That conversation seems a long time ago." My voice faltered. "Stupid, isn't it? To mourn for Arne, more than Carsten?" I tugged at the corners of my eyes to bleed off my tears.

"You considered him a closer friend than you did the other," Zorn said.

"Affection knows no ethics, is that it?" I blinked back the tears which had re-formed.

"Perhaps friendship has its own irrationalities." She gave me one of her considered appraisals.

I took the point. "I suppose you're right."

We both fell silent. I was about to raise with Zorn the questions I had about our departure when a tentative step sounded behind us. Zorn had heard the approach before I did, and had turned. I turned as well. It was Evane.

"Mother was wondering if you were ready to finalize your arrangements for tomorrow." She spoke to include both of us.

"Sure," I said, looking at Zorn for agreement. For answer she started to walk back along the dock.

"Wait," Evane said to her. "I want to say how grateful I am to you. For Lucian. For saving him. I know they would have found him guilty."

I could think of the kind of response I might expect Zorn to give to that, something about claiming no credit for merely bringing out the facts, but she surprised me. She said, "Lucian found himself in difficult circumstances." It wasn't only the accusation of murder that Zorn was referring to and we all knew it.

Evane put her hands together and pressed the edges of her fingers to her lips. She slid her hands down so that her chin rested on her fingertips. "He really does know what he owes you. He would have thanked you. If he could."

Zorn flicked a glance in my direction. There was a gleam of complicity in her eyes. Then she settled her disquietingly level stare on Evane. "I will take your word for that," she said. She walked off toward the house.

I took a step after her, but Evane reached out to me. "Grayall, what do I say?" She put her arms around me. "I'm sorry."

I stepped back and took her by the shoulders. I shook her. "Damn right."

She laughed at me, the laughter of friendship reclaimed.

We followed Zorn back to the house.

Zorn and I left the next morning. It was raining again. At least, this time we were adequately outfitted.

Gwynedd, Torvan, and Evane wished us good speed, each in their own way with affection and genuine concern. And Haslen was there, too, attending to his duties with scrupulous courtesy. Against her inclination, Gwynedd had complied with Zorn's request and had allowed him to stay on as house chamberlain. Unlike Lucian, I think he had the good sense to be more grateful than resentful.

Zorn and I rode to the dock where we would board the boat for the trip down river. We didn't say much. The rain discouraged conversation. But I thought about my companion, Zorn of Northmarch, and about what I had learned of her during the couple of months I had known her.

I learned that she valued the skills and behaviors the Realm had given her, many of which remained to me as chilling as they were intimidating. I learned that, aside from that ariston manner of hers, there wasn't much else about the Realm she did value. How that contradiction in character came about, that I had not learned.

I learned that her upbringing had not hammered out of her either her temper or her sense of humor, no matter how eccentric their manifestations.

I learned to respect her and to trust her. Most of all, I learned to value her friendship as I knew she valued mine.

The Elsewhere Mysteries will continue with…

ZORN AND GRAYALL

DEFY MURDER BY MAGIC

CPSIA information can be obtained at www.ICGtesting.com
Printed in the USA
LVOW11s1054240516

489674LV00001B/111/P

THE
BEGINNING

Date Due